I0603294

# Cinder and Black

## Anchor and the Moon, Volume 1

Maxx Victor

Published by Maxx Victor, 2021.

This is a work of fiction. Similarities to real people, places, or events are entirely coincidental.

CINDER AND BLACK

**First edition. November 1, 2021.**

Copyright © 2021 Maxx Victor.

ISBN: 978-0645325904

Written by Maxx Victor.

# Table of Contents

For Mothers. Yes, even step-mothers.

# Prologue

E arly summer 1856, Vieux Carre, the French quarter of New Orleans. A black-haired man, tries to walk unnoticed through Jackson Square. However, when you are almost eight feet tall, it is difficult to simply just blend in with the crowd. Two children playing with their mammy in the warm evening, whisper to each other and point at the man as he turns down St Peters Street and heads for the river. A group of French sailors on the opposite side of the road stop and eye him in amazement as he ducks under a shop awning.

'Ay monsieur, mind your 'ed,' one sailor jeers.

'Oui, you might hit your 'ed on ze moon,' his friend adds.

'Fais attention,' the voice of a young French woman calls out from behind the tall man.

The man turns to see a tall, beautiful and by all appearances, wealthy woman in a dark blue silk dress and white bonnet walking a few steps behind him.

'Don't you know who dis is?' she addresses the sailors, but places a lace-gloved hand on one of the tall man's enormous arms. 'Dis messieurs, is the giant, Black Angus MacAskill. Tallest and strongest man in ze world.'

The man blushes, smiles and, with a nod, continues on his way.

'I've heard 'e can carry a 300-pound barrel under each arm!' a third sailor speaks up.

'C'est des conneries!' the first sailor calls out in disbelief. The lady in blue crosses the street to talk directly to the sailors.

'It is true, I 'av seen it at Barnum's Circus.'

A young sailor with a blond moustache runs forward.

'Show me, monsieur, lift me up,' he says.

Reluctantly, the man agrees and takes the sailor in his giant hands, lifting him onto his shoulder like a proud father with his infant child. Humid Mississippi delta air forms beads of sweat on his pale skin, but he moves on unperturbed. The crowd erupts into laughter and applause. The young sailor waves his hat in the air, 'Allons-y!'

A second sailor runs forward and shortly a parade of people are following Black Angus, as he walks along the banks of the Mississippi, effortlessly carrying two grown men on his shoulders. The lady in blue leans against a discarded anchor, left to rust against a tree.

'Isn't dis exciting,' she calls to the sailors, removing her bonnet and letting her long red hair cascade down her back. 'So, messieurs,' she continues, using her bonnet to fan her face, 'What shall we get 'im to lift next?'

# Chapter 1

### Old Friends, New Enemies

I *hope your eyes tasted me,*
*A taste worth the entry fee.*
*But we will meet one night quite soon,*
*I'll bring my friend, the harvest moon.*

• • • •

'You're late!' said the voice of a disappointed mother that Cinder had heard too many times to count.

'I was training,' she replied. This made her mother look slightly less irritated.

'I'm glad you're taking your training seriously, but you know I don't like being kept waiting.' Cinder could tell she was flustered because she was slipping back into her French accent.

'Yes, Mother. Sorry, Mother.' Cinder tried her best not to sound sarcastic as she gave her standard reply to her mother's reprimands.

'I have someone waiting to meet you.' These words made Cinder stop mid-stride. She felt like her heart was sinking into her stomach and she clenched her fists so hard that her nails almost broke the skin.

'Please not again, Mother,' she pleaded, 'you know I hate this.'

Her mother was a strikingly beautiful woman, tall and slender with sharp features; her long auburn hair, skin, and nails, meticulously kept by a team of people. Right then, however, no amount of external beauty could hide the foreboding anger rising quickly behind her eyes. She took Cinder firmly by her arm, forcing her to trip and fall uncomfortably against the wall.

'You will do as you're told and you will earn your keep,' she said, her eyes fixed on Cinder's face, unblinking. 'My friends pay handsomely for this opportunity.'

Loosening her grip on Cinder's arm, she pushed her forward into a large, audaciously decorated room. The sitting room was just one of many in a house that, although it was one of the oldest remaining structures in the district, was still one of the largest. It was an impressive example of 19th-century architecture, built by one of the early settlers to show off the fortunes he had made on the goldfields. The original owner adding extra wings and buildings, each time he wanted to impress a new business partner or a woman he wished to court. Sitting high on a large outcrop, to the north it looked out on open green fields and forest that gradually inclined up from white beaches and out into the ocean. On the south, it looked down on the small coastal town of Heathcote. The house's proper name was Berkley's Manor, but now everyone, except her mother, just referred to it as The Big House. When her father was still alive, the sitting room was Cinder's favourite place in all The Big House and for all intents and purpose, her favourite place in her entire world. Now that couldn't be further from the truth. A gigantic, blindingly pristine white couch had replaced her father's worn leather recliners, which made Cinder laugh to herself about a room that her mother did not allow most people to sit down in being called the *sitting room*. Paintings and wall-mounted maps had given way to gold, marble, and jade ornaments, and statues of all shapes and sizes. The smell of an open fire gone, now Clive Christian No. 1 hung thick in the air. Worst of all, the sitting room was the place where her mother introduced Cinder to her friends.

Cinder walked out of the hallway, her arms crossed and her chin jutting forward. An old man with white hair and small dark eyes stood at the far end of the sitting room. Although he was a tall man, he appeared dwarfed by the high ceilings and sheer size of the room. 'Good evening, Louvelle,' he said. Cinder was unsure of which was more surprising–the man's thick European accent, or that he referred to her mother by her first name. Most people addressed her as Lady

Gevaudan or simply 'My lady'. Her mother smiled and replied, 'Good evening, Patru, a pleasure to see you again.' This man must have been a close friend to dare to speak to her so informally.

Louvelle glided across the room, as if rehearsing a set of choreographed dance steps, motioning with her left hand for the old man to sit. Then she sat down herself; crossing her legs, hands crossed on her lap, and her spine perfectly straight.

'Could we offer you something to eat, Patru?' she asked. Patru's attention had shifted from Louvelle to Cinder.

'No, thank you. I had some Chinese in the car on the way here,' he replied, unblinkingly staring at Cinder. 'You know how much I like everything oriental.'

Louvelle gave a polite laugh and nodded.

'Yes, very well then. Down to business. This is my daughter, Cinder. I must apologise for her dreadful appearance; she has just finished her training for the evening.' Louvelle turned her head towards Cinder and motioned with her hand for Cinder to move into the room.

Understanding what they required of her, Cinder walked to a dark corner of the room and stood in front of a large window with her back to Patru. She pulled out a hair-tie that was holding her long red hair in a high ponytail. lifting her sweaty t-shirt over her head, she threw it to the floor. She then dropped her track-pants and stepped out of them, kicking them over to where she had dropped the t-shirt. Finally, she removed her underwear, added it to the pile of clothing, and stood staring at her toes. Louvelle rose slowly, walked to the end of the window, and opened a set of long white drapes.

'Come into the light, darling,' she invited Cinder forward. Cinder paused for a moment, then followed her mother's instruction. On the other side of the room, Patru coughed to clear his throat. His wrinkled mouth crept slowly into a smile, revealing moist, greying teeth.

'Wonderful.'

• • • •

Angus punched Dom in his left shoulder, causing Dom to drop his surfboard on his foot. Dom winced in pain momentarily, then quickly swung at Angus in retaliation. Angus easily sidestepped the blow with a laugh. As Angus removed his own, well-loved surfboard from the roof of his friend's car, the last warm breeze of the day caressed his face, carrying the familiar saltiness to his nostrils and lips. He adjusted his wetsuit and tucked the board under his arm. Dom and Angus were often mistaken for brothers. Both men had the same mop of messy dark hair, pale skin, and tall, muscular frames. The fact that they were both wearing the same black wetsuit only helped to add to the similarity. Angus laughed to himself as he thought about this. Dom was not his brother, but they were related in some distant way that he had never cared to find out exactly. However, if there was anyone in the world he would choose to be his brother, it would be Dom. They had grown up together and shared every good day and bad day. As Dom inspected his foot and retrieved his board from the ground, a second car arrived. Gravelly rocks crushed underfoot as four more young men appeared from the car and greeted them.

They walked in single file, down a set of solid pine steps that cut their way through green shrubs and sand dunes. As the sound of the ocean crashing on the shore grew increasingly louder, they passed other surfers, leaving for the day. Both groups greeted each other with chin raising, but no words. Five years ago, when they first arrived in town, there were confrontations with the local surfers. The *Heathies*, as they called themselves, thought that night surfing was strange and stupid; making a point of letting the newcomers know this at every encounter.

For the first two weeks, Angus had convinced Dom to ignore the Heathies. But after three straight weeks of heckling, Dom snapped. When one of the Heathies pushed past him late one afternoon, calling him a 'pale-skinned freak', Dom grabbed the surfer's board and forced it into his face; breaking his nose and loosening a tooth. A group of the Heathies came to help their friend, and a brawl broke out on the beach.

Dom was only a teenager, but by the time Angus could calm everyone down, Dom had already knocked three grown men unconscious. After that day, there was no kissing and making up, but there was definitely a tone of mutual respect. Since then, the townspeople had come to accept these night-surfing, dairy-farming, day-sleepers, as just a bit different and not something concerning. Angus liked the anonymity that this kind of hiding in plain sight gave them.

The full moon was now shining over the tips of the waves out to the horizon, like millions of silver scales on the back of a black-skinned dragon, shivering in the cool of the evening. Angus caught himself holding his breath; his body's way of stemming the flood of adrenaline. The sight of a full moon filled him with mixed emotions. It gave them light enough to surf well into the night, which was one of the few indulgences they allowed themselves. Unfortunately, it increased the danger and the likelihood of interruptions.

As the first wave crashed over his head, the dark cloud enveloped Angus's senses, the chilling cold on his skin, and a muffled rumble in his ears. He imagined his anxiousness carried away behind him in the churning water and thrown onto the shore. Angus rose from his watery portal, transferred into another world, where all that mattered was him, his board, and the waves. Here, wrapped in this dark blanket, with his best friends – his family – it felt like all his concerns were half a world and a lifetime away. At first, he paddled out past the breakers and just sat floating with his feet dangling in the water.

'You too scared? Need someone to hold ya hand, little girl?' Dom had just caught one of the larger waves and had ridden it most of the way into shore with as many tricks and screams as he could get in – his usual attention-seeking way. He was now paddling quickly out towards Angus, with a stupid, large grin on his face. He continued the heckling. 'Do you need some lessons? I'll give a pretty thing like you the first two lessons for free.' Although he would never tell him, Angus knew that surfing was the one thing that Dom really was better at than him. Dom had the right mix of natural agility, balance, and showmanship. And a general lack of fear. If they didn't live a nocturnal life, Dom might have been able to make it onto the pro tour. Many an early morning drunken argument had started because of Dom's desire to have a life beyond the one they had all been born into.

'Are we surfing or what?' Dom was now next to Angus, bobbing up and down on his board like some kind of crazy-eyed buoy.

'Just letting your head swell enough first so you'll be easier to knock off,' Angus quickly replied, before shoving him hard in the chest, sending him, arms and legs waving uncontrollably, splashing into the water. Angus then paddled as hard as he could to catch the next breaker and rode it in, laughing the whole way.

Angus had been surfing since he was ten years old, but he still marvelled at the feeling. Mother Nature freely giving up her power, wave after wave. Over the past few years, he had spent as much time riding these waves as he had spent with some of his closest friends. But just because this beach with its hills, paths, and dunes were like his second home, that didn't mean he could take the ocean for granted. No wave was the same as the next. One moment he would fly across the ocean's glassy surface, laughing into the wind as his hand trailed through the dark water towering beside him. The next moment he would be rolling around, churning in the foam, eyes stinging and lungs aching until he could work out which way was up. It had been a hot day, and the night was still warm. A gentle, off-shore breeze had been blowing all evening and cleared away any clouds – perfect conditions. As the hours drifted away, Angus spent less time watching the waves and more time watching the hill at the eastern end of the beach; he could see that Dom was doing the same.

Angus paddled out the back of the breakers, to a patch of calm water where Dom was floating face down on his board. Dom's head was laying sideways on his crossed arms so he could see the top of the hill over the waves. 'What time do you think it is?' He called out to Angus when he saw him coming.

'Maybe around 11:30,' Angus answered, looking up at the moon.

'We might make it to midnight without interruption,' Dom said. A small flicker of light appeared, momentary but bright, against the dark backdrop of the hill. Within seconds a warm orange glow was casting trembling shadows into the canopy of the hilltop trees.

'You spoke too soon.' Angus said, then stuck two fingers in his mouth and whistled loudly.

The fire signalled that it was time to go. With military precision, they were all out of the water, up the beach, and at the top of the stairs within a few minutes. They all quickly swapped the boards for balaclavas and weapons. Dom ran up beside Angus with a tomahawk in each hand, the moonlight glistening off the razor-sharp metal and his equally sharp smile.

'Okay, Black,' he called Angus by his nickname, 'time to go hunting!'

. . . .

Cinder walked slowly back down the hallway with her head held high and her shoulders back, her face held resolutely in a look of complete disinterest. Despite her mother's calls from the sitting room behind her, to not be ridiculous and get dressed, she was carrying her clothes bundled up under her arm. Her eyes were getting warm, but her determination held back the tears of rage; she did not want to show her mother any signs that might be mistaken for weakness. She made her way to the end of the hall before turning sharply onto a set of old cobblestone steps that curved down to a solid timber door. Cinder entered a large open space, which before Louvelle had it converted into a gym for Cinder's training, had been the cellar. Louvelle sent Cinder here every afternoon, not that she minded. It was a place to escape and a good stress relief. Down here, she could also keep many of her father's things, so it was the one place in The Big House she still felt at home. She dumped her clothes on a bench just inside the door and pulled on her t-shirt and track pants, before slamming the heavy timber door shut behind her.

A patched and worn boxing-bag hung from a joist in the middle of the large room. Her anger at boiling point, and hands deliberately glove-free, Cinder made straight for the suspended mass. Flesh pulled tight over knuckles, she pummelled the collection of faces mentally imprinting on the dark leather. Louvelle, Patru, Louvelle again. Then a collection of faces she had no name to put to. Stopping to catch her breath, she wiped the sweat and tears out of her eyes with the bottom of her t-shirt; as she did, the face of her father came to mind. She stood for a few seconds listening to her racing heart, her eyes closed to concentrate on his face, his smell, his voice. A small smile crept into the corners of her mouth. As much as she wanted it to stay, her father's face slipped away, replaced by another. A face that woke her in the late hours of the night, with sharp blood-stained teeth, a monster with dead eyes, dark and emotionless like Patru's. Now Patru's face was back. She attacked the bag with increased vigour. The skin on her fingers cracked, leaving small splatters of blood on the bag. The bolt holding the bag to the roof was starting to creak under the strain.

Suddenly, Cinder became aware that someone was coming down the steps into the gym. She wiped her face again with her t-shirt and on seeing smears of blood, realised just how much damage she had done to her hands. 'Oh shi...'

'Language please, Cinder,' her mother had just entered the room. 'A foul mouth is not becoming of a lady, and neither are bloodied hands. How many times have I told you, girl? Wear the gloves. It's imperative that we maintain our outward appearance. Speaking of which, I do wish you would do something with your hair. It's your one redeeming quality when you let Simon do it. Anyway, come over here and let me fix up your hands. We have some things to talk about.' She took Cinder by the elbow and led her over to an old couch that Cinder sometimes used as a bed, even though she had a giant, four-posted bed in her room on the top floor. 'Sit.'

Cinder flopped down on the couch as Louvelle retrieved a warm, moist rag and some bandages from the other side of the room. On her return, she propped herself up on the arm of the couch and began dabbing at Cinder's hands, shaking her head and clicking her tongue.

'Now, my dear, I've come to give you some important news. I need to go away on business with Patru and I'll be gone all month. That means that you will be in charge. Now listen carefully,' She squeezed Cinder's hand and moved her face in close to Cinder's. 'It is very important that you keep going with your training and that you don't do anything... silly. I'm placing a lot of trust in you, do you understand?' Cinder nodded. 'Tell me,' said Louvelle, raising her left eyebrow.

'Yes, Mother, I understand.'

'Good. Now my car's waiting, I've given everyone their instructions and you have my number if you need to call me.' Her mother got up and hastened towards the door, wiping her hands on the rag before dropping it in a bin. Turning to Cinder one last time before leaving, she added, 'Don't do anything stupid.' Leaving the door open, Louvelle disappeared up the stairs.

Cinder sat quietly, wrapping her hands in the bandages, glowering at the blood smears on her t-shirt, waiting for her mother to get out of earshot. When she was sure her mother had gone, she leaped to her feet and ran screaming at the boxing bag, crashing into it with such force that it snapped the chain holding it and came crashing to the floor under her. Cinder rolled off, slightly winded, but now even angrier. Rolling back onto her left side, she continued thumping the bag with her right hand. New, light red blood started seeping through the white bandages. Cinder let out high pitch grunts with every punch, like two tennis players volleying for match point.

'She forgot your birthday again, right?' Someone was standing right behind her! Instinctively, Cinder spun her body around, throwing out her leg to try to knock the intruder off their feet. The other person was too quick however, and simply jumped her leg, sending Cinder spinning and ending up on all fours facing an expensive pair of black leather ankle boots at the end of two long, tanned legs. 'Hey, I'm on your side, sweetie,' came a voice from above. A dark-haired woman with blue eyes bent down to bring her face closer to Cinder. 'Maybe I should call you sweaty, have a look at you.'

Cinder took a moment to catch her breath before answering. 'I should have known it was you Marraine, you're the only one around here that can sneak up on me.'

'You know me, sneaky-sneaky,' Marraine said, reaching down to help Cinder stand.

Marraine was Cinder's godmother; Cinder was not sure how old she was. Although she could pass for a woman in her late twenties, she had been friends with Cinder's mother when Cinder was born, so she must be almost in her forties. 'How do you know she forgot my birthday?' Cinder said once she was on her feet again.

'Well,' Marraine continued, frowning at Cinder's hands, 'she's going away for a month and your $21^{st}$ is in two weeks, so doing the maths she forgot your birthday, again.'

'How do you know she's going away? I just found that out.'

'Like I said, sneaky-sneaky. But don't worry, I didn't forget, I'm taking you out.' Marraine skipped to the couch and slumped herself down with an expression of smug satisfaction.

'Out! What do you mean out? She won't let me out by myself.' Cinder sat down on the fallen boxing bag, nursing her injured hands.

'You won't be by yourself. You'll be with me,' Marraine replied, batting her long eyelashes. Cinder smiled at this and gave a little laugh.

'I think that's worse.'

'Besides,' Marraine continued, 'her ladyship won't be here and, even though she's forgotten, you're going to be 21; she has no say in what you do.'

'But I don't have anything to wear. These were my best pants and now they're, well, a bit spotty.' Cinder looked down at her blood-splattered legs.

'I have an entire ensemble picked out for you already.'

'But...'

'No buts, I've already organised for Bob to drop you off. My place, Friday fortnight, 5:00, bring some of mummy dear's good wine. Maybe her 1907 Heidsieck – that would be fun.' With that, Marraine got up and sauntered out as silently as she had entered.

The door to the farmhouse flung open. Dom was the first to stumble through, followed closely by his 16-year-old sister, Torry.

'Hi, Dad,' they said in unison. A large man with greying black hair was sitting on an old brown leather armchair in front of an open fire. His kind, bushy-browed blue eyes hung heavy with sleep as he finished packing tobacco into a pipe with broad, calloused hands.

'Hi, Uncle Gunn,' Angus said, striding casually in after them. Gunn glanced over his shoulder, then went back to searching for a matchbox in his shirt pocket. He quickly took a second look, jumping out of his seat in alarm. Blood dripped from Dom, Torry, and Angus, covering them from head to toe. Their teeth and eyes, looking abnormally white through their dark red coating.

'Are you hurt? Where are the others? What happened?' Gunn grabbed their arms and inspected their bodies for the source of the blood.

'It's okay,' Torry assured him, 'it's not our blood.'

'Maybe just a little of it's mine,' interrupted Dom, with as much of a laugh as he could muster. 'One of them got my leg pretty good.'

Angus moved in closer to the fire and found a tiled section of the floor to sit, making sure not to drip blood on the floor rug. 'We all made it back fine. The others are getting cleaned up in the shed and the bungalow.' Gunn's expression of concern had now turned to one of confusion.

'But this much blood! You didn't kill any of them, did you? You know that's the first rule, we can't have bodies turning up and police sniffing around.' Dom muttered some indecipherable curses under his breath. Gunn turned quickly and looked his way 'Be careful boy, my eyes might be failing me, but my ears are still sharp.' Angus got gingerly to his feet.

'You can have the bathroom, Tor,' he called out. 'I'm going out the back to get cleaned up. And don't worry, old-man, no bodies.'

'Old man! I can still kick your ass,' Gunn said as he made his way towards Dom, rolling up the sleeves of his worn flannelette shirt, exposing broad tattooed forearms. 'Now let's have a look at this leg.' He crouched down, pulling some thick black-rimmed spectacles from his chest pocket, placing them on the end of his nose.

'I have no doubt you could kick my ass,' said Angus with a cheeky smile. 'But with the way I'm feeling, I think Dom could even kick my ass with that sore leg.'

'What are ya talking about, princess? I could take you on a good day with two sore legs and my arms tied behind my back,' Dom yelled at Angus as he left the room.

Gunn took off his spectacles and rubbed his forehead with his thumb and index finger, as if he was trying to rub away more wrinkles before they formed, then looked seriously into Dom's blood-stained face.

'So boy, why so much blood?'

'There were just so many of them. There must have been three or four of them to every one of us. I'm glad I talked Black into letting Tor come along tonight. It might have been too much. You did a great job tonight.' He turned and winked at Torry, who had been standing in the same place since they entered the house, partly from shock and partly from fatigue.

'Thanks.' She mustered a smile as she left.

'They were hungry too,' Dom continued. 'A lot of this is cow blood. We must have lost a few dozen of the girls tonight. At least that will make the milking quicker for you. Ouch!' Gunn had pushed on the cut on his leg.

'Go get yourself cleaned up and then come back here, that's going to need some stitches. Oh, and I don't want Tor to go out for a while, till things calm down. All right?' Dom nodded in agreement and limped out of the room. Gunn slumped back into his chair, wiped his hands on his handkerchief, lit his pipe, and squinted his eyes as the first light of the day flooded in through the windows. He let out a long breath of smoke and watched it rise to the ceiling. 'I don't think we're ready for this again.'

There were always dozens of people at The Big House. Besides the cleaners, grounds staff, and two chefs, there was also Louvelle's security and countless others that came and went for business. Cinder had learned to trust some of them, but most of the time she felt that there were always prying eyes watching her. Luckily, The Big House was just as the nickname implied, big. The principal building spread out over two wings with three storeys. There were also four more peripheral structures scattered around the hilltop property and over a hundred rooms in total. Over the years, Cinder had learned how to move about the property unseen if she wanted. With her mother away, everyone appeared more relaxed and there were fewer people around for Cinder to avoid.

Louvelle had been on trips before, but never for so long. Cinder started the week keeping up with the normal routine of training and eating how her mother expected, but as the days went on and Cinder's anger at her forgotten birthday increased, she became more and more unmotivated. By the second week, her 5:30 wake time had crept out to 9:00, her morning training hour was non-existent and her evening two hours of training was barely thirty minutes long. She had convinced the chef to replace her protein shakes with regular full cream shakes.

The entire household was under strict instructions to not allow Cinder to leave the property without her mother's permission and a security detail. Feeling particularly noncompliant because of the forgotten birthday, Cinder made plans for an outing. She organised for one of the staff, a man called Bob, to cover for her. Other than to be around to grovel for Louvelle, Cinder wasn't sure what Bob's job actually was. What she did know about Bob was his infatuation with Marraine. He was often eager to bend the rules for Cinder when she promised to put a good word in for him. Like everyone at The Big House, Bob was afraid of Cinder's mother but had demonstrated many times over the years that Cinder could trust him.

On Wednesday morning, she sent her tutors away, claiming she was sick. With Bob as her lookout, she rode her bike – unescorted – into town and bought herself chocolate and soft drinks with some money she had taken from her mother's safe. She regretted this the next morning and had to send her tutors away again, as she had actually made herself feel sick. By Friday, she decided to eat more responsibly and attended her lessons. She was, however, too nervous about going out with Marraine that night to pay very much attention.

The people in the surrounding districts all knew that there were certain places in the forest that you never ventured after dark. Myths and legends had passed from father to son, mother to daughter, older sibling to younger sibling, and classmate to classmate. The tales that had evolved over recent decades were part of the local DNA. For the people of Brookesmarsh at the east end of the Alexander State Forest, it was a family of pumas, kept as mascots at the army base, released in to the forest at the end of World War Two. Further west it was the same story, but with bears, not big cats. And in Heathcote, every school kid knew the tale of the beast and Mr. Loo's chickens.

That being said, it was no surprise that earlier that week when Angus and Dom found themselves standing in the silver glow of a crescent moon filtering down through the trees at the eastern boundary of their property, that there was no sign of any other people. It was also no surprise that the sounds of something large moving and breathing in the shadows was causing them a great deal of apprehension.

Angus turned to look at Dom and seeing the look on his face, asked, 'Are you okay?' Dom didn't take his eyes off the tree-line.

'I don't know'.

'What's wrong?'

'One of them licked me!' Dom was holding his two tomahawks in his right hand while he raised his left hand to his cheek. 'It licked my face.'

# Chapter 2

## New Friends, Old Enemies

Angus wiped perspiration from his brow with the back of his hand. A busy mind had woken him earlier than usual that afternoon. The strange night they had had and the memory of past conversations with Gunn warning him about being cautious when things changed were running through his head, making it impossible to sleep. Deciding some physical activity might clear his head, he made the short walk to a shed at the rear of the property. They had converted the unused building to a gym. There was no electricity, so it was nothing fancy, just a few old boxing bags, a mountain of free weights of all different shapes and sizes, and two large tractor tyres.

Angus dried his hands on the front of his pants, then jumped, taking hold of a length of two-inch pipe, mounted between two of the shed's uprights, and began doing chin-ups. 'One, two, three,' he counted, each number coming out with his breath as he reached the top. 'Four, five, six.'

'Eleven, twenty-six, three,' Dom had just entered, calling out random numbers to make Angus lose count.

'Eighteen, nineteen, twenty.' Angus lowered himself down and dropped to the dirt floor.

'Why are you up so early?' he asked Dom as he bumped past him with his shoulder.

'Who could sleep with you out here, moaning and groaning and huffing and puffing?' He mimicked someone struggling to do chin-ups. 'One oh, two ooow. I thought Tor had bought one of her friends home from school, but then I realised she wouldn't even be friends with someone that pathetic.'

'Ha ha. You should do stand-up, funny guy,' Angus answered, as he squatted and lifted one of the tyres onto its side.

'Why? Cos I'm such a stand-up guy.' Dom had a goofy smile on his face. 'Thank you, thank you I'm here every night, tell your friends.' Angus rested his arms on top of the tyre and shook his head from side to side before dropping the tyre to the floor again. Dom picked up a long metal rod with leather bindings that was sitting on a table in the corner.

'So, can I have a play with your stick?'

'What?' Angus nearly dropped the tyre that he had started to lift again. 'Oh, it's not a stick, it's a naginata.'

'It's only a naginata if you get your blade out.' Dom held the two middle sections of the rod and twisted them in opposite directions. A thirty centimetre double-edged blade shot out of one end. Angus rolled the tyre over one more time.

'The blades are only for emergencies.'

'Maybe you should just give this to me if you're not going to use it properly,' Dom continued as he twirled the naginata around between his hands.

Angus dusted his hands off on the back of his pants and sat down on the tyre.

'You'd miss your tomahawks. You can't exactly go throwing that around… Shit!' Angus ducked with his hands over his head. Dom had just thrown the naginata like a javelin. It stuck out horizontally from one of the shed's timber supports, half a metre away from Angus's head.

'I don't know, that seems to work fine,' Dom said with an evil grin. Angus pulled his naginata out and retracted the blade, placing it back on the table.

'So anyway,' Dom continued, pretending not to notice the unimpressed look on Angus's face. 'Talking about never getting your blade out, that's why I wanted to find you. I've got a plan for Friday night.'

Angus picked up a dumbbell in each hand.

'I'm sure I'm going to regret this later, but please go on. What's your plan?'

'Well,' Dom sat on the tyre, resting his elbows on his spread legs, 'there's a new moon Friday so we won't need to patrol, and as things have been so weird, I think we've earned a break. So... the boys and I are going out in Heathcote, and you're coming.'

Dom could see the look of concern on Angus's face, so he quickly continued.

'Don't think about it, it's just one night. I'm sure you can forget about being "Mr. Serious" for one night.'

Angus reluctantly nodded.

'Okay.'

'Okay?'

'Okay. But what's this got to do with me getting my blade out?' As Angus asked this, the childish look on Dom's face helped him to understand the innuendo. 'You're disgusting. You know that, right?'

'You love me. Actually, is that why you're not interested in girls? Sorry, but you know there could be no future for us?' Dom walked over, placed his hand on Angus's shoulder, and gave him a mock look of concern.

'I like girls fine,' Angus replied, as he pushed the dumbbells into Dom's chest, making him take them. 'I'm just a little more picky than you.'

'I'm picky!' Dom said, feigning offence. 'They need to be female, human, and between sixteen and sixty.'

Angus just smiled and shook his head.

'Okay Mr. Picky, we're going to make a deal,' Dom continued, 'let me know four things you like in a girl. If I can find a girl like that Friday night, you have to talk to her.'

Angus thought this over.

'Alright,' he said reluctantly, 'you know I like girls with red hair and green eyes. That's two things.'

'No way, that's only her looks so that only counts as one thing, you're not getting out of it that easy.'

'Okay, well, she'd need to be tall, so I didn't feel like a giant around her. She'd need to make me laugh, that's three and four, um four, I know, she would need to like surfing.'

'Alright then, a giant, Ranga comedian who has spent too much time in the sun. Easy,' said Dom, putting down the dumbbells. 'Let's shake on it.' They shook hands, then Dom jogged out of the shed, stopping to pummel one of the boxing bags.

'Yes! I'm so psyched, this night's going to change your life man. I can feel it.'

• • • •

Cinder sat staring at the girl in the mirror in front of her. She had similar features, but other than that, she was a stranger. After days of feeling both excited and anxious, Friday afternoon had come. She had just spent the last few hours being attacked by a lovely woman called Tina and a strangely feminine young man who referred to himself as "The Shaz". They had come at her with tweezers, scissors, brushes of all shapes and sizes, and all sorts of lotions and potions. In the meantime, Marraine had fluttered around her flat, calling out instructions and encouragement, a glass of red wine in one hand and the other hand occupied by sorting out the multitude of outfit options that were now scattered unceremoniously over bed, bench tops, and furniture. Cinder was at least glad that The Shaz had left her hair long. Her mother had cut it off after her father died and she had spent the last three years refusing to have it cut. The Shaz had told her he was just going to layer it and give it some body and shape. Cinder was unsure what that meant, but was happy with the result. Not quite as happy as The Shaz appeared to be, who was now crying with joy into a large purple handkerchief.

Tina had used mascara and a pallet of pencils and paints to magically double the size of Cinder's eyes and eyelashes. She put the finishing touches on Cinder's lips.

'There you go, beautiful, all done.'

Cinder stood up with difficulty. The boots Marraine had picked out for her had much taller heels than she was accustomed to. Marraine signalled for her to turn around. Sheepishly tucking her hair behind her ear and biting her now French-polished nail, she did a slow turn. The other three smiled and nodded in approval. Marraine had finally decided to put her in a long black fitted dress with three-quarter length sleeves and a high-low hemline. Cinder wasn't sure about having almost all of her left leg showing, and the scoop neckline revealed more of her chest than she thought was necessary.

'You look amazing, sweetie!' Marraine whispered reassuringly, noticing Cinder fidgeting with the hem at her thigh. 'There's just one more thing I need to give you, to finish off your look.' Marraine disappeared into her room. She returned a moment later, holding a small black box tied with a red ribbon and bow. 'This is your birthday present.'

Cinder noticed some tears welling in Marraine's eyes as she handed her the box.

'Thank you.' Cinder unwrapped the ribbon and slid off the lid. Nestled inside was a round pendant, just slightly smaller than Cinder's palm. It looked very old but well cared for.

The pendant contained three principal parts: a silver loop around the outside, a tree made from seven gold strands intertwined, the roots wrapping around the bottom of the loop and spreading out into seven swirling branches at the top, and a full moon carved from a red garnet, suspended in the branches. Cinder lifted it out of the box, a long silver chain slithering out behind it.

'It's beautiful,' she said.

'It was your mum's,' Marraine said. 'She gave it to me when you were born and asked me to give it to you, when you were ready, and now you're all grown up.' Marraine choked on her words. She wiped her eyes with the back of her hand and said, 'Let's see it on.' Careful not to mess up Cinder's hair, Marraine placed the chain over her head and sat the pendant just below the neckline of Cinder's dress, rubbing her thumb lovingly across it. 'Okay, let me look at you.' Marraine took a step back. 'Perfect, you look just like a queen.' She dabbed away another tear. 'Okay, time to go before I wreck my make-up.'

There was a car waiting for them outside, but Cinder took no notice of what kind it was. She couldn't stop looking at the pendant and moving it between her fingers. Not only was it the most beautiful gift she had ever received, it was also the only thing of her mum's that she hadn't had to steal and hide away.

• • • •

The chosen destination for their night out was a place called Paddy's. There were only two real nightspots in Heathcote and Paddy's was far more popular with the tourists and under-thirties. Paddy's, was a two-storey bluestone building. Built towards the end of the 19th century. Its original name was St Patrick's Guest House. After being vacant for some years, an investor converted the guest house into an Irish pub. Its position at the top end of the esplanade and uninterrupted views over the Heathcote pier made it an overnight success with the tourists that tripled Heathcote's population over the summer months.

As they walked towards the door, Cinder started to grow nervous again. 'Stop,' she said, grabbing Marraine's arm. 'I don't think they're going to let me in. I don't have any ID and everyone always tells me I only look about 16 or 17.'

'They won't even ask us,' Marraine reassured her and placing her hand on the small of her back, lead Cinder in through the door.

Just inside the doorway was a very large Samoan man wearing black jeans and t-shirt. He was sitting in a booth that was almost too small for his very broad shoulders.

'Good evening, ladies,' he greeted them with a nod.

'See, nothing to worry about,' Marraine said after giving the doorman an appreciative smile.

'But how did you do that? I feel like Mother uses mind-control on her men, but not on ordinary, everyday men.' Cinder looked back at the doorman in confusion as they walked further into the already crowded pub.

'Believe me, sweetie, you have all it takes to do a bit of mind-control on most ordinary, everyday men.' Cinder looked back at Marraine, still puzzled.

'What do you mean?'

'Take a look around,' Marraine moved Cinder's head by cradling her cheeks. 'All those eyes aren't just on me. You're a beautiful young woman! A sexy lady! A hot chick!' Cinder pulled Marraine's hands off her face and held them.

'Thank you for saying that, but I'm not. I know I'm not.'

'Who says?'

'My mother, at every possible opportunity.'

Marraine gripped her hands tightly and looked angrier than Cinder had ever seen her look.

'You listen to me. That woman has not acted like your mother since your father died, so I'm putting a ban on you calling her mother for the rest of the night.'

'What should I call her then?'

'I have a few suggestions,' Marraine smiled, 'but maybe it's best if we don't talk about her at all.'

Paddy's was about two-and-a-half times as long as it was wide, with a high wooden bar that ran along the middle half of the south wall. There was an open section near the front windows, with a view out onto the beach. Upturned wine-barrels sat around the polished timber floor for the patrons to use as tables. Although it was still early, many locals and tourists already occupied the stools at the tables and bar. Marraine led Cinder to a spot against the wall opposite the bar, then went to order some drinks.

Cinder looked around the room, smiling nervously at anyone that made eye contact with her and adjusting her dress. Out of the corner of her eye, Cinder glimpsed a group that had just entered the pub. A group of seven men who were noticeably taller than most. One of them in the middle particularly caught her eye. Something in Cinder noticed straight away that he was the leader of the pack. She had had little experience with men her age. The look of his face and the shape of his body was pleasing to Cinder, but it wasn't until she noticed others following him with their eyes, that she realised she was feeling attraction. She became conscious that her heart was now beating a little faster, and her cheeks and her chest were feeling warm. As he came closer, she became even more uncomfortable. He walked tall and confidently through the crowd with his entourage in tow, but he was always at the centre like a sun at the centre of his own solar system, Cinder thought to herself, unable to take her eyes off him, with the others like little planets caught in his gravity. She laughed to herself. *There's Mercury staying nice and close, then Venus, Earth, and Mars together against the wall. And Jupiter and Saturn further out, moving towards me. Oh, no!* Cinder realised that the entire group was now drifting towards her.

Cinder felt like everything had slowed and grown dark – everything except him, the sun. Now she was being pulled into orbit. He was looking straight at her; there was no mistaking he was coming over. *I'm like the next planet now. What's its name?* Her brain spun. He was only a few steps away now. *I'm like... I'm like...* Now he was leaning in to talk to her over the music. *Mercury, Venus, Earth, Mars, Jupiter, Saturn, and I'm like?*

'Hi, I'm Angus,' the sun had spoken.

'I'm like Uranus,' the words escaped uncontrollably from Cinder's mouth.

'You like my what?' Angus asked, a cheeky smile creeping across his face.

'No!' Cinder blurted out.

'No?' Angus had a mock look of hurt on his face and turned to look at his backside.

'No, it's fine, very fine,' she stammered. 'I... the planet... I... I have to go talk to my friend.'

Cinder turned and hurried away, feeling extremely angry with herself. How could she have let a man make her feel like this? She was the strong, intimidating one. She spotted Marraine by the bar and hurried over.

'He's gorgeous. Why are you coming over here? I thought you were making a friend.' Marraine looked over Cinder's shoulder, took her drink from the bar, and raised it in the air, giving Angus a quick wink.

'Don't,' Cinder said through her teeth, as she pulled Marraine's arm down. 'I told him I like Uranus.'

'Wow,' Marraine giggled, 'I do have an exceptional butt, thanks, and talking about another woman's body is defiantly a good way to get a guy's attention.'

'No, he thinks I meant his butt.'

'Well, do you like it? Because it looks pretty good from over here.' She took a sip of her drink, holding her straw with her thumb and index finger and waving at Angus with the remaining fingers.

'No!' Cinder said again, moving in front of Marraine. 'I was talking about the planet.'

'Oh?' Marraine's giggle had now grown into a laugh. 'Probably best to steer clear of the science stuff first up,' she said, leaning in closer. 'Well, whatever you said seemed to work,' she nodded towards Angus. Cinder glanced over her shoulder.

'What do I do?' she asked, seeing him coming towards her.

'Don't worry, just get him talking about something he likes.' Marraine put her drink down on the bar and took a step towards Angus, stretching out her hand to shake his. 'Hi, I'm Marraine, I think you've already met my friend Cinder, she's into astronomy.' She turned with a flick of her hair and a quick wink before returning to her drink.

'Nice to meet you, ladies. I'm Angus. Cinder was it? I'm interested in the night sky too. I like to keep track of the moon cycles.' Cinder swallowed hard, her mind racing for a reply.

'I prefer the stars,' she said after a brief pause, 'I prefer when there's no moon.' *Get him talking about himself,* Cinder thought to herself. 'What else do you like to do when you're not moon gazing or meeting strange girls in bars?'

Angus could feel himself staring into Cinder's eyes, but he couldn't help himself. He had never seen eyes that deep shade of green before. Now those eyes were staring back. *She's looking right at me, oh that's because she said something to me!* Angus's brain was playing catch up. *What did she say?* 'I like surfing,' he said after what he hoped was only a short time.

'I love surfing,' Cinder called out excitedly. 'Well, that is to say I love watching others surf, I can't swim and I'm terrified of water, but I love to watch. There's a surf beach called Tallo's Bluff just down the coast from my house, do you know it?'

'Yes, I've heard of it. We never go that far north, but yeah, I know where it is,' Angus replied, beaming.

'So, I use my telescope to stargaze at night, and to watch the surfers during the day,' Cinder continued before catching Marraine out of the corner of her eye, shaking her head from side to side.

'Do you ever go to the beach or just watch from a distance?' Angus asked, looking puzzled.

'No, I don't get out much and like I said, I'm scared of the water,' Cinder replied as Marraine put her face in one hand and took a long drink with the other.

'You should come watch us some time,' said Angus.

'We'd love to,' Marraine interrupted, coughing slightly as if choking on her drink.

'Well, we won't be going for a few nights now until the moon's back out, but sure come along then.' As soon as he had said this, Angus realised his friends would not like the idea. 'I'll just go let the others know, and then I'll come back and work out the details.' He turned quickly and walked off to find Dom. *What are you doing?* He thought to himself.

Cinder turned on Marraine with an accusatory look.

'What?' said Marraine as she flashed her perfect teeth and battered her eyelids innocently.

'What!' spat Cinder, 'We don't even know these people, and did you hear him? What kind of people surf at night?'

'Exciting ones. And very good-looking ones, apparently.' Marraine's response just angered Cinder further. She could feel her ears and cheeks getting hot.

'And the moon will be out!' she continued. 'My two biggest fears, the ocean and being stuck outside in the moonlight. What are we supposed to do, just hide somewhere and hope for the best?'

'Shhhhh,' Marraine interrupted her. 'Don't worry, I've got an idea, you just worry about enjoying yourself birthday girl, which reminds me, you don't have a drink.' Marraine turned back to the bar and signalled to the bar staff.

In the meantime, Angus had found Dom sitting at a table at the far end of the bar with Duncan and Blair. Duncan, at twenty-nine, was the oldest of their group and at seven foot two, he was also the tallest.

His bald head and bushy brown beard help to add to his commanding presence. Blair, on the other hand, had a cleanly shaven face and light brown shoulder-length hair pulled back in a ponytail. Blair was of average height but looked dwarfed by the other three. 'Did you set this up?' Angus said, giving Dom a friendly punch in the shoulder. Dom looked puzzled as he put his beer down on the table.

'What?'

'I've just been talking to a very nice, tall, red-headed girl, who has the greenest eyes I've ever seen and who says she likes surfing.'

'Nothing to do with me, mate, I swear, but well done.' Dom raised his glass to Angus.

'What are you doing over here with us then?' Blair interrupted.

'Um, well, I thought I should let you all know that I invited her to come watch us surfing.'

Dom, who had just taken a sip of his drink, spat some of his mouthful out and started choking on the rest.

'Ya what? Invited some girl you just met to come watch us, even I know that's a bad idea and you're supposed to be the smart one.'

'She's got a friend,' Angus stepped out of Dom's line of sight and pointed towards the two girls at the bar. Marraine was now sitting cross-legged on a barstool. She pushed her hair behind her ear, laughing at something Cinder had said.

'Great holy mother father!' Dom exclaimed. 'Of course, it's always good to make new friends. In fact, I think we're being very rude leaving them waiting over there.' Dom jumped off his seat and put his arm around Angus's back, patting him on the shoulder before walking off towards the girls, then remembering to grab his drink, said, 'Come on.'

Angus caught up with Dom just as he reached the two girls.

'Marraine, Cinder, this is my friend Dom. He's very excited that you're coming to watch us surf.'

Dom did not attempt to hide the fact that he was looking Marraine up and down.

'Bonjour, mademoiselle,' said Dom, cutting Angus off.

'Bonsoir. Est-ce que vous parlez français?' asked Marraine, raising one of her eyebrows sceptically.

'Oui,' replied Dom confidently, moving his gaze from her eyes to her lips. Marraine ran her tongue slowly along the front of her teeth and leant closer to Dom.

'Êtes-vous un cochon stupide?'

'Oui,' Dom replied again, moving over to lean on the bar in front of Marraine. She looked at him and rested her hand on his.

'Allez-vous continuer à dire oui, dans l'espoir qu'on aille chez vous?' she asked.

Dom now looked far less confident.

'Um... arr... Oui.'

'Interesting,' said Marraine, turning around on her stool to give her attention back to Angus. 'So, Angus, Cinder was just saying she wanted to ask you about your tattoo.'

'Oh, okay,' Angus turned over his right arm to reveal a black anchor that took up most of the space between his palm and elbow on his muscular forearm. Cinder felt slightly embarrassed and could feel her cheeks turning red again.

'It's an anchor obviously, but what does the writing say?' she asked as she took hold of his arm and moved in closer for a better look. Angus's dark stubbled cheeks were now also turning rosy.

'Pride before your pride.' Cinder read aloud the words on a banner that wound its way down the length of the anchor. 'What does it mean?' she asked, looking up into his dark brown eyes.

'I'm going to get some drinks and find us a table,' interrupted Dom. 'What can I get you, ladies?'

'Red wine, please,' replied Cinder, not taking her eyes off Angus.

'Surprise me,' said Marraine, flicking her hand in the air as if to swat away a fly. Dom, looking dejected, disappeared to the other end of the bar. Angus looked over at Marraine.

'J'espère que... er... le loup ne vas pas faire envoler... la maison,' he said.

Marraine laughed.

'Oui,' she replied, nodding at Cinder, 'I like this one, handsome, funny, and smart.' Cinder shot a look of concern at Marraine, but she was listening to Angus continuing about his tattoo.

'The first pride is like a lion's pride. You know your family, friends, loved ones, the people that are important to you. So, it means putting the needs of all those people before your own glory. Your Pride before your pride.'

'I like that. But why the anchor?' Cinder asked, absentmindedly running her finger down Angus's arm. He swallowed hard before continuing.

'My family has a long history of making mistakes while showing off. I'm actually named after one of them, Angus MacAskill is my full name, but Angus MacAskill or Black Angus was the world's tallest natural giant, and some say the world's strongest man. He was seven foot ten and could carry a full beer barrel under each arm. Unfortunately, one day he got too cocky and took a bet to lift a three-thousand-pound anchor. He slipped while he was putting it down and broke his ribs and shoulder and was never the same again. So, the anchor's there to remind me to always make good decisions and not let arrogance get the better of me.' Cinder, who was still holding his arm and looking into his eyes, suddenly realised what she was doing and put Angus's arm down next to his side.

Dom returned with the drinks. 'So, Angus, how did you meet these lovely ladies?' he probed as his eyes traced the shape of Marraine's legs.

'Cinder told me I have a nice bum,' Angus joked. Cinder's eyes widened desperately.

'No!' she called, pointing a finger at Angus, and then, 'No!' again, as she pointed at Marraine, whose lips had curled into a grin. 'I was talking about the planet Uranus,' she clarified with Dom. 'I'm into astronomy.'

'Hey, I hear you. That's cool with me,' Dom answered, leaning on the bar next to Marraine. 'I like watching heavenly bodies too.' He handed Marraine her drink. 'I could stare at Uranus all night.' Marraine studied her drink, unsure of what the liquid under the mess of straws, umbrellas, and fruit actually was.

'I hear they're looking for people to go to Mars. It's a one-way trip, maybe you should volunteer, do the world a favour.'

'Touché,' Dom replied, smiling and handing Cinder her wine.

'Oh wow,' said Marraine, holding up her glass. 'A French word he actually seems to know the meaning of.'

'All right, all right.' Dom flung his arms up in surrender. Angus and Cinder started to laugh.

Dom suggested they sit at the table with the others. As they all agreed and started moving off, Cinder pulled Marraine aside with a look of concern on her face. 'My French isn't very good, but I'm sure I heard Angus say something about a wolf, did he?' Marraine placed her hand reassuringly on Cinder's shoulder.

'It's okay, he just made a joke.' Marraine said. Cinder looked puzzled. 'I may have referred to the obnoxious one, as a pig who was just interested in getting me into bed.' Marraine nodded her head in Dom's direction. 'Your boyfriend there,' she looked at Angus, 'said he hopes that a wolf doesn't blow his house down.'

'Oh,' said Cinder, a smile creeping into the corners of her lips as they continued walking over to the table. 'Hey!' she said, after thinking for a moment. 'He's not my boyfriend,' she called to Marraine as she moved off in front of her.

'Okay good, you won't mind if I take him home with me tonight then,' Marraine replied with a cheeky wink.

'I... um... I,' Cinder didn't know how to reply.

'Come on,' Marraine said, walking backwards with a wide-eyed smile and her hand in front of her face, her index finger moving back and forth, beckoning Cinder forward.

Cinder was above average height, and in heels would usually look down on most men, but as she approached the table and Angus's friends rose to offer their seats and introduce themselves, she couldn't help noticing how tall they all were. 'So?' she said as she sat down on a stool that was still warm from Duncan's rather large backside. 'Are you all related to the other Angus, the giant, um, the anchor man?' She asked. Dom, Blair, and Duncan burst into laughter simultaneously. Duncan's wide chest heaved in and out and a wide smile appeared through his black beard.

'Did you hear that Black, do ya want us to start calling ya 'Anchorman'?' he called to Angus.

'I've been calling him something that rhymes with anchor for years,' blurted out Dom, in between laughs.

'Yes,' interrupted Angus, shaking his head back and forth slowly, 'unfortunately, this comedy trio are all my *very distant* family.'

'Some of us are more distant than others, aren't we hey?' Duncan piped in, whacking Dom on the shoulder and continuing to laugh.

'So, you've all got a bit of giant in you?' Cinder continued when the laughter died down.

'We sure do have a little bit of giant in us. Would you like a little bit of giant in you?' Dom asked, turning to Marraine.

'The giant bit sounds intriguing,' she replied, while reaching out and playing with his top button, 'but your little bit isn't coming anywhere near me.' She pulled her hand slowly back, wiggling her little finger in the air. The entire group erupted with laughter again, even Dom.

'Are any of you strong like the other Angus?' Marraine asked, looking Duncan up and down.

'Yep, I'm most likely the strongest one in here, strong enough to pick you up,' Dom said as he grabbed a stool from another table and wedged it in beside Marraine's.

'Um I think your aftershave's probably the strongest thing in here actually,' she replied while crossing her legs the other way and turning her shoulders so that her back was to Dom. 'What does he do, bath in it?' she asked Blair who laughed and nodded in agreement. Dom pinched his shirt and pulled it up to his nose, giving it a few good sniffs before shrugging his shoulders.

Cinder didn't know if it was the joking, or the alcohol going to her head, but she was really enjoying herself.

'I'm... I'm really... strong...' she called out in a voice much slower than she had expected. 'TOO!' she finished with a giggle. 'Even stronger than Dom's aftershave, which is very nice, so don't listen to her.' She leant across the table and patted Dom on the chest.

'Alright then, prove it,' said Dom, grabbing her hand. 'Let's arm wrestle.'

'I wouldn't want to hurt you,' replied Cinder, trying her best to keep a straight face.

'Hang on, hang on, the other boys'll want to see this,' Duncan called out before putting two fingers in his mouth and whistling loudly, waving with his free arm to the others, who were on another table a few metres away.

'C'mon boys Dom's gonna get 'imself beat by a girl.'

A few minutes later, a small crowd had gathered around the table, all making pretend bets of one, two, or five dollars. Dom and Cinder sat opposite each other, hand in hand, with their elbows on the table, staring fiercely at each other. Blair stood behind Dom, massaging his shoulders, whispering words of encouragement into his ear. 'Don't hurt him, missy. He's got to work tomorrow morning, and he'll use any excuse to get out of it,' Duncan called across the table.

'Okay, on the count of three. One, two, three, go.'

To begin with, Dom was merely playing with Cinder. He was smiling, laughing, and making mock grunting noises. Shortly though, Dom fell silent, his smile replaced by gritted teeth and a furrowed brow. Marraine, noticing that Dom's hand was slowly but surely moving towards the table, sauntered behind Dom. She placed one hand on each of his shoulders and leant in very close, her lips just centimetres from his right ear. She whispered something that only Dom could hear, before running her tongue around the edge of his ear, from lobe to top. Dom sat up straight and his eyes looked as if they might pop out of their sockets. As he did, Cinder pushed his hand down to the table with a thud and rattle of empty glasses. Cheers and laughter erupted from the small crowd of onlookers.

'That's not fair, not fair!' Dom tried to call over the crowd. Angus came over and patted him on the back.

'You know what they say. All's fair in love and war,' he said. Dom looked up at Angus, smiling.

'Yeah, but I'm not really sure which one of those I'm in.'

'What did you say to him?' Cinder asked as Marraine sat back down next to her.

'I told him if he won, you and I would kiss.' Cinder flashed red again.

'I... I wouldn't... I... haven't.'

'It's okay,' Marraine assured her, laughing and poking Cinder's side with her elbow, 'I know you don't kiss girls, I was just joking.' Cinder looked down at her feet and then leant in to whisper in Marraine's ear.

'I've never kissed anyone.' Marraine started to laugh again, but when she saw the look on Cinder's face, she realised she was serious.

'I guess I suspected that, but I had hoped things weren't that bad. We need to fix that, sweetie. Come on, we're dancing.' With that, Marraine took Cinder's arm and pulled her towards the front door of the pub.

In the front right corner, there was a small stage, and an area left free of tables for people to dance. A duo was playing music. A man and a woman in their mid-30s, dressed in all black. He had dark hair, wore a pair of thick-rimmed black glasses, and was playing an acoustic guitar. His partner was a pretty blonde lady playing a variety of percussion instruments, who in Cinder's opinion, was wearing a dress that was slightly too tight for her voluptuous body. Although everyone sitting around the dance floor appeared to be enjoying the music, nobody was dancing. Marraine walked to the middle of the dance floor while Cinder stood at the edge. After waiting for the song to finish and clapping along with the others, Marraine removed a fifty-dollar note from somewhere down her dress, handing it to the woman on stage. 'Hi Tammy, can you give us something to dance to?'

'Something sexy?' asked the guitarist with a smile.

'You know me, Andy,' replied Marraine, winking as she turned and walked back to Cinder.

Cinder looked like a frightened kitten that had climbed too high in a tree. 'What's wrong?' Marraine asked, taking her by both hands and leading her onto the dance floor as the band started the next song.

'I don't know how to dance. I don't want to make a fool of myself.'

'You know what looks worse than someone on a dance floor who can't dance?' Marraine asked as she swayed her hips from side to side. 'Someone standing on the edge of a dance floor, not dancing. Besides, we're two gorgeous women dancing together – no one's going to be looking at your dance moves. The women are going to be looking at how we have too little clothing and too much make-up and the men, well let's just say they're not going to be looking at your moves.' With that, she put one of Cinder's arms up and spun her around, slapping her backside as it went by. Cinder laughed. 'And anyway girlfriend,' Marraine continued, 'surely with all that training you do you've got all sorts of moves.' Marraine did her best impression of a martial-arts-fighting stance and then started karate chopping Cinder's arms. Cinder joined in and after a short time felt like she was doing something that could be considered dancing.

'What are you doing?' Dom asked as he handed Angus another drink. Angus took a long drink and tried to look Dom in the eyes, but his gaze kept on involuntarily going back to Cinder's swaying hips.

'What do you mean?' he asked.

'I mean, why are you over here drinking with us, not over there dancing with them?'

'Have you ever known me to dance?'

'No, but we had a deal.'

'No,' said Angus, shaking his head, 'I said I'd talk to her. I didn't say anything about dancing.' Dom took Angus's drink from him and put both their drinks down on the table.

'We're dancing,' he said, grabbing Angus in a headlock and dragging him towards the dance floor.

Dom put an arm around Marraine's waist and gently pulled her away from Cinder. Cinder felt a different hand on her waist, a much larger, warmer hand. A stubbly cheek brushed against her ear as a deep voice whispered, 'I'm not very good. Can you help me?' Cinder turned to look up into Angus's face, his large brown eyes helping to make him look like a lost puppy. Before she realised what she was doing, Cinder placed her arms around his neck.

'I don't know what I'm doing either, we can look bad together.' Angus put his other hand on her back.

'I don't think you could look bad, I mean you look good, I mean you look like you know what you're doing.' Angus blushed, but Cinder smiled and started swaying along to the music more confidently.

A few minutes later, the song ended, and the duo played a slower song.

• • • •

*If I move too slow, if I move too soon.*
*I'm bewitched by you,*
*And that old devil moon*
*Hand in your hand, stars in the skies*
*Is that the devil or the moon, I see in your eyes?*

• • • •

More couples, encouraged by the occupied dance floor, made their way forward to join them. Angus pulled Cinder in closer and, in doing so, moved his hands lower down her back. Cinder relaxed her hands onto his firm shoulders and brought her head closer to his chest. His heart, like hers was beating fast. She looked back up at his face and could see herself in his eyes. Angus started moving his head down towards hers. Cinder took a deep breath through her nose and held it as she moistened her lips with her tongue. 'Do you want another drink?' Angus asked.

'What?'

'Do you want a drink?' Angus asked again, 'I'm getting one.'

'Um, okay, just another glass of red wine, thanks.'

Angus walked away, leaving Cinder feeling exposed, awkward, and confused. Dom grabbed her hand and spun her around to dance with him and Marraine.

'Where's he going?' he asked.

'Going to get drinks,' Cinder called over the music with a shrug of her shoulders. Dom looked over at Angus at the bar, shaking his head.

'Idiot. Oh well, now I get to dance with two beautiful women, his loss.'

• • • •

A warm breeze rising from the tarmac, flicked strands of auburn hair across a mirrored pair of Gucci sunglasses. Two frown lines appeared on the usually line-free brow above the lenses. The smell of aviation fuel burning in the pre-flight check of the Embraer Legacy 600's Rolls-Royce engines had sparked a memory. A memory that was quickly smouldering into a thought.

The frown lines faded, and the lenses turned slowly to reveal two large men looking remarkably cool and calm for people who had been standing in the scorching sun in black suits and ties.

'Is he ready for us?' Louvelle asked, in a tone that sounded more like an order than a question.

'Shortly, Lady Gevaudan,' Tibult, the nearer of the two brothers, answered in his deep Caribbean accent. 'Do you think we will have a warmer welcome this time?'

Louvelle strolled gracefully towards a large metal chest that was waiting to be loaded onto her aircraft.

'Are you worried about me, Tibult?'

'It is my job to worry about you, my queen, and my pleasure,' Tibult replied, with a small bow of his head. A smile curved the ends of Louvelle's blood-red lips, and she ran her hands over the cold metal lid.

'What would I do without you two?' she asked. 'I wouldn't worry so much, my dear; we are bringing a gift this time.' Louvelle unclipped two large twist-latch clamps, opening the lid with a hiss of escaping air. At the bottom of the chest, lying in an S shape, was a petite, young woman with long silky black hair and pale skin. She was motionless except for the shallow rise and fall of her chest as she breathed.

Tibult's head twisted towards a sound coming from the small black device concealed in his right ear.

'They are ready for you now, my lady,' he announced.

Louvelle closed the lid and secured the latches.

'Thank you, Tibult. Can you make sure this finds its place?' She tapped her long fingernails on the metal lid. 'Lysander, you can stay with me.'

With a nod of Louvelle's head and a wave of her hand, Tibult rolled the chest towards the waiting aircraft. Lysander walked closer to his queen, standing tall and straight with his hands held behind his back.

'Can I help you, my lady?'

'Yes,' Louvelle replied, resting her hand on Lysander's wide, firm chest.

'Is there something you need me to do when we get to Bucharest, my lady?'

Louvelle smiled, tapping her index finger on the top button of Lysander's shirt.

'No, in fact, you won't be coming with us.'

'No?'

'No, all this talk of gifts has reminded me that there is a birthday I have overlooked.'

# Chapter 3

**Old Devil Moon**

M*y heart it leads and beckons me*
*to follow him and be free.*
*Where ocean and darkness entwine thee,*
*both slave and master to the sea.*

• • • •

A short, middle-aged man with balding black hair looked about anxiously, as a cigarette ashed slowly towards his stubby fingers. He stood at the rear corner of The Big House, running his eyes expectantly along the tree line. A woman in a long, black coat and hood shadowing her face appeared beside the trunk of one of the larger trees. After taking one last look around, the man indicated for her to come forward, with a slight movement of his unoccupied hand. The woman strolled confidently across the lush, green lawns, her hands buried deep in large pockets at her hips.

'Good afternoon, Marraine.' The man said when she has close enough to hear his hushed voice.

'Good afternoon, Bob,' Marraine replied, pulling back her hood. 'Anyone sniffing around here today?' she asked.

'They are all busy in the west wing.' Bob nodded towards the front of the property.

'Thanks, Bob. You're a sweetheart.' Marraine leant in and kissed his cheek. Bob opened his mouth but could not form any words.

Marraine went inside and made her way quickly and silently to the top floor of the neglected east wing of The Big House. Cinder made sure that the library on the second floor was clean and organised, but most of the rooms at this end were used for storage or had become moth-eaten and mouldy. Cinder didn't mind though, it meant that visitors were not invited to this end of the house and her mother rarely ventured out of the west wing. Between the permanent staff, Louvelle's security detail, and the comings and goings of her business dealings, there could be up to sixty people shuffling around busily in the renovated and maintained western end of The Big House. Other than her maid, the occasional cleaner, or nervous, sweaty lackey sent to search through dusty old boxes, Cinder usually had the east wing to herself. She also liked the view of the ocean from this end of the house. Marraine walked to a door at the far end of the hall. She knocked three times quickly and then three times slowly.

Cinder's bedroom was a contradiction. It was small, but Louvelle had converted the adjoining room into a walk-in robe and ensuite. Her bed, which took up most of the room, was like something out of a fairy tale. A white four-poster with lacey curtains and covered with silk sheets and fluffy pink cushions. The bed was Louvelle's contribution to the room, an attempt to make Cinder a lady. Each morning a maid arranged the pillows and cushions perfectly. Not that Louvelle ever came to check. The colour of the rest of Cinder's room was predominantly black, because Cinder had painted the walls with chalkboard paint; smuggled in by Bob. There were no more perfectly placed cushions around, instead, there were random piles of books and magazines, covered in a layer of chalk dust from the ever-changing murals and poetry on her walls. Besides the telescope and the bed, there was one other piece of furniture, an old armchair that was the partner of the couch that Cinder used in the basement gym. This is where Cinder was sitting, one eye looking through her telescope and one leg tucked up to her chest, supporting her chin.

'Come in,' she responded to Marraine's knock.

Cinder smiled with excited anticipation. For the week that followed their night out in Heathcote, her normal routine had gone completely out the window. Cinder, Marraine, and the boys had laughed and danced into the early hours of Saturday morning. She had awoken in Marraine's bed with a sore head and no voice, but feeling more excited than she could ever remember. She had tried to concentrate on her studies and training with little success. Any words she tried to read seemed to turn into the songs that she was humming to herself and on more than one occasion, she found herself holding onto her boxing bag, swaying with her head resting against it, remembering the feeling of Angus's chest. They had made plans to meet up with the boys again at sunset the following Saturday, and although Marraine assured her everything would be fine, Cinder was still worried about going out in the night with people she didn't know. The week seemed to last a lifetime, but the day had finally arrived.

'Are you ready to go?' Marraine asked, looking Cinder up and down.

'Yep,' replied Cinder, standing up to reveal the bloodstains that were still visible on her old track pants.

'No sweetie, you're not,' said Marraine, walking into Cinder's wardrobe. 'I'm sure you've got some jeans in here somewhere and those boots I gave you last Christmas... Ah, here they are.' She lifted the boots and threw some jeans at Cinder. 'And these too.'

Two tops came flying at Cinder's head and she caught them just before they hit her in the face.

'We're just going to sit on a beach, hidden in the dark somewhere. Why do I need to dress nicely?' Cinder asked as she inspected the clothes on her lap. 'And why are you looking in there?' Cinder got up and pushed closed her underwear draw.

'You never know what might happen,' said Marraine, as she sat down on the bed smirking. 'Come on, get dressed.'

Cinder shuffled into her wardrobe and started putting on the clothes that Marraine had picked out. 'I still don't know why I need to get changed,' she complained.

'Because,' Marraine answered as she drew a stick figure hanging from a noose on one of the blackboard walls, 'tonight is going to be one of the most important nights of your life.' She drew long red hair on the stick figure. 'Hopefully for more than just one reason.' She dusted the chalk off her hands, looking very pleased about her work. 'Now, most importantly,' she picked Cinder's tree and moon pendant up off one of the book piles, 'you need to keep this on and hidden at all times.' She hung the pendant over Cinder's head and ignored the questioning look on her face. 'Come on, come on,' she pushed Cinder out of the door.

· · · ·

The surf beach was at the west end of Heathcote. Cinder wanted to ride her bike and offered one to Marraine. Marraine refused and organised a taxi. When they arrived, the sun had already disappeared behind the hills. A few people were using the remaining pink-orange light to catch their last few waves, and a couple played fetch with a chubby, old Labrador. Off to her right, Cinder could see a large concave in a stone wall that rose from the beach. Centuries of water had washed away the bottom of the wall, creating a shadowy overhang that Cinder thought would make a perfect place to sit and hide in the darkness. However, despite Cinder's growing apprehension, Marraine appeared in no hurry to move out of the carpark and down onto the beach. 'Shouldn't we get out of the open? It will be dark soon.' Cinder had a pleading tone in her voice, but Marraine simply answered, 'Trust me.'

Five minutes later, two surfboard-topped cars arrived. Duncan was the first to get out and came straight over to them, lifting both of them off the ground in one giant-armed bear hug.

'Evening ladies. These three here,' he pointed to the others who got out of the car with him, 'be the brothers. Ya didn't meet them lot last time. The two carrot tops are the twins, Rory and Tavish, and pretty boy blondie there is their little brother, Bowie.' The three brothers waved and then unloaded the car. In the meantime, Angus, Dom, and

Blair had emerged from the second car. Dom whispered something in Angus's ear before pushing him towards where Cinder and Marraine were standing.

Angus's stubbly, pale face lit up when he saw the girls waiting, but flashed pink when Dom and Blair showered him with a chorus of wolf-whistling as he approached Cinder. 'I was worried that you weren't going to come,' he said, trying not to get lost in Cinder's eyes again, which was made more difficult by the fact that they looked even more amazing in the twilight than they did under the lights of Paddy's.

'We wouldn't miss it,' replied Marraine, bringing Angus back to reality. 'Night surfing, you're either stupid or brave.' She looked over at Dom. 'I think I know which one of those he is but the jury's still out with you.'

'Isn't it dangerous?' interrupted Cinder, fidgeting nervously.

'Well, that's kind of the point,' answered Angus with a smile. 'That's what makes it more exci...' he stopped because Cinder had just pulled her hood over her head and pulled her sleeves over her hands. 'Are you cold? I'll go get you a blanket.' Angus jogged back to the car.

'What are you doing?' Marraine asked. 'I said to trust me, you look petrified.'

'I do trust you, but it's dark out now.' Marraine reached her hand towards her neck. Taking hold of a gold link chain, she pulled it up slowly, revealing a pendant from under her collar. Except for boasting a blue moon instead of red, it was identical to the one she had given Cinder. She quickly tucked her pendant away, then pulled off Cinder's hood with a flick of her wrist.

'Trust me,' she said again. Cinder looked at Marraine, completely bewildered.

'How's that going to help us?'

Before Marraine could answer, Angus returned and wrapped a blanket around Cinder's shoulders.

'Thank you,' said Cinder. Marraine just smiled and gave her a wink.

'You coming, lover boy?' yelled Dom from the top of the steps leading down to the beach.

'After you, ladies,' said Angus as he motioned towards the ocean.

Cinder and Marraine sat huddled together under the blanket. Angus sat a short distance away. Cinder watched as the breeze ruffled Angus's thick black hair and the moonlight played at the corners of his eyes. The joy on his face as he watched his friends on the ocean, was remedial to her fears. 'Do you want to have a go?' Angus asked, spotting Cinder looking at him.

'No, no, no,' Cinder replied, turning quickly to look out at the others paddling on top of the black water. 'I'm happy watching.'

Cinder watched as the dark figures bobbed up and down amongst the silver shimmer on the surface of the ocean. Someone she couldn't recognise caught a large, rolling wave and raced towards the shore. 'I can't believe you really do this. I mean, when you told me about night surfing, this is what I imagined, but then I thought it must be something different.'

'So, you've been thinking about me?' Angus asked.

'Fantasizing, I would say,' Marraine interrupted.

'No, I've been thinking about all of them,' Cinder corrected her.

'Kinky,' Marraine teased. Cinder nudged her.

'If you two are going to pick on me, I won't say anything,' Cinder said, crossing her arms over her chest.

'I'm sorry, I'll be good,' Angus said, shuffling closer to her. 'What did you think would be different about it?'

'I guess I thought you might have a boat with lots of lights or maybe that you might just splash around in the shallows,' Cinder said with a shrug of her shoulders. 'But this is real surfing, real danger.'

'Is it better watching up close, instead of through your telescope?' Angus asked, shooting her a sideways grin.

'It's much better up close,' she replied, holding eye contact with him for a few heartbeats. Angus picked up a small stick of driftwood and drew circles in the sand.

'We're all glad you could make it. You two definitely made an impression. You have been the topic of conversation all week.'

'Oh, really?' Cinder asked. 'Now who has been fantasizing?'

Angus smiled and stuck the stick in the sand in front of him.

'Guilty as charged,' he admitted, throwing his hands up in the air. 'So, what would you two usually be doing on a Saturday night, anyway?' He asked, changing the subject.

'Stargazing, reading, hitting the gym,' Cinder replied.

'International espionage and domestic duties,' Marraine said with a wink.

The edge of the water slowly inched further away as the tide receded; the water-smoothed sand, glimmering in the silver glow of the waxing moon. Powerful waves rose and crashed, echoing off the cliff faces that bounded both ends of the beach. The surfers laughed and yelled, their words indecipherable to the three spectators on the sand.

'You can join them if you want. You don't need to babysit us,' Cinder said to Angus, seeing the joy that the sounds of his friends gave him.

'I'm fine here,' Angus said, laying down and leaning on his elbow so that his head moved even closer to Cinder.

'Are you sure?' she asked.

'Yep. This is my happy place.' He looked around the beach, the ocean, and the lights of Heathcote in the hills behind them. 'Where is your happy place?' he asked, watching her hair flick and dance around her shoulders. Cinder turned her head towards where she knew her house was. No happiness there, she thought.

'I know,' she said, after thinking for a moment. 'Out there.' She pointed up to the stars.

'It would be better without the moon,' Cinder and Angus said at the same time. Then they burst into laughter.

Rory and Tavish emerged from the water, carrying their boards up the beach. 'They're going to start getting a fire ready,' Angus explained. 'Their skin is so pale that they are worried about getting moon burn.' He joked. Cinder laughed again.

'I'm going to take a closer look.' Marraine said, taking Cinder's laughter as her cue. She stood up, brushing off the sand as she walked down to the water's edge; slipping off her shoes and rolling up the bottom of her jeans. Cinder had been sitting close to Marraine. Now that she was in the breeze, she shivered. Angus moved next to her and put his arm around her shoulder.

'Thanks,' Cinder said, smiling and putting her head on his shoulder. Remembering how nice his chest felt, she started moving her hand towards him.

Down at the water's edge, Dom was excited to see Marraine standing closer to the water. He splashed his way out of the shallows.

'Hello beautiful,' he said, standing his board up in the sand and shaking water out of his messy, dark hair.

'Bonjour, Monsieur Dom,' she replied sarcastically.

'You know I can't actually speak French, don't you?' asked Dom as he deliberately unzipped his wetsuit to show off his muscular torso. Marraine continued to stare out into the ocean, apparently unimpressed.

'Oui,' she replied with a slight smile and momentary glance. Dom turned to look up the beach at Cinder and Angus.

'You coming in or what?' he yelled out, with his hands cupped around his mouth.

'Yeah, yeah alright, I'm coming.' Angus hollered back. As he stood up to get his board, Cinder's hand brushed against his chest. 'I'd better go. Will you be okay here?' he asked.

'Yep, sure, I'm fine,' Cinder lied.

'Imbecile,' spat Marraine, as she kicked water up in Dom's face, turned, and walked back up the beach, shaking her head at Angus as she passed him coming the other way.

'What did I do?' Dom called out to her. 'What did I do?' he asked Angus when he was next to him. Angus just shrugged his shoulders. 'What about you? Looked like things were going well,' Dom asked as he walked back into the ocean. Angus just shrugged again. Seeing the moonlit look of disappointment on Cinder's face, Marraine sat down and climbed back under the blanket with her.

'Don't worry,' she said, pulling Cinder's head onto her shoulder, 'the night is still young.'

'It's okay, it will give us a chance to talk.' Cinder leant closer to Marraine. 'What the hell's going on here?'

'We're sitting on the beach enjoying the company of some nice people,' Marraine replied, looking down at her with a grin. Cinder sat up.

'I'm serious. Here we are, all hanging outside on a moonlit night, and everyone's fine with it. I'm okay and you're okay and they...' she pointed to their new friends, 'they what? Do this all the time?' Marraine pulled Cinder's head back onto her shoulder.

'It will all make sense in time, sweetie.'

Cinder sat her hand on Marraine's lap.

'I feel like my whole life's been a lie. It has something to do with this, doesn't it?' Cinder pulled out her pendant. It had an almost unnatural glow in the light of the crescent moon, which was now high in the sky. But before Marraine could say anything, Cinder turned to look back up the beach. They had both sensed it. Someone was coming down the stairs. A large dark figure was moving slowly towards them.

'Don't worry, it's just me, Uncle Gunn,' said an old, kind-sounding voice from the shadows. When Gunn's face was in the moonlight, Cinder could see him put his thumb and little finger in his mouth before he let out a remarkably loud whistle. 'Ello boys,' he waved, and the surfers waved back. 'Well now, you two must be the young ladies I've been hearing about.'

'Good things I hope,' said Marraine, flashing her perfect teeth in the moonlight.

'Good's just a matter of opinion, I always say. But I did hear that one of you beat my boy in an arm wrestle and anything that puts him in his place is good in my opinion.' Gunn's large belly wobbled up and down as he chuckled to himself.

'That would be Cinder here, and I'm Marraine,' Marraine said, holding out her hand. Gunn lent down and shook their hands in turn.

'You can call me Uncle Gunn, everyone else around here does. That's a nice pendant you have there, lass.'

Cinder had forgotten that she had taken the pendant out.

'Oh, thank you,' she said as she tucked it back under her top. 'I got it last week for my birthday, my 18$^{th}$.' She wasn't sure why she lied; people just often mistook her for being younger.

'Well, happy birthday, love.'

Gunn stood, looking proudly out into the ocean. 'So, I have heard Dom's side of the story about the arm wrestling, but how did you all come to meet?' Cinder and Marraine recounted their recollection of the events from the week before. Gunn listened intently and chuckled to himself. He looked like he was about to ask something else, but a fire that had sprung up on the cliff above distracted him. 'Looks like the twins have got the fire going. They're going to finish up now and just do some boy stuff. If you girls want to hang around, our place is only fifteen minutes' walk, well twenty for me these days, and I make a mean hot chocolate.'

'A hot chocolate sounds fabulous,' said Marraine as she stood up and dusted the sand off her cold backside. 'It's getting very chilly out here now.'

Gunn whistled again, waving one of his large hands above his head. Cupping his hands around his mouth, he yelled towards the ocean, 'Hey lads! I'm taking these young ladies back to the house!' Angus waved back to acknowledge that he had received the message. Gunn gave him a thumbs up before pointing towards the fire on the hill. 'Okay let's go.'

Marraine helped Cinder to her feet, and they followed Gunn as he made his way slowly up the soft sand and the wooden steps.

Cinder had never met someone who could talk so much. Gunn talked continually the whole walk back to the farm. Cinder felt like she learned more in those 20 minutes than she had all year from her tutors. Gunn talked about everything from dairy farming to politics, sport, and some fascinating things that Cinder had never heard about local history. In what felt like no time at all, they were sitting down in time-worn armchairs, sipping hot chocolate in front of an open fire. Although everything here looked far more rustic and lived-in than anything in The Big House, Uncle Gunn's family room reminded Cinder of how the sitting room felt when her father was alive. It was relieving to be warm and inside out of the dark.

'Do you mind if I smoke?' asked Gunn, holding up his pipe.

'No, not at all,' Marraine answered, smiling. 'The hot chocolate is lovely, thank you.' Gunn nodded in reply as he lit his pipe. Cinder had been staring at an old black-and-white photo on the wall above the fireplace.

'Is that the other Angus, the giant one?'

'Ah yes,' answered Gunn, standing up and pointing his pipe towards the photo. 'They told you about Black Angus, did they?' Marraine and Cinder nodded in unison. Gunn walked over to the photo. 'Angus MacAskill, born on the Isle of Berneray, Scotland and immigrated to Nova Scotia. He was the world's largest "true" giant, eventually reaching seven feet ten and weighing almost six hundred pounds. He was in show business, you know?' Gunn turned and looked at the others. 'He worked for P. T. Barnum's circus, with Tom Thumb. They say he could carry barrels weighing over 300 pounds apiece under each arm. You must be pretty strong yourself?' Gunn turned and looked at Cinder.

'Me?' replied Cinder, surprised.

'Yes, beating my boy in an arm wrestle.'

'That was teamwork, actually,' interrupted Marraine.

'Teamwork?'

'Yes, I distracted him, if you know what I mean?' Marraine explained.

'Oh yes, I understand,' replied Gunn, laughing to himself. 'That's the story of my boy's life, unfortunately. I can see it on his headstone, "Dominic James Kinnaird. Died young. Distracted by a beautiful woman."'

'I think he's a very nice young man,' said Cinder in Dom's defence. Gunn smiled.

'And that's just what he'd like you to think. Don't get me wrong, I'm very proud of him. He's extremely loyal and has always excelled at whatever he puts his mind to. But... let's just say that there are a lot of young ladies out there that thought he was a nice young man when they met him but wouldn't feel that way now.'

Marraine smiled to herself, finishing her hot chocolate. 'He's very handsome, I'll give him that,' she said as she put her cup down.

'Yes,' said Gunn as he sat back in his seat, 'he got his good looks from his mother, obviously.' A look of sadness came over his face as he watched smoke rise slowly from his mouth. 'Now you ladies,' he said, a warm smile returning to his face, 'we always have guest rooms made up and we would be more than happy for you to stay.'

'Oh, I'm not sure,' said Cinder, moving her head slowly from side to side.

'Nonsense,' Marraine interrupted her, 'of course we'll stay. I couldn't possibly leave without another of these hot chocolates in the morning.'

'Good, good,' said Gunn, smiling at Marraine and then turning to raise his large eyebrows questioningly at Cinder.

'Okay, I guess we're staying then,' said Cinder, shrugging her shoulders.

• • • •

Angus was leaning with his back against a tree stump, his chin resting on top of his naginata. He watched as a translucent white cloud drifted over the crescent moon, giving the impression that it was actually the moon moving through the cloud. He smiled to himself as he thought about how rarely he could just sit and enjoy the night. Dom walked up to him, spinning his tomahawks around his fingers like a spaghetti western gunslinger.

'What are we even doing here, Black?' He blew imaginary smoke off the end of the tomahawk handles, before tucking them into his belt. 'They haven't attacked in weeks.'

Angus stood up straight and put his weapon across his shoulders.

'Gunn says when they start acting different, good or bad, is when we have to be most vigilant.'

'Well, have fun with that,' Dom started walking off.

'What are you doing?' Angus asked, coming after him.

'Black! There's two hot chicks sitting at home right now, and we're here watching playtime at the zoo. I'm sure you'll be okay without me.'

'Dom?'

Dom walked off into the darkness, leaving Angus standing by himself. A few metres away, hidden in the shadows of the forest, a large brown creature was scratching its back against a tree.

# Chapter 4

**No Place Like Home**

T*here's no place like home, no place like home, no place...*
*Thank God for that.*

• • • •

Cinder awoke in a panic, her sleepy mind processing the unfamiliar sounds, smells, and textures. Once she had orientated herself, she could see Marraine, naked and fast asleep in the bed on the other side of the room. Trying not to wake her, Cinder pulled her hair back into a ponytail and fumbled around on the floor to find where she had thrown her clothes. She had slept well for being in a strange place. The nightly visions of teeth, hair, and blood only woke her once. She slipped on her jeans and t-shirt, decided that her shoes were too hard to find, and shuffled her way to the door. Stretching and squinting, she pulled the door open quietly and walked outside. A cold, overcast morning greeted her.

Rolling green paddocks extended out in front of Cinder, lined with stone walls and old oak trees. She could smell coffee brewing, fresh bread baking, and the fire that Uncle Gunn had just lit inside the main house. Over the distant rumble of the ocean, she could hear birds looking for food. Other than that, everything was still and quiet. A gentle chilly breeze blew over the paddocks towards her and made goosebumps on her bare arms. As she tucked a stray hair behind her ear, she took a deep breath of the morning air. The grey clouds that framed the surrounding hills carried the promise of rain, but that did not dampen her mood. To Cinder, this whole place smelled of something she had not experienced for a long time; 'freedom,' she whispered to herself as she breathed the word out. It was ironic, she thought, feeling more at home here among strangers than she had felt for many years in her own house. Another breeze blew over her face. She breathed it in and felt the joy roll through her body and bubble up inside her stomach. Tears welled in her eyes, her cheeks involuntarily creasing at the ends of her mouth.

'Tea or coffee?' Surprised that someone had walked up behind her, Cinder turned to see Torry holding a tray with two steaming pots, four mismatched old cups, and a jam jar full of milk. 'I bought both. I wasn't sure which you liked, and I couldn't wake Angus to ask him.' Torry placed the tray down on an old wooden chair sitting on the porch, just outside the door of Cinder's room. 'There's sugar too,' she said, holding up one of the cups to show the sugar cubes contained inside. 'I'm Torry, by the way, Tor,' she said, shaking Cinder's hand.

'Nice to meet you Tor, I'm Cinder and I'd kill for a cup of tea. That smells great.'

'How do you have it?' asked Torry, pouring the tea into two of the cups.

'Black with two thanks,' Cinder said. Torry looked up with an enormous smile.

'Just like me, I knew we'd have heaps in common.'

'Thanks,' said Cinder, taking the cup from Torry and sipping. 'Ah perfect. I was wondering if there were any girls around here.'

Torry blew the steam off the top of her drink as she strolled out into the green paddock.

'Just me,' she said.

'There are some good-looking guys here. That must be nice?' Cinder asked, following her. Torry laughed and turned to give Cinder a funny look.

'Well, they're all older than me and they're all either my cousins or uncles and Dom's my brother, so no, not nice. Anyway, talking about good-looking guys, are you Angus's girlfriend?'

'How do you know I'm here with Angus?' Cinder tried to avoid the question. 'I might have come here for Dom.'

'No, I don't think so,' said Torry, sitting down on a low section of one of the stone walls, 'girls that came back here with Dom usually slink out while it's still dark and they're in less clothes and more make-up than you. Besides, my dad's inside making breakfast right now and he never makes breakfast for one of Dom's girls.'

'Dom's girls?' asked Cinder, as she sat beside her, raising her eyebrows. 'There's been a few of them?'

'Let's just say I've lost count,' answered Torry, taking another sip of her tea.

They sat quietly together, sipping their warm beverages for a few minutes before Torry broke the silence, 'The red hair gave it away too, like his mum's.'

'What?'

'Your hair, Angus likes girls with red hair like his mum had.'

'Had?' asked Cinder, lowering her cup.

'When Angus was only about ten, he was staying with us. His mum and dad and his little sister Katie, she'd be about my age now. They were driving to pick him up, and a tree fell across the road. Then there was a fire, and they couldn't get out.' Cinder didn't know what to say. She sat, looking down into her cup.

'I lost my dad when I was about that age,' she said after a few moments of silence. 'There was a fire, too. He saved me, but he couldn't...' she trailed off. 'What about your mum?' she turned to look at Torry, unsure if she wanted to know the answer.

'Cancer, two years ago.' Cinder put her hand on Torry's lap.

'I'm so sorry.'

'It's okay,' Torry forced a smile. 'It happened pretty quick really, and now I've got a guardian angel watching over me. There's been other women here too.' Torry changed the subject. 'My aunts Jill and Beth, they've moved out west somewhere. I think it was too hard for them here without my mum. So now it's just me and my boys,' Torry smiled. 'What about you? Is that girl, that girl that's here with you, your sister?'

'Marraine?' replied Cinder. 'No, she's just my, just a friend. No sisters for me either, or brothers for that matter. I've always wished I had a little sister.'

'We could be sisters, you and me,' said Torry, suddenly excited. 'I've always wanted a big sister.'

'I'd like that,' said Cinder with a smile, 'but I'm not sure what sisters do?'

'They borrow each other's clothes.' Torry jumped up and tipped the remainder of her drink on the ground. 'Come on.' She grabbed Cinder's cup and tipped it out too, pulling her up off the wall. 'If you let me try on your boots, I'll find some of my clothes for you to change into.'

'How do you know I was wearing boots?' asked Cinder, laughing.

'Oh, I found your boots outside your door early this morning and put them in my room. You know, to keep them safe.' Torry looked a bit embarrassed.

'Thanks, little sis,' said Cinder, putting her arm around Torry's shoulder. 'I was wondering where I left those.'

They walked off together, collecting the tray from the chair on the way past.

'There's just one other thing I want to know. How often does your dad cook breakfast for visiting girls?' Cinder asked as they walked towards the main house.

'Oh, this is the first time,' replied Torry, smiling. Cinder smiled too.

Although Torry was a few years younger than Cinder, she was tall like the rest of her family, so they found Cinder was able to fit into many of Torry's clothes. Satisfied with their selection, they dragged Marraine out of bed and went to get breakfast. It was almost midday by the time they walked into the kitchen, where Gunn and another man greeted them.

'Hey finally, good morning, ladies. Come in, help yourselves.' Gunn said.

Cinder's stomach rumbled. She had had nothing but a hot chocolate and half a cup of tea since last night. The sounds and smells of the food cooking were almost too much to bear. Torry motioned for Cinder and Marraine to sit down at a long wooden table in the middle of the room. Steam rose from a pile of pancakes and homemade bread, fresh out of the oven.

Over at the stove, a man that looked remarkably like Gunn was busying himself with a large sizzling pan of sausages, eggs, and bacon.

'This is my brother Dand. You've met his boys, Bowie and the twins,' said Gunn as he took a jug of orange juice from the refrigerator and placed it on the table. 'Dand, this is Cinder and Mar, Marraine, I think I got that right.' Marraine nodded. 'And this, as you know,' he continued while placing a hand heavily on Torry's shoulder and kissing the top of her head, 'is Her Royal Highness, Princess Stephany.'

'Stephany?' asked Cinder.

'My middle name,' answered Torry, looking mortified.

'Don't worry,' said Marraine, pouring herself a glass of juice, 'my middle name is Beatrice, and don't tell anyone,' she leant in and pretended to whisper, 'but we're both real, actual princesses.' She pointed to Cinder and herself with a wink.

'So where are the boys?' asked Cinder, who was still trying to decide what to eat first.

Gunn and Dand smiled at each other.

'Ya won't see them till late this afternoon now, lass,' said Dand, bringing the pan of hot food over to the table.

'They stayed up all night and then took care of the milking early this morning,' explained Gunn.

When they had finished breakfast, they all agreed that they had eaten too much.

'Thank you very much for your hospitality,' said Marraine as she got up from the table, holding her stomach. 'It's been a pleasure meeting you all, but now I really should get home.'

'Going? Now?' asked Torry, looking deflated. 'But I wanted to show Cinder around the farm.'

'That's fine, she's staying.'

'I am?' Cinder asked, confused.

'There's plenty of room and it would be nice for Torry to have some company,' Gunn interrupted. 'You're both welcome to stay as long as you like.'

'Great,' Torry jumped up out of her chair, 'you can help me with my jobs.' Cinder looked from Marraine to Torry, feeling a bit perplexed.

'Okay, sure, I guess.'

Marraine pulled her phone from her pocket. 'I'm just going to organise a ride. What's the name of the road out the front?'

'Jasmine Lane,' answered Gunn.

'Thanks again. Cinder, can you walk me out to the gate?' Marraine put her arm around Cinder and started moving to show her it was more instruction than request.

A long, gravel driveway edged by low green hedgerows led away from the main house up to an old wrought-iron gate. When they were out of earshot of the house, Cinder turned to Marraine.

'What did you mean I'm staying? I can't stay here without you. I hardly know these people.'

'These are good people, sweetie. I feel better about leaving you with them than I ever feel leaving you with Louvelle.'

'Then why don't you stay with me?'

'Someone needs to hold down the fort back at The Big House and make sure no one contacts her ladyship.' Marraine said and continued walking.

About three-quarters of the way up the drive, Cinder took Marraine by the arm and stopped her. 'What if they're rapists or murderers?' she asked.

'Or worse, vegans?' Marraine interrupted sarcastically.

'I'm serious, they might try to hurt me!'

'Then let's just hope for their sake they have good hospital cover.' Marraine took hold of Cinder's hands, holding them to her chest, and looked into Cinder's eyes. 'Cinder, there are very few things in this world that you should be afraid of, but if you don't like it here, we can go right now, you and me. Now stop using your head and tell me what your heart says. Do you like it here?'

'Yes.'

'Do you feel safe?'

'Yes.'

'Do you want to go home?'

'No.'

'That's settled then, you're staying.' Marraine gave Cinder a reassuring smile. 'Now you need to listen because this is very important,' Marraine was suddenly looking very serious. 'I will try to make it back here before the full moon, but if I'm not, you need to be gone before midnight.'

'Why?' asked Cinder, concerned. 'What happens at midnight on the full moon?'

'Our pendants,' Marraine said, putting her hand on Cinder's chest, where the moon pendant was sitting under her clothes, 'they stop working.'

'What do you mean, stop working?' Cinder's anxiety rose again.

'I mean, they stop keeping the monsters away. I mean, you need to be home and safe,' Marraine moved her hand from Cinder's chest to her head, stroking her hair.

'How long for?' Cinder asked.

'Half an hour... Or so.'

'Half an hour or so?' Cinder looked unimpressed with the answer.

'Well, it's not science, it's magic sweetie, there's a lot of variables and it's different for everyone.' Seeing that Cinder still looked confused, Marraine continued. 'For me, my pendant stops working for exactly 31.4 minutes, but this is your mum's. It was different for her and it will be different for you.'

Marraine's car arrived at the gate. They hugged and Marraine kissed Cinder on the forehead. 'I'll send some clothes back and we'll talk soon. Remember, full moon, midnight.' She walked to the car and turned back as she opened the door. 'Don't do anything I wouldn't do... Which gives you a lot of options, really.' She gave one last cheeky wink before she disappeared behind the tinted windows, and then she was gone.

Cinder stood watching the car as it shrank into a small dust cloud in the distance. She was unsure how she felt. She walked slowly back to the house, holding her mother's pendant in her hand. *I still don't even know what this really is,* she thought to herself. All the reasons why staying here was a bad idea were running through her head, but when she got back to the house, she instantly felt better. Torry was sitting astride a quad bike with two helmets and an enormous smile on her face.

'Here,' Torry passed Cinder a helmet, get on.'

• • • •

Torry spent the entire day driving Cinder around the farm. Cinder helped feed, clean, and fix things, while Torry told her all sorts of funny stories about Dom and Angus. In the late afternoon, they stopped under a tree on top of a large hill. Cinder was sunburnt and very dirty. She had a sore backside from riding on the back of the quad bike and sore ribs from laughing. Torry was, she had decided, the funniest person she had ever met.

Cinder lay down on the grass, looking up at the patches of blue sky breaking through the green leaves as they danced in the breeze. She was still laughing about the story she had just heard. Apparently, when Dom was at school, he had started dating one girl at recess and then another at lunchtime. He ended up sandwiched between them both at a school assembly that afternoon. Torry came and sat beside her and handed her a bottle of water. Sitting up to drink, Cinder looked all around.

'How much of it is your farm?'

'Just under 300 acres,' replied Torry. 'North to Grass Tree Creek,' she pointed behind them, 'then along Bramley's river in the west down to Harvey's inlet. And over in the east,' she pointed to a dense area of trees away to their left, 'we go right up to the state forest. What about you, where do you live?'

'Oh me? Um, I live on the other side of Tallo's Bluff,' Cinder lied. She knew very well that The Big House was just the other side of the Alexander State Forest, but she didn't think she should let Torry know that.

'Have you always lived here?' Cinder asked, changing the subject.

'No,' said Torry, picking up her helmet, 'we've only been here about five years. Anyway, we should get back, the boys will be up now.' A flash of excitement shot up from Cinder's stomach and must have changed her expression because Torry laughed when she looked at her and said, 'Come on, I'm sure he'll be excited to see you too.'

Angus was lifting his surfboard onto the roof rack of Dom's car when he heard the quad bike coming up behind him. It confused him to see two girls. He didn't know who Torry's passenger was. He nearly dropped his board when Cinder took off her helmet and shook out her long red hair.

'You're still here,' he said as he tried unsuccessfully to not let his excitement show. 'We're going to head off soon. Do you wanna come again?'

'I'd like to,' Cinder said, leaning on the car next to Angus, 'but I'm starving. We haven't eaten since breakfast.' She held her stomach and nodded in Torry's direction. Torry nodded back in agreement.

'Okay then,' said Angus as he turned around and leant with his arms crossed on top of the car. 'How about I don't surf with the others and we have a fire and a picnic on the beach and watch them together?' Cinder's smile grew even bigger.

'That sounds really nice.'

'How about you, squirt? You wanna come too?' Angus turned and looked at Torry.

'I ... um ... no I'm too tired.' She pretended to stretch and yawn. 'You guys go, I just want an early night.'

'Okay then,' said Angus as he turned back to Cinder, 'looks like it's just the two of us.' Torry gave Cinder a wink and two thumbs up behind Angus's back. Angus lifted his board back off the roof of Dom's car. 'I'll go sort out some food and blankets.'

'I can help,' said Cinder enthusiastically.

'Oh,' replied Angus, smiling and nodding towards Cinder's reflection in the car window, 'you don't want to get cleaned up a bit first?' he asked. It mortified Cinder to see her reflection looking back at her. Dirt and grease were smudged across her face and clothes, and her hair was sticking out in all sorts of unnatural ways. Worse than that, she realised that she probably smelt as bad as she looked.

'Yes, good idea,' she said, walking off quickly to find Torry. 'I'll meet you back here after I have a shower.'

Cinder returned later to find Dom and Angus waiting at the car. Torry had done her hair for her and loaned her a skirt and t-shirt. Although she had argued that it was too little clothing for a night on the beach, Torry assured her it was perfect. Dom wolf-whistled as she approached.

'Looking very cute.' He called out.

'Really?' Cinder replied, smiling. 'These are your sister's clothes. Does that mean you think your sister's cute?' Angus laughed and opened the door for her. As Cinder got in, he said.

'You do look nice. I kind of liked the dirt and helmet hair look though.'

# Chapter 5

## Beaches and Speeches

*The fire burns, burns bright and free.*
*A spark was all it needed.*
*Now I cannot, will not, do not wish to put it out.*
*I desire now to bathe in its warmth*
*And take joy from its light.*

. . . .

It was much colder on the beach than it had been the previous night, so Cinder was very thankful for the small fire that Angus had made. She sat under a blanket, twirling her mother's pendant in her fingers, thinking happily about the day she had shared with Torry. Slipping off her shoes, she pushed her feet into the sand. The warmth of the day still lingered beneath the surface. Through the gaps in the flames that danced in front of her face, she could see Angus collecting more driftwood from the sand, with Dom walking along beside him.

'So, Marraine just left and she stayed?' Dom asked as he threw a pebble into the ocean. Angus nodded and picked up another piece of wood, placing it in the pile balanced on his left arm.

'Apparently. That's what Cinder said.'

Dom threw another pebble.

'I don't trust them.'

'Who?'

'Her and her friend.' Dom nodded his head in Cinder's direction.

'Cinder and Marraine?' Angus stopped to process what Dom was saying. 'You mean the two girls that you walked off on me to see last night? You mean the two girls you've been pushing me to spend time with? You mean those two?'

'Yep, I don't trust them,' Dom replied, looking out to the ocean with his back to Angus.

'Hang on,' Angus started walking again, 'are you just pissed because the one I liked stayed and the one you like,' he pointed a piece of driftwood at Dom, 'didn't stay?'

'No, of course not. I like when they leave,' Dom answered defensively. 'There's just something strange about them and I don't think they should be hanging around.'

Angus shook his head.

'As much as you'd like every girl to be drunken bimbos, they're not all like that. That doesn't make them strange, mate.'

'Hey, how shallow do you think I am?' Dom feigned offence. 'I like sober bimbos too.' Angus laughed and looked back up the beach. He could just see Cinder's eyes flickering in the firelight.

'Well, Cinder's not either of those, but I still think she's alright. I thought you'd be happy that I was spending time with someone?'

'I am, I am. I'm just saying I don't think we should be mixing business with pleasure. We don't know anything about her.' Angus stopped and looked at Dom.

'Wow,' he said in a mocking tone, 'that's so grown up of you, Dom.'

'Yeah, yeah, whatever. You better get back before the fire goes out. I'm going up to talk to the twins.' Dom continued along the beach to find Rory and Tavish, who were getting the signal fire ready on top of the hill.

Angus dropped the pile of driftwood and added a few pieces to the fire before sitting next to Cinder. 'You haven't eaten anything yet. Is something wrong with it?' he asked, seeing that the basket he had packed remained undisturbed.

'I was waiting for you and I couldn't see any cutlery, anyway,' Cinder said, looking around.

'Cutlery?' Angus laughed. 'You mean forks and plates and stuff? God gave us all the cutlery we need,' he said, wiggling his fingers in the air. He reached into the basket and pulled out a chicken drumstick in one hand and some carrot sticks in the other.

'Evolution gave us thumbs so that we could grip tools,' said Cinder, looking a bit disturbed.

'You can't tell me you never eat with your hands?'

'I eat some things with my hands, appropriate things. Not meat and salad, at least not without them being held between two pieces of bread.'

'You don't know what you're missing.' Angus picked up a handful of chicken breast. 'Here, try this.' He handed it to Cinder. Cinder took it, and after she had swallowed, she said,

'Mother would not approve.'

'Would she approve of you sitting on a beach in the dark with a strange man?' Angus asked, smiling.

'NO!' laughed Cinder. 'I'm sure she wouldn't approve of a lot of things I've been doing lately.'

'Oh, really?' asked Angus, raising his eyebrows. 'I never picked you as a bad girl. We might have to start calling you Cin.' Cinder blushed.

'Well, if you're giving me a nickname, I'm going to call you Black, like Dom does. It does suit you.' She reached out and ruffled her hand in his thick dark hair. Angus suddenly became very unsure of what to do with his hands. He picked up the basket and offered Cinder some more food to give them something to do. Cinder picked up a carrot stick and held it to her mouth like a cigarette.

'Hey Black,' she said, trying to do her best tough girl impression, 'Cin needs a light, what ya gonna do 'bout it?'

Angus added some more driftwood to the flames and then stoked up the fire with a stick, sending sparks shooting into the dark sky, like a jar full of fireflies escaping into the night. Cinder held her pendant lovingly to her breast as she watched the last of the sparks disappear in front of the moon. Angus pulled the stick out of the fire now glowing red on the end, and pretended to light a carrot stick in his mouth. He took a few puffs of imaginary smoke and, closing one eye to keep out the non-existent smoke, he turned to Cinder and said,

'Ya can light yours off mine, Cin.' Cinder leant in close to Angus's face, trying hard to keep her carrot stick still in her mouth as she giggled. In the end, the giggling became too much, and she dropped her carrot stick in the sand. Laughing, she lent in closer still to Angus and bit his carrot stick, pulling it out of his mouth.

'I'll just take yours,' she mumbled, with the carrot still protruding from her teeth.

They spent the next half hour joking and trying to set carrot sticks on fire. Feeling sleepy, Cinder stretched and lay her head down on Angus's lap. The crackling of the fire and the rhythmic crashing of the waves were like a natural lullaby in her ears.

'I'm sorry,' Angus said, pushing some hair behind her ear. 'I forgot you have been up all day. Let's go back.' Cinder rolled over and looked up into his face

'I think I'll just stay here,' she said sleepily before closing her eyes.

'Come on,' Angus lifted her head, 'I'll piggyback you.' As he picked up the picnic basket and blanket, Cinder nodded in silent agreement, then climbed onto his back.

'Do you think you can carry me? It's a long way.'

'I'll be fine,' Angus said as he checked the hill out of the corner of his eye. 'Good, no fire yet.' He thought to himself.

Cinder tried to stay awake on the way home by repeating some of the local histories that Gunn had told her the night before. Her head rested on Angus's shoulder and her arms wrapped tightly around his warm, firm chest. As much as he was enjoying her hands brushing against him, Angus hoped Cinder couldn't feel his heart pounding against his ribcage. It was not due to fatigue; he had carried things three times as heavy as Cinder for three times as long as this in his training.

This was, embarrassingly, he thought to himself, the closest he had been to a pretty girl for a long time. The closer they got to the farm, the less coherent Cinder's rambling became.

'You awake?' asked Angus, giving his passenger a bit of a shake.

'Yeah,' came Cinder's airy, unconvincing reply. 'You're good, you're a good man. My dad would have liked you.' Angus turned his head as best he could to see Cinder's face. She was smiling widely, but her eyes were closed. Angus kissed her arm, and she squeezed him tighter.

'I'd like to meet your dad.' Angus said.

'But you can't silly.'

'Why can't I meet your dad?' But Cinder didn't answer. She just breathed heavily in Angus's ear. 'Hey, you still with me?' He shook her again.

'Yep!' she said, patting him on the chest.

The night had become cool and foggy when they returned to the farm. Angus placed Cinder carefully down on the chair outside the guestroom, before opening the door. The cool night air against Cinder's skin roused her back to consciousness.

'Did I fall asleep?' she asked, opening only one eye and stretching. Angus smiled, walked back, and crouched down next to her.

'Just for a little bit,' he said. Cinder yawned and reached out, sitting her hand on his chest.

'Sorry, I hope I didn't say anything too embarrassing.'

'No.' said Angus, putting his hands on her knees to steady himself. 'Just that you have a crush on someone you just met.'

'Oh yeah, and who did I say that was?' Angus leant in putting his hand up to his mouth and whispered.

'Uncle Gunn. But don't worry, your secret's safe with me.' Cinder laughed. 'It's the eyebrows,' she said. 'I just want to run my fingers through them.' She yawned again and Angus smiled.

'Okay then, I'd better let you get some sleep. Goodnight.'

'Goodnight,' she replied, leaning and resting her forehead against his.

Angus's heart was pounding again, and he was once more falling into those amazing eyes. He could feel Cinder's lips only centimetres from his. All he needed to do was change the angle of his face by a few degrees and they would touch. He moved so that the side of his nose brushed against hers, but then a tidal wave of doubt flooded over him. *I've only just met her and she's half asleep. What if she doesn't want this?* Angus stood up and stretched out his hand to help Cinder up.

'Well, I'd better go check on the boys.'

'Oh, okay,' she said, taking hold of his hand and standing up. 'Thanks for a nice night and thanks for getting me home safely.' She shook his hand and walked to the door. 'Good night, Black,' she said as she shut the door.

'Goodnight Cin,' he called behind her.

• • • •

The following morning, Torry invited Cinder to look at the automated milking systems. Cinder had slept in through morning milking and the cows were being led out to feed by Gunn and Dand. Angus and the others had already gone to bed.

It was Torry's job that day to do the maintenance and cleaning. For her young age, Torry had a great deal of technical knowledge of how the machinery worked and how to maintain it. If thoughts of the night before were not distracting Cinder, she might have been an expert herself by the time they needed to get ready for the afternoon milking. It amazed Cinder that the cows knew to start moving to the yard by themselves at the right time.

Perching herself on a stone wall, Cinder watched as the beautiful animals ambled in and lined up. Gunn, Dand, and Torry sang along to relaxing tunes as they fitted the suction cups to each teat. When one cow finished, it moved off and the next one took its place. Looking at how smoothly it all happened, Cinder wondered what was different about the morning milking that needed so many more hands. Cinder walked along the edge of the milking yard, running her fingers through some long grass. Stopping to lean on the top rung of a weather-beaten timber fence that ran down the northern side of the property, she imagined Angus and his mates working while they sang to the cows. *Maybe they harmonise like a barbershop quartet,* she thought to herself, smiling.

At the west end of the milking yard, under the shadows of a sprawling old oak, Cinder spotted a cute little wooden building she had not noticed before. With a single door and two dusty windows, it was only slightly larger than a child's playhouse. Making her way towards it for a better look, Cinder noticed two large gas bottles attached to the wall and a thick power cable running to the roof. The old timber porch creaked noisily under her boots as she tried to look through one of the small windows. From inside, she could hear a low mechanical hum and smell a familiar smell that she couldn't quite put her finger on. Cupping her hands at the side of her head to block out the daylight, she peered into the darkness. The dust on the inside of the window made it impossible to see anything other than some dark outlines of the objects within. Cinder tried the door, but found it locked.

'Hey,' called Torry's voice from behind. 'You don't want to go in there, sis.'

Cinder turned to see Torry jogging towards her, stomping in her tall rubber boots.

'Why?' she asked, 'What's in there?'

Torry stopped jogging and started walking towards her with long strides. Her hands out in front of her, with fingers twisted.

'That's where we keep the bodies of the other girls,' she said with an evil laugh and a crazy look on her face.

'Oh, my!' Cinder gasped, placing her hand over her mouth. Torry laughed and started jogging again. 'No really,' Cinder said, 'what's in there? It smells familiar.'

'Smell?' Torry asked in surprise, stepping up onto the porch next to her. 'It's um... chemicals and stuff, you know? Stuff we need to keep locked up. Don't you have stuff locked up at your place?'

'Only me.' Cinder said with a laugh.

'What?'

'Oh, nothing. Don't worry.'

'Come on,' Torry grabbed Cinder's hand and started leading her away, 'let's get some food, I'm starving.'

The timber deck creaked once more, as Cinder stepped off. Turning to take one more look at the little building, a shiver inched slowly up her spine. Her father's anguished face flashed into her mind. *'Stay back, Cinder!'* His last words flooded her mind. Cinder shook her head as if she could somehow dislodge the memory from her brain.

'You alright?' Torry asked, feeling Cinder grip her hand tightly.

'Yes, yes fine,' Cinder lied, 'just excited about eating.'

• • • •

Cinder sat barefoot on the sand in the light of the waxing moon. Around her shoulders, she had draped a brown velour blanket that smelt slightly of grease and mothballs. After an early dinner, Cinder and Torry had decided to walk to the beach, leaving before the boys woke. Torry took Cinder the long way through the town so that they could look in some shop windows and get themselves an ice-cream from the ice-cream shop that always stayed open late in the summer months.

The sound of inflated rubber pushing on the carpark gravel above announced the arrival of Angus and his friends. Cinder made one last frantic effort to clean the drop of chocolate ice-cream from the front of her t-shirt, to no avail. Accepting defeat, she pulled the blanket further across her chest to hide the stain.

'Good evening, ladies,' Duncan's bellowing voice echoed through the sand dunes. Cinder turned to see him at the top of the walkway, the moon reflecting off his bald head. Cinder stood up, holding the blanket against her chest with one hand and using the other to dust off the sand from her pants.

'Hey Duncan,' she called back. Duncan ran down the steps with his surfboard above his head, planting it nose-first in the sand when he reached the bottom. Torry, who had been sitting next to Cinder, sprang to her feet and ran at Duncan. Yelling loudly, she launched herself at Duncan, grabbing him around the neck in a bear hug.

'Arrr she's got me!' Duncan yelled, then without even breaking his stride, he lifted Cinder off the sand over his other shoulder. 'Time for a swim, girls!'

'No!' Cinder and Torry called in unison. Cinder pulled the blanket free of Duncan's grip and wrapped it around his face.

'Go for the legs!' Torry cried.

The two girls swung their legs behind Duncan and pushed hard against the back of his knees. All three tumbled to the sand in laughter. Duncan pulled the blanket from his head and threw it at Torry. Cinder got to her knees, brushing off the sand from her face and arms.

'Do you need some help?' Angus was standing next to her with his hand held out. Cinder took his hand and pulled herself to her feet.

'No thanks, sis and I have got this.'

Torry handed Cinder the blanket and jumped on top of Duncan, tickling him. Grabbing her in both arms, Duncan pinned Torry to his chest and struggled to his feet. Cinder and Angus watched on in amusement as Duncan stomped down the beach with Torry kicking her legs frantically to free herself. Just as they got to the edge of the water, Torry pulled her legs up in front of her and pushed herself free. She hit the ground running.

'Ha!' she yelled, running back up to the dry sand. 'No one can hold me!'

She ran up into the dunes, before doing a backflip, down onto the dry sand. Cinder and Angus burst into laughter and applause. Dom who had also arrived wolf-whistled.

'Nice work, sis!' he called before placing two fingers in his mouth and whistling again. Torry flexed her muscles and boxed the air.

'You're my hero!' Cinder yelled, holding her hands up to her mouth.

'I thought that was me,' Angus said, pretending to look hurt and putting his arm around Cinder's shoulder.

'Ha, you wish,' Cinder pushed him away playfully and walked ahead of him. 'I don't really even know you. You're always in bed.' Angus jogged to catch up to her.

'What do you want to know?'

'Hmmm,' Cinder continued to walk away from him along the beach, tapping her index finger thoughtfully against her chin.

'What's your girlfriend's name?' Angus picked up a smooth, flat stone and turned it over in his fingers.

'Which one?' he asked.

'Which one?' Cinder echoed, raising her eyebrows. 'How many are there?' Angus linked his fingers and pushed his hands out in front of him, cracking his knuckles.

'Six. One for each day of the week, and I have Sundays off,' he said. Cinder glanced at him, noticing a childish grin forming on the corner of his mouth.

'That's nothing,' she jeered, collecting her hair into a ponytail. 'I have 364 boyfriends. I get one day a year to myself.'

Angus laughed as he walked closer to the water, preparing to skim the stone on the ocean. Cinder stayed hesitantly on the dry sand.

'Are you okay?' Angus asked, noticing the gap between them widening.

'Yep, fine,' Cinder tried to smile unconvincingly. Angus grinned at her poorly-veiled act.

'Come put your feet in the water.'

'No, no, I'm fine here thanks.' Cinder crossed her arms and pushed her toes into the sand. Taking a few steps closer, Angus held out his hand for Cinder to hold.

'I thought you liked the ocean?'

'I like the ocean fine,' Cinder answered, while turning to look back up the beach towards the sand dunes. 'It's all the things in the ocean I'm not keen on.'

'Come on,' Angus insisted, taking her by the hand and leading her forward.

As the foamy, cold water rushed over her toes, Cinder grit her teeth and tried her best to keep smiling. Angus guided her further into the shallows.

'See? It's fine.'

'Yep, fine,' Cinder replied, her heart quickening its rhythm. 'This is far enough now,' she declared, squeezing his hand.

The water was icy, but Cinder found it surprising how quickly her feet had grown accustomed to the temperature. She was caught off guard when a wave crashed against her, sending cold water up her thighs and wetting the hem of her shorts. Startled, she went to step back, unaware that her feet had sunk into the wet sand. Angus caught her as she began to fall.

'You all right?' Angus asked, helping her up.

'Yes, I'm fine, just a bit embarrassed.' Cinder rested her hands on his chest to steady herself. Angus took her hand again.

'Let's go a little deeper,' he said. Cinder swallowed hard and walked forward with him. Gripping Angus's hand tightly, she stood in the dark water as it rose and fell; sometimes at her knees, sometimes lapping against her shorts.

'Nope, nope, this is too much,' Cinder protested, hurrying back up the beach. 'Something touched my foot.'

'You are a very strange girl,' Angus laughed, following her out of the water.

'You think I'm strange?' replied Cinder, feeling a little insulted. 'What about all of you? This isn't normal.' She motioned with her head towards the silhouettes of Dom and the others bobbing up and down on the dark ocean. 'You think my fear of the water is strange? I think it's strange that you don't appear to be afraid of anything.'

Angus joined her on the dry sand.

'What's there to be afraid of?'

'Oh, I don't know, drowning, sharks, things lurking in the darkness, monsters under the bed.'

Angus looked up at the moon. 'I'm not afraid of monsters. I've got you to protect me,' he joked and put his arm around her shoulder. Cinder turned and surveyed the gloomy shadows of the forest at the far end of the beach.

'Maybe you should be,' she said, more to herself than to Angus. Angus laughed.

'And why's that?' he asked.

Cinder leant her head into his chest and looked down at the water lapping against the shore. She was convinced the ocean was trying to move closer to her with each wave.

She breathed Angus in through her nose. He had a pleasant mix of sweetness and saltiness. But what was most interesting to Cinder, was what was missing. All the men that her mother had paraded her in front of over the years all had the same smell, a smell that made her feel sick until she had come to realise it was fear. This man, she thought, has no fear.

'Surely you have heard the stories? Everyone around here knows it's not safe to be out late at night, yet you have all made a life of it.' She paused to think. 'Why is that?' she asked, looking up into Angus's face. Cinder felt his muscles tense. His arm dropped away from her and he took a step back.

'Torry's coming,' he said, becoming rigid.

'Oh? Okay,' Cinder replied, fixing her stray hairs. She suddenly felt the need to occupy her hands. Angus gave an overly enthusiastic wave to Torry, who was still sitting back near the carpark steps. Springing to her feet and dusting herself off, Torry jogged and stumbled across the soft sand to talk to them.

'What's up mi amigos?' she asked, draping her arm over Cinder's shoulder. Angus smiled and rubbed the back of his neck.

'Cinder was asking me what we think about the dangers of being out at night around here. Have you two been telling ghost stories?' Torry and Angus exchange a look that Cinder couldn't read.

'No, no, we've just been feeding our faces. Isn't that right, sis?' Torry looked into Cinder's eyes.

'Sounds good,' Angus replied. 'Well, I'm going to get in the water. Maybe you two should head home soon.' he added. Cinder reached up and took hold of Torry's hand that was resting on her shoulder.

'Okay, sure. I guess I will see you tomorrow then?' she said, trying to hide the disappointment in her voice. Angus wrapped his large arms around both the girls and kissed Torry's cheek.

'Goodnight girls.' Angus turned and jogged away along the wet sand. Cinder watched him run off to find his surfboard, before lifting Torry's arm from her shoulder.

'What was that?' she asked, turning to look at Torry's face.

'I don't know Cin. Boys are weird.'

'Yes, I am starting to work that out. I'm not sure I like it.'

'Are you okay?' Torry asked, placing her hand back on Cinder's shoulder.

'Yes, I'm fine,' Cinder lied again. '*This is becoming a habit,*' she thought.

Torry asked Duncan to walk them home. Torry explained she didn't really like surfing and preferred to ride dirt bikes. Duncan listened as she talked about the pros and cons of different bikes. Cinder's mind was elsewhere. She kept an eye on the shadows and tried to figure out Angus.

That night, in her little bed in the guesthouse, Cinder's nightmares returned with a vengeance. The cast tonight, however, had a new player. Angus stood, watching, impassive as her father's blood speckled her pink bed sheets.

# Chapter 6

### Heart's Like the Moon

'Cinder, Cinder, wake up!' Torry pleaded with concern as she leant over Cinder's bed, shaking her shoulder gently.

Cinder's eyes shot open as she sent her pillow flying in Torry's direction. 'Let him go!' she yelled. Torry ducked out of the way. The pillow continued past her at great speed, collecting a small hall table with a thud. Sitting on the table, a small yellow vase that had been busy holding dried flowers and dust, suddenly moved for the first time in decades. The vase teetered backwards, releasing the years of dust, before falling forwards and rolling in a semicircle across the top of the table. The sound reminded Torry of a bowling ball rolling down its lane. She tried to get to the table, but it was too late. The vase fell to the timber floor, popping open into a dozen shards of porcelain and a cloud of dust. The sound startling Cinder to full consciousness.

'I'm so sorry,' Cinder offered, sitting up and holding her hand to her mouth, her eyebrows raised and her pupils large.

'It's fine.' Torry laughed as she picked up the pieces. 'It was an ugly old thing, anyway.' Cinder smiled apologetically.

'I'm sorry I threw the pillow at you too?' she said.

'Oh, that bloody pillow had it coming.' Torry picked up the pillow above her head to show Cinder. There were tears in the slip, and stuffing squeezing out of some of the larger holes. 'It looks like it was giving you trouble all night.' Torry sat the pillow on the table and continued to collect the shards. 'You okay, sis?' she asked.

'I'm embarrassed, but I'm fine. I should be asking you that. You're the one that just had a pillow missile launched at you by a crazy woman.'

'It's all good,' Torry called out, as she carried the vase and flowers into the ensuite, placing them in a bin under the sink. 'What were you dreaming about?'

Cinder yawned and stretched as she tried to think. 'Um, I'm not sure. I think Angus was in it.'

'Oh?' Torry strutted back into the room and sat on the end of the bed. 'And I thought all the moaning and calling out you were doing was a bad dream. I'm sorry I disturbed you now.' A cheeky grin spread across her face.

'You know,' Cinder said, looking at her young friend. 'This is the first time I've really seen the resemblance between you and Dom.'

'Hey lady!' Torry yelled, pulling off Cinder's bedding, 'I'm nothing like my brother, thanks. I'll throw something at you if you're not careful.' Cinder noticed the dust floating in a beam of sunlight coming through a crack at the side of one of the window blinds.

'What time is it?' She asked.

'About midday.' Torry said as she stood up and opened the blinds. Cinder squinted her eyes as they adjusted to the change in light.

'I'm sorry I slept in, I should have been helping you out with your jobs.'

'It's okay, I have a day off, *we* have the day off,' Torry corrected herself.

'Oh, why's that?' Cinder asked, stretching her arms above her head.

'There're storms coming and it will be overcast for most of the night.' Torry motioned with her head towards the greyish daylight entering the window she had just uncovered. 'It means that the boys won't go out tonight so there will be some extra helpers around this afternoon.'

Cinder scratched the back of her head, ruffling her messy mop of red hair, then flopped her hands down on the bed with a sigh. Torry took hold of her hand and looked her in the eye. 'Are you really okay?' She asked.

'I'm fine, just bad dreams. You know?' Cinder squeezed Torry's hand and smiled.

'Yep, I know.' Torry mirrored Cinder's expression. She paused for a beat before continuing. 'Now come on, get up, I'm taking you shopping.'

'Oh, nice!' Cinder was genuinely excited about the idea. She had only ever been shopping with her mother, which was never an enjoyable experience. Shopping with a friend would be a pleasant change. Cinder lifted her quilt and threw it over Torry's head. 'I'll go get cleaned up.' She said. Torry pulled off the bedding to see Cinder disappear into the ensuite.

'Okay, I will be in my room when you're ready!' she called out, flattening her ruffled hair.

Although there was still some summer warmth in the air, Cinder could feel that the weather was changing. Grey clouds hung thick and low over the farm and as she walked to meet Torry, she could see black storm clouds over the ocean and the telltale streaks of rain striping the horizon. Moisture collected on the exposed skin of her arms and face, and the scent of the dry ground, gratefully receiving some water, filled the air.

Uncle Gunn and Dand were about 100 metres up the driveway, arguing as they unloaded some bags from the back of a flatbed truck. Cinder waved as she entered the main house.

'Hello?' she called out, closing the door gently behind her, feeling a little like she was intruding.

'I'm just in my room,' Torry called out in reply, 'come down.' Cinder followed the voice down the hallway. Her footsteps drumming on the timber floor, loud against the contrast of the otherwise silent house.

Torry was rummaging through her wardrobe; she turned and greeted Cinder with a smile as she entered. 'I'm trying to find a coat for you. Here it is. It's a bit old but it will keep you warm.'

'Oh, thanks.' Cinder accepted the puffy, black jacket. 'But I'm not cold,' she continued, sounding a bit confused.

'Yes, but it gets cold on the back of my bike,' Torry answered.

'Bike, like a bicycle?'

'No,' Torry laughed. 'I'm not going to peddle all the way to the bluff, hauling your fat ass up those hills.'

'Hey!' Cinder protested, throwing the jacket back at Torry. 'I'll have you know my body is perfectly proportioned, thank you very much.'

'I seem to remember Black saying that to me when he first told me about you.' Torry threw the jacket back. Cinder felt her cheeks warming.

'Anyway,' she said, changing the subject. 'What bike do you mean, then?'

'A dirt bike, MY bike!'

'Oh, a motorcycle?'

Torry laughed and mimicked Cinder's voice,

'Yes, a motorcycle.'

'Is that even legal? You're only 16.'

Torry got down on her knees, and after pushing some clothes out of the way, retrieved two helmets from under her bed.

'Well,' she said, getting to her feet, 'I have been riding the roads between here and the bluff since I was twelve, so I guess maybe it's less illegal now.' She shrugged her shoulders.

'Less illegal?' Cinder asked, with one eyebrow raised. 'You know that's not even a thing, right?'

'Look Miss-do-right,' Torry continued, handing one of the helmets to Cinder, 'there is the sum-total of three police officers for this whole district. I think they have better things to do than chase a couple of unlicensed girls around the coast. Besides, they couldn't catch me if they tried.' She placed the remaining helmet under her arm, holding her hands out in front of her, turning the throttle on an imaginary set of handlebars.

'Okay then.' Cinder conceded.

Torry eyed the satchel that Cinder had hung low from her right shoulder.

'Hmm, here I think we might need this.' She reached into her wardrobe and produced a black, hessian backpack, with two thick shoulder straps on one side and two thinner straps on the front, with buckles to hold down a top flap. 'Put whatever you need in that. You can leave your other bag here if you want.'

They left the farm and Heathcote behind and made their way out onto the coastal road. Cinder had travelled this way before, but it was a far more terrifying and exhilarating experience on the back of a motorcycle. The road between Heathcote and Tallo's Bluff followed the undulating twists and turns of the coastline. Cinder had never been so aware of the great wall of stone that flanked one side of the road and the sheer drop to the rocks and ocean on the other side. Torry seemed to take each new turn faster than the last. Cinder gripped tightly around her waist, involuntarily squealing more times than she would like to admit.

Other than Cinder's racing heart and sore backside, they arrived safely in Tallo's Bluff just after 2 pm.

'Is one of these yours?' Torry asked, gesturing towards a row of large, audacious homes; each with second-storey balconies that looked out over the ocean. Cinder handed her helmet to Torry.

'My what?' she asked, confused.

'Your house. You live here, right?'

'Oh yes and no,' Cinder replied, 'None of these are my place. I live, um, further back from the beach.'

'We could go to your place if you want?' Torry said, hanging the helmets over the handlebars.

'NO!' Cinder blurted out in a voice far more dramatic than she meant. 'I mean no, it's a long way back, and we don't need to waste time. There's nobody home, anyway.'

'Okay then,' Torry agreed. 'Maybe next time.'

Unlike Heathcote, that had a small section of shops along the esplanade, Tallo's Bluff had a larger variety of stores, positioned along three streets, running from east to west, perpendicular to the ocean. Torry and Cinder spent the next few hours browsing, snaking their way along the three streets. When Cinder's stomach rumbled audibly, they grabbed a sandwich and a slice of carrot cake from the bakery to share.

Although there was still a thick covering of dark clouds, the afternoon had grown warm and sticky. The heat rising from the road and the concrete paths also added a few degrees. Tory suggested they sit on the shaded steps at the entrance to the cinema. They watched people go by as Cinder did her best to avoid more questions about her home life.

'Okay, let's keep going,' Torry said, licking cream cheese icing from her fingers and scrunching up the brown paper bags that had contained their food.

'Help me up?' Cinder asked, holding out one hand and picking up the backpack with the other. Torry pulled her up, then tossed the ball of brown paper, basketball style, into a bin a few metres away. Throwing one of the straps over her left shoulder and brushing some crumbs from her chest, Cinder froze, her hand held over her heart. A tall man in a black suit and dark sunglasses stepped inside the second-hand store three doors down.

'Are you okay?' Torry asked, seeing the look on Cinder's face. Cinder dropped her hand to her side.

'Oh, yep I'm fine I just thought I saw someone.'

'Who?' Torry turned and looked towards the second-hand store.

'One of my, um... my old teachers,' Cinder lied.

'Oh okay, yeah it's weird when you see them out of their natural habitat, hey?'

'Yes, very weird,' Cinder agreed. Torry took her hand and pulled her along to the next shop.

'Come on, let's go before they see you and try to talk to you.'

In the last street, there was a small boutique that sold new and retro women's clothing. Torry was not a big fan of dresses. In fact, the only one she owned was her school uniform, but a dress for Cinder was a different story. Torry had spotted a blue dress in the shop window and goaded Cinder to try it on. On seeing that it fit perfectly, she had set out to convince her to buy it.

'You need to get this,' Torry pleaded with Cinder, standing behind her as they both looked at the reflection in the change room mirror. Cinder turned from side to side.

'I don't know, it's $85 for a second-hand dress.' Cinder inspected the price tag to confirm what she already knew.

'It's not second-hand,' Torry argued, 'it's re-claimed, it's retro.' Cinder stood on her toes to try to see what the dress would look like if she were in heels.

'I only have $50 cash on me, anyway.'

'So?' Torry asked. 'They take other forms of payment; not everything here is retro.' Cinder walked into the dressing room and pulled the door closed behind her.

'I know, it's just I, um... I left my phone and things back at the farm.' Cinder didn't know if her mother kept track of her bank account, but she assumed she did. She reached inside the backpack that she had left on the change room floor, retrieving the money from her phone, before pushing the phone deeper into the backpack.

Torry leant against the change room door. 'I thought I saw you put your phone in. What was that?'

'Just my notepad.' Cinder pulled a small, black leather-covered book from the backpack and held it above the door before unzipping the side of the dress. 'I take it everywhere.'

'What's in it?'

'Just thoughts, poetry, stuff like that.'

'Can I read it?' Torry asked.

'No way, no, no, no.' Cinder said, quickly pulling her diary down and putting it away again.

'Okay then,' Torry laughed. 'Don't you trust me, sis?' Cinder slipped the dress off and draped it over the door. 'I don't let anyone read it, sorry.'

'That's fine,' Torry said, taking the dress off the door. 'So are you getting this?'

'No, I told you I don't have enough money.' Cinder said as she pulled the last of her clothes back on and opened the door. Torry freed some of Cinder's hair caught under her collar.

'We could just take it; it would fit in the backpack. I've done it before.' Torry said. Cinder didn't acknowledge what Torry was saying. Someone walking past the front of the boutique distracted her. 'Cinder?' Torry asked, holding up the dress.

'No, what? No, we're not going to shoplift.' Cinder took the dress. 'I, um... I think I want to go now, I'm getting tired.'

Placing the dress on the counter and thanking the shop assistant, Cinder made her way quickly out onto the footpath, looking nervously up and down the street.

They walked back to Torry's bike in silence. When Torry handed Cinder her helmet, she noticed Cinder looking around anxiously. 'Hey it's okay,' she said. 'We didn't steal anything.' Cinder just smiled and put on her helmet.

• • • •

It was early evening when Cinder and Torry arrived back at the farm. Dark clouds hung thick in the sky, promising rain but, as yet, not delivering. After dumping their things in Torry's room, they found Torry's father and Uncle Dand both half asleep in their armchairs. Gunn informed them that Angus and Dom were already awake and had a fire going just the other side of the milking shed. Torry collected up some snacks and warmer clothes. After both kissing Gunn on the top of his head, they ran off to find the boys.

Rain was falling again, so Cinder and Torry walked briskly, their collars pulled high around their necks. A large campfire was burning under a tall, wall-less structure. Although the structure appeared pieced together with repurposed logs, timber, and roofing iron, it had managed to stay upright for fifty or more years. Brown volcanic rocks edged an oval-shaped firepit, shallowly dug and just over a metre across at its widest point. Half a dozen chainsaw-cut logs had been placed around the pit as makeshift seating. Dom and Angus sat on two of the log seats, talking and warming their hands. A third log was occupied by an acoustic guitar.

'Oh yes!' Torry said with excitement, as she and Cinder approached the fire. 'Dom has his guitar.' Torry ran up to the fire. Cinder approached a little slower and sat down on the empty seat next to Angus. Torry moved the guitar off the woodblock next to Dom and handed it to him before sitting down. 'Play us a song!' she demanded.

'Okay then,' Dom said. 'Good evening to you too.'

'Oh yeah, hi,' Torry laughed. Angus and Cinder exchanged smiles and waves. 'Play,' Torry demanded again. Dom played a few strings to check if the guitar was still in tune.

'Fine, but the price of a song is a kiss.' Torry leant over and pecked him on the cheek. 'From everyone,' Dom continued, 'Black?'

'I'm not kissing you, mate,' Angus replied, shaking his head.

'I will collect on that later,' Dom said, winking at Angus. 'Cinder?' he asked, pointing to his cheek.

'Um, okay,' Cinder said, getting up and walking over to Dom. As she bent down to kiss his cheek, Dom moved his head so that their lips touched briefly.

'Hey!' Cinder protested, before whacking him on the shoulder. Torry leant over and whacked his other shoulder. Angus shook his head again.

'You're such a jerk.' He said.

'Yes, but I am a happy jerk.' Dom said, smiling and strumming the guitar.

'You okay, sis?' Torry called out to Cinder as she sat back down.

'Yes,' Cinder called back as she adjusted her hair. 'Not exactly how I imagined our first kiss, Dom,' she added. *My first kiss ever,* she thought to herself with a smile.

'I could try again if you want?' Dom said, standing up.

'No, no.' Cinder held up her hand. 'That's enough excitement for one day. You owe us a song.'

The sound of Dom's guitar was hard to hear at first over the sprinkling of rain on the tin roof, but as he committed more to the emotion of the song, his volume increased. Then he started to sing. Cinder shot Torry a look that said, *'he's pretty good'.* Torry held her hands against her heart and mouthed the words, *'I love it'.*

Cinder watched the flames, the fire warming her body as the song warmed her heart. Orangey-red reflections danced in her glassy eyes, as memories of home filled her thoughts; good memories from when her father was alive. As though it had been waiting for its cue, the rain began to clear as Dom's song was ending. He repeated one last phrase, about a boy gathering his courage to be with a girl.

'That was beautiful,' Cinder said as Dom placed the guitar down across his lap. Torry, however, just gave her brother a strange look. Was it disappointment? Cinder couldn't be sure. She stood up to walk over to Torry, but Angus stood up with her.

'The rain has stopped. Maybe we should go for a walk,' he said, moving closer to her. 'Who wants to come?' He asked.

'No, I want to hear another song.' Torry said, shaking her head.

'Looks like I'm staying here, mate,' Dom said. 'But come over here, I have something to tell you.' Angus walked over to Dom, then seeing Dom cup one side of his mouth with his hand, Angus leant in to hear Dom whisper.

'If you're going to do something, this is your chance. Get it over and done with tonight, so things can get back to normal.' Then Dom kissed Angus on the cheek. 'Yes!' Dom called out triumphantly. 'I got my kiss.'

Angus gave Dom's shoulder its third whack for the evening and said, 'Well, Cin, looks like it's just the two of us.'

'Fine with me,' Cinder said, turning and walking away with Angus, leaving the siblings by the fire.

When Angus and Cinder were out of earshot, Torry turned to Dom. 'Interesting choice of song. That was Dermot Kennedy, right?' she asked.

'Yep, it's called Closeness, I think,' Dom said, beginning to strum again. 'Don't you like it?'

'I like it fine. I just found some of the lyrics... well, interesting.' Torry stared at Dom, her left eyebrow raised, inviting an answer to her unasked question. Dom smiled, his white teeth glowing orange in the firelight.

'I don't know what you mean.'

'Come on,' Angus said with a sideways nod of his head. Cinder followed as he led her across the damp grass. The warm orange glow of the fire slowly drifted away into darkness. For a time, Cinder followed Angus blindly until her eyes adjusted to the washed-out, grey of the moon as it struggled to pierce through the water-heavy clouds above. The crackle of the fire and the twang of guitar strings drifted slowly away as they walked towards the tree line, replaced by nature's own melody of the low growling of frogs and the high pitch squeaks of bats and many other unseen orchestra members who joined in with the nightly chorus.

Cinder had her arms crossed in front of her chest to block the cool night air, but Angus reached out his hand. Cinder understood the gesture and took hold of it.

'There is a creek just up ahead,' he explained. 'You might want to watch your step.' Cinder could hear the muffled trickle of water but could not make out where the creek was in the darkness. 'Okay, stop there,' Angus said, squeezing Cinder's hand and stretching his right leg out, before dropping it firmly on the other side of the water. 'Here, I'll lift you over.' Before Cinder could protest, Angus placed both of his large hands on either side of her waist, lifting her into the air.

'Oh, okay!' Cinder called out, taking hold of his shoulders. 'Are you alright? I'm not small.'

'You're fine,' Angus replied, holding her out in front of him, then lifting her higher still.

'Okay, okay, show-off,' Cinder tapped Angus on the shoulder. 'This isn't dirty dancing, buddy; Baby is happy to go back in her corner.' Cinder laughed. Angus smiled and placed her down gently on the other side.

'What?' Angus asked.

'I could have just stepped over that, you know.' Cinder adjusted her clothes and shook her head. 'I would hardly call it a creek.' She looked down at the narrow stream of water. 'And my legs aren't that much shorter than yours.' Angus held his hands to his chest.

'I was just trying to help.' his reply dripped with sarcasm.

'Trying to show off your muscles more like it.'

'Well, were you impressed?' he asked. Cinder turned and continued walking towards the forest.

'I wasn't unimpressed,' she said with a shrug of her shoulders.

A line of tall, thinly-trunked trees loomed in the darkness just ahead of Cinder. She recognised their familiar pine scent before she could properly see their rough, patchy bark and long needles. These remnants of a long-forgotten pine plantation became more abundant around The Big House. She walked forward and pulled aside a branch, looking deeper into the forest, visions of home flooding her thoughts.

Angus moved slowly up behind her, removing something long and metallic from a leather pouch on his hip. Out of the corner of her eye, Cinder caught the glint of a blade. Instinctively, she grabbed Angus's wrist and forced it firmly against the tree trunk. 'Hey!' Angus protested. 'What are you doing?'

'What am I doing?' Cinder replied, with her eyes wide open. 'What are you doing?' she asked, pointing with her free hand at the hunting knife in Angus's restrained fist. A look of realisation grew on Angus's face.

'Oh, yes, I see how this looks bad.'

'Yes, it does,' Cinder agreed. 'It looks like you have taken a girl into the forest at night and pulled a knife on her.' Cinder was trying to appear calm on the outside, but inside her heart was racing. Her hand was shaking on Angus's wrist. Angus held his free hand up reassuringly.

'I was just going to suggest we carve our initials into the tree.' Angus loosened his grip on the handle. 'You can go first.'

Cinder cautiously took the knife out of Angus's hand. 'Sorry,' she offered, loosening her grip on his wrist, 'you just surprised me.' Angus retrieved his hand, smiling and rubbing his wrist.

'That's okay.' He said. 'Good reflexes, by the way.' Cinder flipped the knife over in her hand and stabbed it into the trunk of the nearest tree.

'Were you impressed?' she baited, carving a line in the bark.

'I wasn't unimpressed,' Angus replied, leaning against the tree. Cinder forced a smile but struggled to keep eye contact with Angus. 'What are you writing?' he asked, squinting his eyes.

'CIN + BLACK.' She said.

'Are you going to put a love heart around it?'

'Sure am,' Cinder replied enthusiastically. 'Then we're going to play kiss chasey,' she added sarcastically. 'What are you, 10?' Angus dropped his bottom lip and crossed his arms high on his chest.

'Don't you love me?' he asked.

'Well, Angus MacAskill.' Cinder said, holding the knife by the blade and offering the handle to Angus. 'I don't even know you. I did think I was starting to like you, before you pulled a knife on me.'

Angus took the knife from her and slipped it back into his belt.

'I'm never going to live that down, am I?' he asked. Cinder traced her carving with her fingers.

'No,' she replied, 'and you need to finish this.' Angus took the knife out again and continued to carve out the letters.

'Did you really think I was pulling a knife on you?' he asked in a more serious tone.

'No. I guess I'm just a bit jumpy because of what might be out there, in the dark.' Cinder looked around the dark forest and then up to the cloudy sky. Angus stopped for a moment, turning his head to search the darkness.

'What do you think is out there, Cin?'

Cinder wanted to say, *I know exactly what is out there,* but that was a conversation for another time and place. She simply said, 'You've heard the stories.'

'Yes, I have,' Angus said, returning to the carving. 'But I can tell you this,' he stepped back to admire their handiwork, 'I have never come across anything in there I couldn't explain.'

'Just because you can explain something doesn't mean it's not dangerous.' Cinder said, moving next to Angus, crossing her arms, and nodding her approval of the finished product. Angus ran his eyes up and down the beautiful, mysterious woman next to him.

'I think you might be dangerous. I'm not sure I can explain you yet,' he said, sliding the knife back into his belt. Cinder took a few steps backwards before turning and walking deeper into the forest.

'Maybe a woman likes to maintain a bit of mystery, Black,' she said seductively, channelling Marraine. Angus took one last look at the carving before turning to follow her.

'I didn't say I don't like it. I'm okay with mystery and danger.'

'Are you flirting with me, Black?'

'I'm not *not* flirting.'

Walking quicker, Cinder weaved in and out between the trees, making it hard for Angus to keep up with her. 'You know, Danger is my middle name,' she called back to him

'Really?' Angus asked, jogging a little to catch up.

'No, not really.'

'What is it then?'

'That's just going to have to be one of those mysteries.' Cinder said, letting Angus catch up and then running ahead again.

'Be careful,' Angus called out 'you're getting close to a cliff up ahead.'

The darkness of the forest canopy opened up again to the grey light of the illuminated clouds far above. The tree line stopped suddenly, a few steps back from a drop of about five metres. Cinder slowed down and walked cautiously to the edge. Leaning over, she could see a wall of smooth rock that fell at a slight angle, down to the continuing forest below. Patches of moss and blackberries grew in the spots that were not polished clean by wind and rain.

'How do you like that view?' Angus asked, walking up close beside her. Cinder looked across the top of the trees below. They stretched out to the lights of Heathcote. Beyond that, she could see the ocean and the distant twinkling of the towns that dotted the coastline. She looked up at the sky before answering.

'It's beautiful; I just wish I could see the stars too.'

'I will have to bring you back on a clear night.' Angus said, looking up.

'I'd like that,' Cinder answered, looking at the glow of The Big House, on top of the hill at the far end of Heathcote. Anxiety built in her stomach. She shook off the feeling and focused on the lights further along. An idea popped into her head. She leant sideways, bringing her head down near her knees so it was almost upside down.

'What are you doing?' Angus laughed.

'Hang on,' Cinder replied, standing up straight again and looking around. 'I have an idea – come over here.' She took his hand and walked over to the trunk of a large, fallen tree that was lying near the edge of the cliff. Climbing on and laying on her back, Cinder positioned herself so that her head could hang off the end and she could look out over the coastline. 'Come on,' she called again, lifting her head and beckoning with her hand. 'Lay down.' She slapped the trunk next to her. Bewildered but compliant, Angus lay down next to her on the trunk. It was cold and hard, but he enjoyed laying close to her.

'Okay,' Cinder said excitedly, 'lay your head back like this.' Wordlessly, Angus followed her example and they both hung their heads off the end of the fallen tree. Cinder turned to look at him, smiling shyly when she realised how close their faces were to each other. 'Okay, now squint your eyes and look out at the coastline.' She waited a moment. 'Can you see it?' Angus laughed.

'See what?' he asked. Cinder took hold of his hand and looked again.

'It looks like the stars,' she announced proudly. 'I can see some of the constellations in the lights of the coast.'

Twinkling lights dotted the serpentine coastline – blues, yellows, and warm-white- with the occasional traffic lights rhythmically performing their amber, green, and red dance. The water mirrored some lights as shivering points on the black canvas, while other light cast bands of colour, stretching out onto the dark ocean, shimmering with the rise and fall of the waves.

'You don't get out much, do you?' Angus teased. Cinder started to laugh, making her chest move up and down awkwardly, which only made her laugh further.

'No, I don't get out much.' She took a breath. 'I don't get out much at all. Although...' she paused to wipe away a tear that had made it to her hairline. 'My mother once took me to Paris, when I was a little girl. She was hosting some enormous ball and told me that Paris was the only place to find the right dress. I knew Marraine had an apartment in Paris at the time, so I tried to run away. She never took me away again after that.' Angus turned his head to look at her.

'How old were you?' he asked.

'Seven or eight, I think. I didn't get very far before they found me.'

Angus watched her lips moving and the joy sparkling in her eyes. Even hanging upside down like this, she was beautiful. 'Who are you?' His thought came out as words. Cinder turned her head to look into his eyes.

'I'm just me, Black, nothing special.'

'I think you're someone special.' Angus, embarrassed, turned to look back at the lights. 'I mean, fancy balls and trips to Paris. Are you a celebrity and I just don't realise?'

'What haven't you seen any of my films?' she joked, 'I did wonder why you hadn't asked me for an autograph.'

'Sorry,' Angus said, trying to keep a straight face. 'I only watch black and white, Romanian art films.'

'Oh good,' Cinder replied. 'Then you might have seen some of my earlier work.' Angus noticed the lights of The Big House.

'I bet you live somewhere fancy like that. With servants and stuff,' he joked. The memory of recognising someone in Tallo's Bluff earlier in the day flashed into Cinder's mind.

'I'd rather live somewhere like this,' she said, trying to change the subject, wriggling down the log and looking up at the sky. Angus moved with her and started to sing:

*'Just rest your weary head, it's time we went to bed.'*

Cinder smiled and rested her head against his chest, listening to his heart rhythmically pushing blood around his large, warm body. 'That was nice,' she said, placing her arm around him. 'But Dom's song was better,' she teased, giggling. Angus propped his head up with his right hand and wrapped his free arm around her back, sitting his hand on her hip.

'Whatever,' he laughed, squeezing her hip. 'He had a guitar.' Cinder relaxed her body further into his embrace, her heart falling into tempo with his.

'Yes, he did have a guitar,' she conceded. 'And talent, good looks, great hair,' she continued. Angus shifted his weight slightly so that his hand could drop to Cinder's thigh.

'Now you're just being mean,' he said as he breathed in the scent of her hair. Cinder played with the hem of his shirt.

'Sorry, I'm being naughty,' she teased. Angus could feel the coldness of her fingers as they occasionally found the skin of his stomach.

'I'm okay with naughty,' he uttered, his voice hindered by a lump in his throat.

A short distance away, in the thick night of the dense forest, something large and dark moved along on its two hind legs. Misty warm air rushed from its nostrils as they flared, sniffing the air, searching.

Lifting Angus's shirt a few centimetres, Cinder ran her fingers along the skin just above his waistband. She smiled when she felt his body stiffen and his hand gripping her thigh. His heart rate quickened, and she crept her hand up towards his chest. The hairs on the back of Angus's neck stood up, but not because of the movement of Cinder's hand. Angus was focused on the movements of something else – something large and unseen in the darkness. It was difficult to pick out above the other noises of the night, but Angus was convinced he could hear the heavy footsteps of something moving closer to them. As quickly as he could politely move out from under Cinder, he did. 'I think we should head back now,' he said, standing up.

'What? Why?' Cinder asked, still laying on the log, unaware of the strange sounds. Angus held out his hand to lift her up.

'I just think the others will be wondering where we are.' He answered. Cinder stood up without taking his hand.

'If that's what you want.' She said, brushing off her clothes and starting to walk back to the farm.

From behind them, a crack of twigs caught their attention. This time, Cinder heard it too.

'Did you hear that?' she asked, squinting her eyes to pierce the black veil of the forest.

'Yep.' Angus's reply was short and sharp. 'Probably just a fox.' He placed his arm around her, gently but purposely moving her forward and quickening his pace. A pair of dark eyes, unblinking, watched as the two young people hurried out of the trees and back towards the distant glow of the fire.

Arriving at the fire, Cinder sat down next to Torry with her arms crossed. Angus stood next to Dom, placing a hand on his shoulder. 'Can you go get the others?' he asked. 'I think we might have a fox problem.'

'A fox?' Dom asked, turning so he could see Angus's face.

'Yep, over near Vivien's Ridge.' Angus said. The boys exchanged glances that Cinder couldn't read. Then the girls shared their own looks, leaving Angus guessing. All four stood for a few minutes in uncomfortable silence. Although no one spoke a word, a multitude of information passed between them.

Saying nothing, Dom picked up his guitar and walked away. The others watched him go. Torry was the first to break the silence. 'Well, I'm ready for bed,' she announced, stretching her arms above her head and yawning. 'I'll leave you two to it.' She made to walk away, but Cinder interrupted her.

'I'm going to bed now, anyway.'

'Are you sure?' Torry asked. 'The fire will still be going for a while yet.'

'Yep,' Cinder said, standing up and walking away from the fire. 'I'm very sleepy'

'Okay, sis, do you want me to walk you?' Torry asked, sending Cinder another look.

'No, it's okay. I'll talk to you tomorrow. Goodnight.' Cinder said.

'Goodnight.' Torry said, jumping up and hugging her.

'Goodnight, Black. Sleep well.' Cinder said, looking at Angus and hugging Torry.

Angus looked down at her and smiled.

'Goodnight Cin,' he said, 'sweet dreams.' Cinder stood up straight, stretching and yawning before taking Torry's hands, squeezing them as she walked away.

Angus watched Cinder walk towards the guesthouse until she was out of view. Torry whacked him on the chest. 'Hey!' Angus protested. 'What was that for?'

'What did you do?' Torry asked, pointing her finger at him.

'I didn't do anything.'

'Oh, you did something, and you need to figure it out.'

'I have no idea.' Angus stood, bewildered.

Torry left to go to bed. Turning once more as she walked, she said, 'Figure it out!' Angus stepped forward to warm his hands by the fire, left standing alone and confused.

• • • •

Back at Vivien's Ridge, a large, black figure emerged from the trees. Stopping first to sniff the air, it climbed onto the fallen tree and smelled the spot where Angus and Cinder had been lying.

# Chapter 7

**What's wrong?**

'Is there something wrong with me?' Cinder asked as she hosed mud off a shed floor. She was having one of the most enjoyable times she could remember, but Cinder couldn't help but wish that Angus would take their relationship further. Her growing unease about the secretiveness of Angus and her mother's voice of disapproval echoed around in her mind. Torry, who had been sweeping, stopped and leant against the broom.

'Well, you seem to enjoy doing this, so yeah, I'd say that's pretty wrong,' she said. Cinder smiled.

'No, I mean am I... do I look okay?'

'Are you serious?' laughed Torry. 'You're wearing my dad's old overalls and boots, you're covered in mud and cow crap, and you still look twice as beautiful as I ever will.'

'Thanks.' Cinder blushed. 'That's a real compliment because I think you're the cutest farm girl I've ever met.'

'Aww shucks,' replied Torry, putting her hands against her chest and batting her eyelids wildly. 'It's the mud, it's great for my complexion.' She put a comical emphasis on the last word and then bent down, wiping her hand in the mud and using it to paint stripes on her cheeks like war paint. Cinder laughed and mimicked Torry with her own muddy face-paint.

'At least we both agree that we're the hottest girls around here,' she said, striking a pose.

'Yes, yes,' said Torry, walking along an imaginary catwalk dragging her broom behind her, stopping and posing for non-existent photographers.

Uncle Gunn walked past the shed door with a bale of hay in his arms. He stopped and looked at the two muddy faced girls, who were now blowing kisses to their adoring fans. Gunn just smiled and walked away, shaking his head. Cinder and Torry cracked up laughing. 'I wish Angus thought the way you do,' Cinder said when she caught her breath.

'What are you talking about?' said Torry, going back to sweeping. 'He can't take his eyes off you.'

'If that's the case, why won't he, you know, take things further?' Cinder asked. Torry walked over to the door to see if her dad was out of ear-shot, before running back to Cinder.

'Are you going to sleep with Black?' She whispered.

'No!' Cinder replied, becoming very embarrassed. 'I'm just talking about kissing.' Torry dropped her broom and her jaw.

'What!? You haven't kissed yet?' She covered her mouth to stop herself from giggling. Cinder frowned at her. 'I'm sorry,' Torry continued. 'We all just assumed... what have you guys been doing on your walks together then?'

'Nice to know everyone's talking about us,' Cinder grumped as she picked up Torry's broom. 'We've been talking and getting to know each other, if everyone must know.' She pushed the broom back into Torry's hands.

'It's not like that,' said Torry, sweeping the floor again but stopping almost immediately to lean her chin on the broom handle. 'Well, it is actually,' she laughed, 'but you've got to understand that it's usually so boring around here. You're the most exciting thing that's happened in ages.' Cinder gave her an embarrassed sideways grin.

'This is the most exciting time I've had in a long time too.' Cinder said. 'I guess I'd just like it to, well, keep getting better.' Torry had stopped and was staring at Cinder with a stupid grin on her face. 'What?' Cinder questioned irritably.

'Nothing, nothing.' Torry put down her head and started sweeping again. 'It's just, well,' she continued, smiling again, 'it's just that this is the most girly talk I think I've ever had.'

'I'm sorry,' Cinder apologised.

'That's okay,' replied Torry, leaning her broom up against the wall and walking over to take Cinder's broom. 'What are sisters for?' Torry placed Cinder's broom with hers, before interlocking her fingers and stretching her arms up over her head. 'I'm gonna talk to Black when he gets up this afternoon.' Cinder began making objections to Torry's statement, but Gunn returned.

'Hello girls, 'tis looking very nice in here.' Gunn said as he entered the shed.

'Dad! You're interrupting secret girls' business,' Torry complained.

'I'm sorry, princess.' Gunn placed a large hairy arm around his daughter and squeezed her into his chest. 'I've been doing some girly stuff too. See this?' He held up an old dusty book. 'This has a whole chapter about jewellery in it and I thought I might read up on it again.' Cinder suddenly became uncomfortably aware that Uncle Gunn kept glancing at her chest. She crossed her arms in front of her and gave him an embarrassed smile.

'Dad, you stink,' Torry protested as she tried fruitlessly to work her way free of Gunn's arms.

'Alright, alright,' he said, letting her go. 'It's lunchtime anyway, girls. Come in and get cleaned up.'

Cinder had a strange feeling in her stomach for the rest of the afternoon. She was anxious about what Torry might say to Angus, and something about the way Gunn had looked at her was making her feel uncomfortable. Something at the back of her mind that she couldn't put her finger on was causing an alarm bell to ring. There was also another feeling that grew as the afternoon crept by, one that she had never expected: homesickness. Her home life was not great, but at least it was predictable and familiar. Here, as nice as everyone was, she was never sure how to behave or what anyone was thinking about her. She tried to talk to Torry several times during the afternoon, but Torry kept her busy. There was always another task for them to do whenever Cinder tried to talk about Angus. In the late afternoon, Torry slipped away, leaving Cinder peeling some potatoes with Uncle Dand, who was talking to Cinder about hunting quail. Cinder hoped she was nodding and smiling at the right points in his story because she really wasn't listening.

A few hundred metres south of the main house was a wooden cabin that was the original farmhouse. This was where Dom and Angus and some of the others now slept. Torry found Angus still in bed.

'Wake up, princess!' she yelled, as she pulled his pillow out from under his head. Angus ran his hand over his crumpled face and through his messy hair before slowly opening one eye.

'Seriously?' he mumbled. 'I thought your brother was bad, but you, you're the worst kind of person.' He closed his eye again. Torry whacked him with the pillow.

'Oy, wake up, I need to talk to you.' She made to hit him again, but he grabbed the pillow and pulled it away from her, covering his ear.

'Make an appointment with my secretary,' Angus grumped.

'I'm serious,' Torry pushed on, 'I need to talk to you about Cinder before she finds a way to get away from Uncle Dand.'

'Alright, alright, I'm awake.' Angus rolled over and hugged the pillow to his chest, still only able to open one eye. 'What's wrong with Cinder? I thought she was having a good time here. You two seem to be getting along.'

'It's not what's wrong with *her*, it's what's wrong with *you*.' Torry flopped down on the end of his bed. Angus finally opened his other eye and raised his eyebrows. He opened his mouth, but Torry continued. 'Do you like her or what? Are you just stringing her along? Because if you hurt her, you'll have to answer to me.'

'Okay, okay. Down girl.' Angus sat up in his bed, stretching and yawning. 'I like her just fine and I don't even know what you mean by stringing her along.'

'I mean,' she said angrily, grabbing his pillow and hitting him again. 'Inviting her to stay here and then avoiding all the opportunities you've had to... to... to get with her.'

'Get with her?' Angus laughed but also looked embarrassed.

Dom yawned loudly from the other side of the room to announce that he was awake and listening in on their conversation. 'She's got a point, mate,' he said

'Not you too. I thought you were on my side,' Angus protested.

'I am on your side, Black, but seriously, you need to make a move and then move on. We can't have this chick hanging around here.'

'That chick?' Torry glared at Dom. 'That *chick* is a friend of mine and she has a name.'

'She has a home too, and it's time she went there.' Dom sat up in bed and threw off his covers to expose his naked body. He yawned, scratching his chest hair before standing and searching through a basket of clothes beside his bed. Torry held her hand in front of her eyes, as if to block out bright sunlight.

'Firstly, put it away. Secondly, why have you suddenly got something against Cinder?' she asked. Dom sniffed a pair of black boxer shorts he had just pulled out of the basket.

'I don't have anything against her, I just wish he,' he pointed his hand still holding the boxer shorts, towards Angus, 'would hurry up and put something against her, so then she can leave.' Torry, still holding up her hand to block out Dom's nakedness, rolled her eyes and shook her head from side to side.

'I don't want her to leave. It's been nice to have another girl around here. What about you Black, what do you want?'

Angus looked from Dom to Torry and then shrugged his shoulders.

'You don't know? Really?' Torry asked. 'No wonder she's pissed with you. And you,' she turned on Dom, 'put some bloody clothes on.'

'Hey, what's wrong with you? It's not like you've never seen it before. We used to have baths together.' Dom said, picking up a towel that was draped over the back of an old chair in the corner.

'That was a long time ago,' Torry answered. 'Back before all the hair and... man... stuff.'

'Hang on,' said Angus, suddenly looking very awake. 'She's angry with me?'

'Yes, silly,' Torry walked over and put her hands on Angus's shoulders. 'That's what I've been trying to tell you. She's going to find you soon to talk to you.'

'That's good,' Dom interrupted. 'If she gets angry enough, she might leave.' Angus and Torry both turned and glowered at him. 'What?' asked Dom, heading for the door. 'It's two days till the full moon. Do we really want some girl we don't even know hanging around then?'

'I think we should tell her, tell her what we are,' Torry replied. Dom's eyebrows shot up and his mouth dropped open.

'Are you serious? You want to endanger all of us and break thousands of years of tradition just so Black can get a bit? That's the stupidest thing I've ever heard and trust me,' he pointed at his bare chest, 'I know stupid.'

Angus sat quietly, deep in thought for a few moments. 'Let her know I'm up and I want to talk to her.'

'If she's coming in here, I'll help you clean up a bit first,' Torry said, looking around at the piles of clothes, empty bottles, food wrappers, and other unrecognisable objects.

'What's wrong with our room?' Dom asked, looking hurt. Torry crossed her arms and raised an eyebrow.

'You know it smells like armpit and ass in here, don't you?' she replied in disgust. Angus laughed to himself and walked to the door.

'I'll go get some garbage bags.'

'And some rubber gloves please,' Torry called after him. Dom followed Angus, shaking his head in disbelief.

'I'm going to have a shower. Don't let him tell her!' he said, as he left the room and slammed the door behind him.

Half an hour later, Torry returned to the boy's room with Cinder. With a reassuring nod from Torry, Cinder knocked nervously on the bedroom door.

'Come in,' came Angus's muffled invitation. Cinder entered the room slowly, followed by Torry. Unbeknownst to her, the room was now far more organised and better smelling than it was earlier that evening.

'Dom, can you help me with this stuff?' Torry pointed to the basket full of dirty washing and three large green garbage bags that were sitting against the wall just inside the door. Dom begrudgingly agreed, picked up the garbage, and squeezed his way out of the door. Torry followed him out with the washing basket, winking at Cinder as she pulled the door shut with her foot.

Cinder looked around the room. To her left, mounted on the wall, were two halves of a yellow surfboard above a metal-framed bed. Randomly hung posters of people surfing and women in bikinis covered the remaining wall space. Next to the bed were an old wooden chair and a section of wall containing photos of girls Cinder didn't recognise. Dom's side of the room, she thought to herself. On the right, Angus's side, there were three simple pieces of matching timber furniture: a corner desk, a bookcase, and a bed.

The room fell silent the moment Torry shut the door behind her. Angus stood cross-legged by his desk, fumbling with a book. Cinder walked over to the bookcase, her eyes darting over the covers of the books, searching for something. 'La petite Pantoufle de Verre,' she read the title of one of the books. 'A lot of these are French,' she said, running her fingers along the spines of several books.

'Yes,' Angus said, sitting on his desk. 'Oui, I should say.'

Cinder smiled and looked down at her fingertips, that were now covered in dust.

'Do you read them?' she asked.

'I try to. My French isn't great,' Angus said, placing the book down. These were my dad's books.' A boyish softness in his eyes as he talked about his father, made Cinder feel she could melt into his arms. 'He lived in France for a while as a boy,' Angus continued. 'I can still remember him translating these into English for me and Katie.' The softness evaporated at the mention of his sister's name. Replaced with a new emotion. Sorrow, loss, despair? Cinder felt her eyes becoming glassy in unanimity with his. Now all she wanted to do was wrap him up in her arms. She swallowed hard to stem the tide of emotion welling up inside and walked over to an open window at the far end of the room. Long shadows had grown on the green paddocks. The sun had almost disappeared over the horizon, casting a pink canvas behind fluffy grey clouds. Far off in the distance, a flock of seabirds did their last hunting in the quickly retreating daylight. Cinder placed her hands on the sill and leant out of the window, taking a deep breath.

'It really is beautiful out there,' she said.

Angus turned to see her framed by the window. His eyes moved up the curves of her body. Leaning on the window frame had exposed a small section of skin on her lower back, and her hair seemed to move in slow motion as it caught the wind.

'It's beautiful in here too,' he said with some difficulty because of a lump in his throat. Cinder turned and sat on the windowsill, looking down at the floor.

'What is this? What am I to you?' she asked. 'I feel like there's something here and then there's not, and then Tor tells me that she thinks I'm pretty and that you do too, but I don't know. I don't know what you think.' She looked up, searching his eyes as if she was looking for a puzzle piece buried behind them.

Angus approached her and put his hand against her cheek. 'You're the most intriguing girl – woman – that I've ever met, and yes, I find you attractive, very attractive. But this is all new to me. I don't know what this is either,' he said. Cinder put her hand over Angus's.

'Just tell me what you want this to be. I'm happy to follow your lead,' she said, smiling into his large, dark eyes.

'I... I want,' but Dom interrupted him, coming back into the room.

'Time to go, Black.' Dom called. Angus quickly dropped his hand to his side.

'Alright, I'm coming,' he called back to Dom. 'Sorry, can we talk about this later? I have to go.' He turned back to Cinder and could see by the look on her face that it was anything but okay. She crossed her arms, pushed past him, and sat down on his bed.

'You have to go? Surfing?' she asked.

'There's more to it than that, Cin,' he said, walking over to his desk again and playing with the cover of a book.

'I know there is, Black. I'm not stupid.' Cinder got up and turned towards the door. 'What I don't know is why you're not telling me.' Angus grabbed her by the hand and turned her around.

'I'm sorry,' he apologised again. 'It's complicated.' Cinder stared into his pleading face for several seconds. She was furious with him, but what else could she do? It wasn't her place to pry any further.

'Okay, whatever,' she said finally. 'Let's go surfing.'

Dom, who was still standing in the doorway, cleared his throat and raised his eyebrows. Angus let go of Cinder's hand and turned back to the book on his desk. 'I, um, I think you should stay here tonight,' he said, flicking the pages.

'Sure thing!' Cinder shouted, as she saluted Angus and stormed out of the room, bumping Dom out of the way as she went.

'I think that went well, don't you?' Dom said, rubbing his shoulder.

'Shut up,' Angus said, as he walked out and bumped hard into his other shoulder.

'Hey!' Dom called out, throwing his arms in the air. 'How hard is it to say excuse me?' He followed Angus out, shaking his head. 'Sometimes I think I'm the only one around here with any manners.'

• • • •

Cinder sat alone in the dark on an old tractor tire. A crack in the tin sheet walls was allowing moonlight to fall across her hands. She didn't know how long she had been staring at her hands, but it had been long enough for the blood coming from the dozens of small cuts and cracks on her knuckles to coagulate. It had been long enough for the boxing bag behind her, that she had beaten so violently that it was a wonder the old building she was in was still standing, was now completely still. It had been long enough for Cinder to come to the depressing realisation that the pain in her hands gave her some kind of comforting familiarity. The sweat on her back was getting cold. She retrieved a hair-tie gingerly from her jeans pocket and pulled her hair into a ponytail.

As she wiped the perspiration from the back of her neck, she realised that in her anger she had not only lost track of time; she wasn't sure where on the farm she was. She had stormed off from Angus's room and wandered around the farm before retreating to the guest house. Hours went by as she tried fruitlessly to fall asleep. Finally, she got out of bed and sat at the bottom of the shower, letting the hot water run over her until the shower went cold. After getting dressed again, she went back into the night, trying to find something to occupy her mind so she could stop thinking about Angus's stupid face. Eventually, she spotted a punching bag hanging from the rafters of an old shed.

Stepping away from the bag and wiping her palms on her jeans, she looked around the shed. Hanging from hooks just in front of her were a few old pairs of boxing gloves and a skipping rope. Scattered around the dirt floor were free weights, barbells, and other various exercise paraphernalia. Further down towards one end where it was darker, there were objects hanging from the wall that Cinder couldn't quite make out. She walked forward out of the moonlight to let her eyes adjust to the darkness. *'Hunting equipment?'* she thought to herself. She could see a compound bow with a quiver of arrows and some other metallic objects and... a sword? She moved in for a closer look, squinting her eyes, but then she became aware of some strange noises coming from the main house.

• • • •

Dom crashed in through the front door, rattling framed photos of his mother on the wall. 'Dad, get your med-kit!'

Blair stumbled into the room next, supporting a half-conscious Angus, who let out painful moans with each awkward step. All three men were blood-stained and out of breath.

'What the hell happened?' Gunn called out, as he pushed his body to move as fast as it could.

'They got Black,' Dom called out, as Gunn left the room.

'Who got him?' Cinder was standing frozen in the doorway. Her large green eyes appeared to have doubled in size and the colour had drained from her face.

# Chapter 8

### 'Fore the Sun Wakes

'The rocks,' Gunn said quickly, as he returned with his old, brown Gladstone bag. 'He came off his board onto the rocks,' he continued, gently peeling back Angus's torn t-shirt. 'Could you get us a chair from the kitchen, love?'

Cinder ran into the kitchen and returned with a wooden chair in her trembling hands. Dom and Blair sat Angus down, as Gunn pulled out his spectacles and placed them on the end of his nose. He got slowly down on one knee and sat his bag on the floor. Rummaging in the bag for a moment, he produced some small stainless-steel scissors. 'Okay then, let's see what we have here.'

Cinder walked slowly around behind Angus, as Gunn cut away the ripped and bloody material around the wound. On seeing the full extent of Angus's injuries, she took a sharp breath in and held her hand over her mouth. 'Shouldn't he go to the hospital?' she asked. Five dark red scratches of various depths ran from his left shoulder, across his back, and finished just under his right armpit.

'He'll be fine.' Gunn said, pulling out some gauze and a bottle of green liquid. 'Can you hold him, boys?' he motioned with a flick of his head to Dom and Blair. They both took a hold of an arm each and placed their other hands on his legs. Gunn soaked the gauze in the green liquid and wiped the blood away from Angus's back. Angus flung his head back and let out a throaty groan. Sweat appeared around his hairline and his feet started to shake wildly. Cinder watched as the perspiration rolled down his neck, mixing with the blood and green liquid. That was when something strange dawned on her.

'Why isn't he in his wetsuit, and why is his hair dry?' she asked. Dom and Blair gave each other curious sideways glances.

'We needed to get him warm, to stop him going into shock,' Blair answered. Cinder turned this over in her mind. She was just about to ask why his t-shirt had rips in it too, when Gunn must have hit a tender spot on Angus's back. Angus lurched up out of the chair, yelling and thrashing about. Dom was able to hold on to his arm, but Angus was too strong for Blair. He fell back, landing on the floor, and narrowly missed hitting his head on the fireplace. Cinder moved quickly to grab Angus's arm and help Dom sit him back down. She held his trembling wrist and stroked his face with her free hand. Slowly, his eyes came back into focus.

'Sorry,' he said, taking hold of her hand and trying to smile.

'No, no,' Cinder protested. 'I'm sorry. This is my fault.'

Blair picked himself up and straightened his clothes.

'Where's my sorry, jerk?' he asked. Angus forced a laugh.

Torry entered from the hallway, wearing pyjamas. She had been asleep, but the commotion woke her. She opened her mouth to ask what was happening, but on reading the expression on Gunn's face, she made her way silently over to Cinder. 'Come on, let's give Dad some space,' she said, as she placed her hands on Cinder's back and shoulder. 'Black's going to be fine.'

Cinder watched the steam dance on top of the dark liquid in the mug that Torry had just handed her. She ran her finger along the brown lines that formed a geometric pattern around the rim while Torry took a seat on the bed next to her, trying not to spill her own hot cup of tea. A smile pulled at the ends of Cinder's mouth when she thought about how fond she had grown of this girl she had shared a first pot of tea with, only a week ago. She took a sip, closing her eyes and letting out a long breath. Torry, understanding her unspoken concern, placed her free hand on her shoulder. 'He's going to be okay,' she reassured her. Cinder nodded and looked around Torry's room. It was about twice the size of her bedroom at home, but no tidier. There was a narrow walkway around piles of clothes, shoes, and magazines, and

Cinder could see from the reflection in the mirror on the inside of the open wardrobe door, that the only clothes hanging up were Torry's school and football uniforms. It did, however, smell clean and fresh, like Torry, Cinder thought, reminiscent of grass and sunshine with a hint of vanilla.

Cinder took another sip of her tea, looking down at her feet. 'I feel like it's my fault he fell off his board. I was angry with him and I wanted him to hurt like I was hurting.'

'You know that's not possible, right?' Torry spluttered, almost choking on her tea. 'They have a dangerous hobby; they're going to get hurt sometimes.'

'So why do they do it?' Cinder asked, her face still grimaced with concern. Torry looked up at the ceiling as if the answer to the question might be hovering in the air above her head.

'Um, I don't know. It's just something we've always done.' She gave Cinder another reassuring smile and continued, 'We're nocturnal people and we like to live by the ocean, so I guess it just happened.'

Cinder could feel a jumble of emotions welling up inside. She was worried about Angus, but angry with herself that she cared. She placed her cup down on Torry's bedside table and hugged her legs up under her chin. 'Well, I think it's stupid,' she spat. Torry placed her cup down next to Cinder's and lay her head on Cinder's shoulder, looking up at her with puppy-dog eyes.

'It's stupid, or *he's* stupid?' she asked.

'It, him, us, all this. I don't know,' said Cinder, moaning and looking up at the ceiling. 'I just feel like he's holding back, you know, like there's stuff he's not telling me.'

Torry laughed.

'You haven't spent much time around boys, have you?' she asked.

'No, why?'

'Boys, don't talk,' Torry said, placing her hand on Cinder's knee. 'Not about important stuff anyway, especially not their feelings. I'm actually amazed that Angus has talked to you as much as he has.'

'I guess I just wish it didn't feel like he was hiding something from me.' Cinder said, smiling and shrugging. Torry leant forward and arched her neck around so that she could make eye contact with Cinder.

'Why? We all have secrets Cinder. I'm sure there's more to you than meets the eye. Have you told him all your secrets, opened up your closet, and let all the skeletons out? No?' Torry smiled while she looked into Cinder's eyes, one after the other. 'Hey, I don't even know your last name, and I don't care. All I need to know is that you're a good person and a good friend.'

Cinder sat thinking about what Torry had said, her cheeks warming with embarrassment. Torry was right. She had shared nothing about her real-life with Angus, but she was expecting him to share everything with her. 'Delacourt,' she said, to break the silence.

'What?' Torry asked, smiling with confusion.

'That's my last name, Delacourt.'

'Oh, a pleasure to meet you, Miss Delacourt.' Torry presented her right hand and Cinder reciprocated, shaking her hand firmly.

'The pleasure is all mine.' Cinder stood up and looked at herself in a small mirror that hung on Torry's bedroom door. She imagined the word 'liar' tattooed across her forehead. 'Thank you, Tor.' She said as she looked back at the amazing young girl who, although she really knew nothing about her, had accepted her as family. 'You've given me a lot to think about.' Cinder flopped down on the bed next to Torry and kissed her cheek. 'I'll see you later,' she said, then jumped up and left the room.

The sun was just a semicircle, poking its sleepy head over the green paddocks as Cinder left the main house. She folded her arms across her chest to fight the cool of the morning, but smiled at the beauty of the pinks and reds that were stretching across the sky. By the time she got back to her room, she had made up her mind; she was going to tell Angus the truth, all of it.

Torry watched the last drop of water fall from the tattered flannelette cloth she was holding, before shaking her hands and returning to the table. Angus sat uncomfortably at one end. Gunn studied his wounds, peering over the dark rims of his spectacles set low on his nose. Torry wiped the sweat from his brow, noticing with relief that some colour had returned to his cheeks. 'How does it feel?' she asked as she rested her other hand on his cheek.

'Like my back is on fire. How's Cin?' Angus asked, forcing his lips into a smile.

'I gave her a cup of tea and that seemed to help. She's got a lot of questions, though,' Torry said.

'I've got some questions for her too,' Gunn interrupted. Angus and Torry both raised their eyebrows questioningly. 'Another time maybe,' Gunn continued. 'I think I've done all I can for the moment. What he needs now is some music and a drink.'

'Whiskey?' Angus inquired.

'For me, yes, but for you, my boy, something more medicinal I think.' Gunn nodded to Torry, who responded with her own nod of understanding. She leant down, kissed the top of Angus's head, turned on her heel, and left the room. Gunn made his way into the sitting room and opened an old wooden cupboard. Getting slowly down onto one knee, he pulled out a long black case and a small silver hip flask. From the flask, he took a long sip and from the case, he took *Mildred,* his banjo. He deposited the flask into his shirt pocket, freeing up a hand to pull himself up on the cupboard. 'Okay,' he exclaimed to no one in particular. 'Here we go.' He began playing as he walked back to the kitchen to sit at the table. Then he sang:

• • • •

*The daylight will show us all our mistakes.*
*So, drink in the moonshine 'fore the sun even wakes.*

• • • •

Torry returned with a large glass of thick, dark red liquid and handed it to Angus. 'Thanks,' he said, closed his eyes, and then swallowed it in four loud gulps.

# Chapter 9

### Flight, Fight, and Fire Light.

Cinder walked slowly, feeling the soft grass under her feet, the moonlight guiding her. She had a blanket around her shoulders, pulled up over her head to fight the cold and nervous energy that was snaking its way down her spine. She had never been one to like flowers, but she was trying to find some small white bell-shaped ones she had seen growing wild around the farm. After spending most of the day sleeping, she ate an early dinner before taking an afternoon walk in the trees to collect her thoughts. Pulling the blanket closer to her face, she could smell Torry. She had pilfered it from Torry's room earlier when she left her a note explaining her plan for the night.

The full moon made it easier to find contributions to her posy, but it was a reminder that she was working to a deadline. Come midnight, she either needed to have worked up the courage to speak to Angus, or given in to her fear and made her way home. A tingling feeling she had had in her stomach all evening intensified, and her breathing became more rapid. Fight or flight? Either way, she knew she would need that extra adrenaline tonight. 'Okay,' she said aloud to herself, as she picked half a dozen more flowers. She held the blanket to her chest with her chin as she arranged the stems. Standing up, she took a deep breath and looked up at the moon. 'Okay,' she said again, as if she hadn't convinced herself the first time. She made her way past the old trees and stone fences out on to the dirt road, hoping she could remember the way to the beach by herself.

Torry closed her bedroom door firmly behind her and flopped onto her bed. The inner-springs of her mattress noisily protesting their sudden change of shape. After not being able to wake Cinder in the morning, she had decided to let her sleep and do her jobs by herself; a decision she was now regretting. She was stiff, exhausted, and ready for the day to be over. Forcing herself to sit up in bed, she started to take off her boots. She had one boot off before she noticed a folded piece of paper on her bedside table. She plucked the note off the table and flopped back on her bed. Unfolding it, she read:

*Dear Tor,*

*Thank you for your acceptance and friendship. I have never had someone like you in my life before. You are truly the closest to a little sister that I have ever known. I am going to talk to Black tonight and explain some things to him that I have never told anyone outside of my family. If all goes to plan and Black is the kind of man I think he is, then our friendship will be able to continue. If things don't go well, this may be the last night I can spend with your family. I wish I could tell you more and I hope I soon will be able to, but I think it is only fair that I should talk to Black first.*

*Thank you again for everything you have done for me. I hope to see you soon.*

*Love your big sis.*

*Cinder.*

Torry dropped the note and blundered out of her room, struggling to put her boot back on and snatching a jacket off the floor as she did.

It was a mild night, but the ocean breeze was enough to send a chill down Cinder's spine as it roared in her ears and sent wisps of loose hair across her face. She pulled the blanket around her cheeks and descended the steps that snaked down through the grassy dunes. Silver light from the full moon accorded her an unobstructed view of the beach. Whispering winds picked up plumes of dry sand and carried them away, like ghostly apparitions searching for a place to rest. The ocean stretched out flat and calm before her, foamy waves lapping gently against the shore and displacing previously deposited seaweed and driftwood. The moon shone bright, white, and clear on the ocean's surface and it didn't take long for Cinder to realise that no one was in the water.

Anxiety and self-doubt spiralled in Cinder's head. What if they had already gone home and she couldn't find Angus before midnight? What if he was lying and had just told her he was surfing to get away from her? She could feel her chest vibrating under the force of her heart pounding against her ribcage. 'Don't be stupid,' she said to herself, shaking the thought from her head. 'No time to panic now.' She made her way back up the steps. When she reached the gravel of the empty carpark at the top, her footsteps crunched loudly in the night's quiet. There were spaces for about five cars, six at a push, and a second bluestone road disappeared off to the right, behind a thick growth of peppercorn trees. Knowing better than most the dangers that lurk in the night-covered corners of the world, she convinced herself that it was safe for her to venture into the dark alone. As she followed the road, the sounds of crickets, bats, and other unseen creatures of the night replaced the rumble of the ocean. She had to be careful with her footing in the shadowed darkness, stumbling a few times on the ruts worn by the vehicles of countless beachgoers. To Cinder's relief, it wasn't long before the canopy opened again, and the road broadened into another parking area.

The unmistakable round headlights of Blair's 1971 VW station wagon gleamed like two large, smiling eyes in the moonlight. In the daylight, it was a bright canary yellow, but it now appeared a ghostly white against the dark backdrop of dense trees and shrubs. On closer inspection, Cinder found that there were four surfboards strapped to the roof rack but no sign of the owners. Looking around was fruitless. A dark wall of branches and leaves surrounded her. Cinder closed her eyes and sat on the bonnet, hoping her other senses might give her some direction. The hairs on the back of her neck stood up. Something was wrong. Cinder suddenly had the distinct feeling that she was being followed. Her eyes involuntarily shot open, and she whipped her head around from left to right. Nothing, no movement other than dark talons of the trees cavorting in the breeze that swirled in eddies around the canopy.

Cinder forced her eyes closed again. The tingle in her neck had now taken up residence in the small of her back, forcing her entire body to sit forward, ridged, ready for flight or fight. It took a few moments for her to calm her heartbeat enough to be able to hear anything else, but when she had calmed a little, the other sounds started to build a picture in her mind. The wind up above, the rustle of leaves in the undergrowth, the distant rumble of the ocean, a man laughing further off, and the footsteps of something large on the road, still some way off, but coming closer. As quickly as she could, while trying to remain quiet and navigate her way in the darkness, Cinder ran. She decided to head towards the laughter. It seemed a safer option to head towards a cheerful person than towards the unknown thing that was following her.

The gravel road wound its way along the edge of a hill another six or seven hundred metres, before turning into a sandy walking track that made straight up the hill. The trees beside the track thinned, and Cinder was glad of more moonlight to help her find her way. It concerned her that her footprints would be easier to see in the sand. As much as possible, she tried to walk on the grassy edges of the track to conceal her prints. At the back of her mind, she couldn't help thinking that, if the thing she feared was following her, really was, it wouldn't need to follow tracks. The sweat that was now creating a large damp patch on her back would be more than enough to leave a scent behind. With this thought, she sniffed the air herself. There was something new – smoke – another good sign. A fire could provide light or a weapon and usually meant people. Quickening her pace, she abandoned the plan of staying off the sand. The new plan was simply to outrun her unseen pursuer. '*Not a great plan, Cinder,*' she thought to herself. '*You don't even know who you're running to, and you're running out of time.*'

At the top of the hill, the trees all but disappeared, replaced by tall grass and a few large rocks. The red glow of the flames appeared to her left and she could hear the fire crackling and the muffled voices of people talking. Pausing to catch her breath, Cinder dared a quick glance down the hill behind her. There was movement everywhere, but nothing to suggest it was because of anything more than the breeze. The longer she looked, however, the more her fear augmented her perception. Every moonlit reflection became a pair of eyes peering through the trees. Every sway of the grass was something crawling up the hill. Every shadow of the rocks was a menacing silhouette.

Shaking these thoughts from her head, Cinder moved on towards the fire, trying as best she could to stay in the shadows until she could see who the owners of the muffled voices were. A handful of figures sat scattered around the smoky orange glow, their faces unrecognisably silhouetted against the flames. The figure closest to Cinder rose and lifted a bottle into the air. The bottle looked dwarfed by the giant hand and arm holding it, and when Cinder noticed the moonlight reflecting off a bald head, she was all but convinced that she was looking at Duncan. She was preparing to call out to him when his name froze in her throat. Something out of the corner of her eye had caught her attention. Emerging from the tree line below, were two tall, dark, humanoid figures.

Blair shielded his face from the heat of the fire with his left hand and forearm. A flurry of sparks rose on the hot currents and escaped into the darkness. He stabbed at the red coals with an old branch. The distant streetlights of Heathcote loomed like dozens of cat's eyes in the darkness behind him. Blissfully ignorant of the two new shadows appearing stealthily behind him, he took a seat on a log at the edge of the warmth. Blair studied the end of the branch, red embers slowly

turning one by one into blackness. The crackling of the fire and the
chatter of his companions were more than enough to conceal the
sounds of dry grass crunching, the snap of a twig, or the shuffling of
gravel underfoot of the skilled predator that was now just one more
leap away.

He heard his attacker move before he saw it, but Blair was too
slow. Two large, powerful arms wrapped around his chest as something
pulled him aggressively to the dirt. Trying desperately to turn the
situation around, he scrambled to get his free arm between himself
and the ground, but his attacker pulled his arms back, stretching his
shoulder painfully. 'Arrr, shit!' Blair yelled before snapping the end of
the branch still clasped in his free hand. He glimpsed his attacker's leg
and swung wildly at it. He was about to make contact when a second set
of hands grabbed his arm and pried the branch from his grip. Unable
to move and his heart thumping in his chest, which was pushed against
the ground, Blair heard a familiar giggle in his ear, followed by a wet
tongue on his earlobe.

'Say you're my bitch,' Dom whispered, breathing into Blair's ear.
'Say you're my bitch and I'll let you go.'

'Alright, alright, I'm your bitch,' Blair conceded.

Dom sat up and ruffled Blair's hair as he pushed his face into the
ground. 'Good bitch,' he said as he climbed off Blair and patted him on
the back.

Getting slowly to his feet, Blair dusted himself off and spat into
the fire. The firelight glowed red in his eyes as he glared at Dom.
His tongue gathered the last traces of dirt from his mouth before he
spat again. In a flash, he whirled around and punched Dom in the
left cheek. Dom stumbled back as the rest of the group erupted into
laughter. 'What the hell? I almost stabbed you,' Blair yelled, pointing
at the broken branch in Angus's hand. Dom sat down on the log and
wriggled his chin to check that everything was intact. He forced a grin
and looked up into Blair's contorted face.

'That would have been funny,' Dom said. They all burst into laughter again, including Blair and Dom.

'Here you go, boys,' the twins Rory and Tavish called out in unison, throwing a duffle bag each to Dom and Angus. Dom stood up and placed his bag on the log. He gave his cheek a rub and then unzipped his wetsuit.

Cinder had found a bush large enough to conceal her when she crouched down. She had watched the two dark figures make their way stealthily up the hill and had been preparing to run and help Blair when she realised with relief that it was just Angus and Dom playing a prank on their mates. Now that their play fighting was over, Cinder made to go talk to Angus. She stood up and notice that Dom was halfway through removing his wetsuit. With embarrassment, she ducked back behind the bush. She was desperate to talk to Angus, but thought she should wait until Dom had some clothes on. Glancing through the leaves of the bush, she could see Dom's large chest and rippled stomach glistening in the firelight. She turned away again quickly, instinctively looking around to see that no one was watching her. Cinder had never seen a naked man in the flesh before. She looked down at the ground and up at the sky, trying to look anywhere but at Dom. A smile crept onto her face as she shrugged her shoulders and turned back to peep through the bush. Dom was now completely naked. He had his back to her, showing a black, Celtic thistle tattoo that took up most of his back. Cinder covered her mouth and laughed to herself as she watched him warming his round white butt cheeks. Angus appeared from the other side of the fire to stand next to Dom, mimicking his goofy smile.

Cinder could hear their laughter, but couldn't distinguish what was being said. She watched as Angus turned to face the fire. The reflection of the flames danced in his large dark eyes above his strong cheekbones, and his thick hair hung in wet thickets. Reaching slowly over his shoulder, he unzipped his wetsuit, unfolding it from his back and sliding off his muscular arms. Cinder could feel herself becoming uncomfortable again, but made no attempt to look away. This time there was more interest and excitement mixed in with the embarrassment. Angus peeled the suit off his torso and let it hang around his waist. Cinder noted his chest was larger and hairier than Dom's, more manly, she thought as she watched him run his hand through the dark hair around his naval.

Angus watched a small blue flame pirouette out of a hole in a large log, then turned to see Dom's pale backside bobbing next to him. Smiling, he turned to see if Dom was watching him. Dom was making a joke with Bowie about blondes and redheads, when he jumped forward, cursing at the top of his voice and clutching his backside. 'What the hell?' he cried, inspecting the red handprint that was materialising on his left buttock. Angus had slapped him so hard that the sound had echoed through the chilly night air. 'Look at what you did,' Dom yelled at Angus, who was laughing. Raised white lines appeared between the red finger marks. Looking at his handy work only made Angus laugh harder, the others joining in as well. In retaliation, Dom took a swipe at him. Quickly sidestepping, Angus narrowly avoided Dom's fist making contact with his left shoulder blade.

'Not his back, stupid.' Duncan moved swiftly on his long legs to stand in between his two friends. 'You'll open his wound up again. Give us a look at it.' Duncan took Angus by his shoulders and angled him so that the fire illuminated the wounds on his back.

Even from a distance, Cinder could see that his injuries were healing very well. Whatever Gunn had done to him must have worked, she thought. Duncan placed his hand on Angus's shoulder and motioned something to the twins. Tavish walked over to Angus and handed him a glass bottle. He accepted it with a nod and unscrewed the lid. Eyeing the thick, dark liquid, he took a swig, wiping the residue from his lips with his thumb and index finger.

Cinder moved her head from side to side to get a better view of what it was he was drinking. It resembled red wine, but with a strange consistency. If she didn't know better, she would think it was... 'No, it can't be,' she said to herself and took a deep breath in through her nose. Even from this distance, she recognised the smell, mostly because of the sick feeling it gave her in her stomach. It was the same smell that was on the breath of Patru and her mother's other friends. It was the smell that had stayed in her nostrils for weeks after her father's death and continued to return in her nightmares for years after. It was the smell she had left all over her boxing bag only a few weeks earlier. Cinder fell to her knees behind the bushes, unable to take a breath, hardly able to think. The blanket fell slowly from her shoulders, briefly bobbing up and down on a branch before flopping to the ground. Shaking uncontrollably, Cinder sat for several minutes, trying to piece together the thoughts spinning wildly around her mind.

Then she ran.

She ran like the night would close in around her if she didn't keep ahead of it. She felt like a scream was trying to escape from her chest, trapped by the lump growing in her throat. Warm tears started rolling down her cold cheeks and she could taste their saltiness in her mouth as she gasped for air. How could she have been so stupid? She ran down the hill, stumbling in the soft sand dunes at the bottom. Then up a dirt road, past fences and trees, through a gate into open fields and kept running. When she finally had to stop to catch her breath, she realised she didn't know where she was. It must be getting close to midnight, she thought to herself. Her heart pounding and her eyes and lungs hurting, she looked frantically around for somewhere to get away, get under cover, hide. The clouds overhead drifted past the moon and like two giant white eyelids they slowly parted to reveal a glowing white eye. Silver beams of light flooded over Cinder. She felt a familiar tingle shooting up her spine and her clothes felt tight and constricting. She gasped for breath as panic set in. Fighting to steady her shaking hand, she pulled her phone from her pocket, almost dropping it twice while she tried to call Marraine.

'Hello, sweetie. Are you okay?' Marraine's voice sounded serious and concerned.

'No,' was all Cinder could say between her breaths.

'Are you hurt? Are you safe? Who's with you? Can you talk?' Marraine shot a volley of questions at her.

'I'm not hurt, I just need you.' Cinder had finally caught her breath.

'I'm sorry sweetie, I'm about half an hour away, but I will get there as soon as I can.'

'Where are you?' Cinder asked, desperately.

'I'm at the airstrip. I've been trying to get in contact with my friend here. He keeps an eye on things for me. I can't find him, sweetie, and it looks like someone's been here before me. You need to make sure you stay in your room or the library, stay out of sight. Something's going down.'

'I'm not home yet,' Cinder admitted. 'I'm going there now.'

'Oh, my god sweetie!' Marraine exclaimed. 'You need to get home now. Don't let anyone see you, you're not safe. I'll get there when I can. Now go!' Marraine hung up. Cinder slipped her phone back in her pocket and looked around.

Up ahead, she spotted the forest across a paddock. She ran on desperately, but growing discomfort in her feet compelled her to pause and try to kick off her shoes. With one foot free and struggling with the other shoe, she thought she heard something over her distressed breathing.

Torry was leaning over with her hands on her hips. She had a stitch in her side and there was perspiration pooling on her back. She felt concerned for Cinder, but also impressed with how quickly she could run in the dark.

After reading the note, Torry had decided that she should warn Angus that Cinder was coming. She had made her way to the fire as quickly as possible to get to the boys before Cinder found them. There were other troubling things that Cinder might find in the dark. Torry had spotted Cinder just as she was making her way up the hill towards the fire and had tried to sneak around to the top before her. When she noticed Cinder stop behind the bushes, she stopped too, almost giving her hiding place away when she laughed out loud at Cinder watching Dom and Angus getting undressed. When she saw Cinder running off, she was still some distance away, but close enough for her to tell that Cinder was upset. Torry decided to follow her and had kept up for a while, but now couldn't see where she'd gone.

The full moon came out from behind the clouds and she could see a female figure who appeared to be hopping around in the middle of one of the paddocks. 'Cinder, come back! Cin!' she called, with what breath she could muster.

Cinder ripped off her other shoe and looked around in the direction of the noise.

'Cinder!' This time, she clearly heard Torry's voice. She put her hand up above her eyes to block out the moonlight, carefully studying her shaking hand. She wanted to run to Torry and tell her to go home, but it was too late; it was midnight, and she needed to get home. She turned, stumbled to the ground, and, running on all fours, escaped into the forest.

# Chapter 10

**Sometime, Somewhere, Someone Might Just Love You to Death**

Torry decided that she should go home to get help. Not only would it be too hard for her to find Cinder in the forest by herself, it would also be too dangerous tonight. She ran back to the main house as quickly as her tired legs would take her. The full moon overhead made her progress easier. Gunn, Dom, and Angus were all just walking up to the front door when she got back. Angus was still in his wetsuit.

'Where've you been short stuff?' Dom asked when they heard her running along the gravel road. 'We saw you running away from the fire and we've been looking for you.'

Torry sat down in the dirt, taking a few moments to catch her breath before she recounted her story of seeing Cinder running away from the fire.

'Why would she run away like that?' Angus asked, staring off towards the forest, his brow creased with concern.

'Sounds like she might have seen you naked, mate,' Dom said with a laugh. 'Maybe she didn't like what she saw.' Angus's nostrils flared, and he glared at Dom.

'This is no joke. We need to find her before something else does. It's not safe out there tonight.'

'She might not be in as much danger as you think,' interrupted Gunn.

'Huh?' Angus looked at the old man in confusion.

'That pendant of hers, the one with the moonstone and tree,' Gunn continued. 'I think she might be one of us, part of another family.'

'What are you talking about, Dad?' Torry asked, her face twisted with confusion.

'Around three hundred years ago, there was a time of peace between us and the beasts,' Gunn continued. 'We agreed to stop hunting them and they agreed to stop praying on humans. As you can imagine, there was a very long period of negotiations before both sides could trust each other. The thing that turned the tide was a gift from one of the queens to the heads of our families. Seven moon pendants with the power to stop them changing. Their delegates agreed to have the pendants locked around their necks during the negotiation and that was how we brokered peace.'

'And you think Cinder is part of one of these families?' Angus asked, still looking desperate to get moving.

'She did tell me her mum makes her train all the time. I thought she just meant dancing or something.' Torry got up and dusted herself off.

'And she's strong too,' mumbled Dom.

'What?' the other three all asked together.

'She beat me in that arm wrestle when we first met her.'

'I thought that was only because you got distracted,' said Angus, smiling.

'Yeah, of course,' Dom defended himself. 'But she was putting up a good fight even before that.'

Even in the moonlight, the others could see that Dom's face had become flushed. Torry walked over and patted her brother on the back.

'Don't feel bad, I've beaten plenty of boys in an arm wrestle before.'

Dom gave her a sarcastic smile.

'Okay, okay, let's not get caught up on how many girls are stronger than Dom,' interrupted Gunn, coughing into his hand to conceal a laugh. 'Look at this, it's a copy I made of a drawing of one of the pendants.' He took a crumpled piece of paper out of his chest pocket and unfolded it in front of Angus. 'Is this like hers?'

'Exactly,' Angus said after looking at it for a short time. 'But how do we know she's one of us?'

'Well, you had better go ask her, boy,' answered Gunn, folding the paper up again. 'Off you go.'

'Okay,' Angus nodded and started jogging in the direction that Torry had just come from. 'Can you show me where you saw her?' he called out to Torry.

'Sure, hang on,' she replied, running into the house to get a torch before running after him. Gunn watched them until they disappeared into the darkness, then turned to Dom.

'You go and let the others know what's happening and stay sharp. Something doesn't feel right about tonight.'

'Hey, you know me!' shouted Dom as he ran off. Gunn smiled and walked to the front door, shaking his head.

'Yes, yes, I do.'

Torry had walked along this tree line many times in the daylight, but now in her torchlight, the trees looked unfamiliar and unwelcoming. 'I think this is where she went in,' she said, stopping between two thick trunks that leant into each other like a large gothic arch.

'Can I have that for a second?' Angus reached back for the torch while continuing to peer into the darkness. Torry handed it to him and crossed her arms over her chest. Now that she had stopped moving, she was starting to feel the cold in the night air. 'Can you see that?' Angus asked, shining the torchlight on a bush about five metres ahead of them. Something small and shiny was reflecting the light. Angus pushed quickly past some low-hanging branches, holding them out of the way long enough for Torry to follow. They must have both realised what the shiny object was at the same time because just as he was opening his mouth, Torry called out what he was going to say.

'That's Cinder's pendant!' Torry rushed past and plucked it off the bush, turning it over in the light to make sure. She looked desperately around in the darkness, running her thumb gently over the smooth moonstone. 'Cinder! Cinder, where are you?' she called out into the trees.

'Sh,' Angus interrupted her. She turned to see him with a worried expression and his index figure in front of his lips. 'Look,' he said and pointed to the ground. It took a moment for Torry's eyes to adjust, but then her heart skipped a beat when she saw what he meant. In the moist soil and rotting leaves of the forest floor was the print of a large dog-like animal. They moved deeper into the forest, quietly searching for any signs of where Cinder had gone. When the undergrowth grew thicker, Angus handed the torch to Torry. 'Here, take this and go back and get help,' he said 'I think it's going to be safer for me to go alone in the dark.'

'But I want to find her,' she protested.

'I know,' he replied, placing a reassuring hand on her shoulder and taking the pendant from her with his other. 'I do too. That's why we need help.'

Torry took one more look around the forest. 'Okay, okay'. She turned and made her way back the way they had come.

'Hey!' Angus called from behind her. 'Go straight home.' Torry nodded in agreement and left Angus in the dark.

Torry moved quickly through the trees but tried to stay quiet, all the while on the lookout for any sign of her friend. She was almost back at the forest's edge when she spotted something out of place. Further back into the forest to her left, something white was flapping in the breeze. 'Go straight home,' Angus's voice repeated in her head. *It would only take a few seconds to check*, she convinced herself, so she ventured back into the trees to investigate.

The object was a large piece of cotton material. It had a long tear in the centre and hung on a broken branch of one of the smaller trees. Torry's hands shook as she picked it up, and the colour drained from her face so that she was nearly the same shade as the material itself. She recognised it instantly because it belonged to her. It was a t-shirt she had given Cinder to wear a few days earlier. Torry took the t-shirt from the tree and clenched it to her chest, her eyes straining, desperately searching the dark. Hearing a rustle behind her, she turned quickly, 'Cin? Cin, is that you?' she called but froze on the spot, the t-shirt dropping to her feet.

# Chapter 11

### Dark Fairy Tail

Less than 10 metres in front of Torry, two large cat-like green eyes had appeared through the trees. They seemed impossibly high off the ground. A puff of misty breath formed just under the eyes, accompanied by a deep, throaty growl. A drop of sweat ran down Torry's spine as an enormous creature moved slowly into her torchlight. Although she had seen many of these creatures, she had never seen one this big before and she had never faced one alone. Her heart pounded and her mind raced. The creature must be at least eight feet tall, with a body that looked like a giant, muscular woman with a layer of orange hair. It had human-like hair on its head, but its face, ears, feet, and tail resembled a lion's. A small part of her brain was screaming at her to turn and run, but Torry knew from the look of the beast's long powerful legs there was no way she could outrun it. She needed to make the first move; injure or distract it before she made her escape.

The beast snarled and opened its mouth wide to show an abundance of razor-sharp teeth, so white that they appeared to glow in the moonlight. Then it ran straight at Torry. 'Move!' Torry yelled out loud to herself. Then she saw them: two low thick branches just off to her left between her and the beast. She threw her torch at the beast and sprinted toward the branches with all her might, jumping onto the lowest branch with her left foot and then landing her right foot on the next higher branch just as a large, hairy, clawed hand smashed through the first branch with a thundering crack, sending dozens of splinters into the air. Torry continued over her attacker's head, turning 180 degrees and grabbing one of the thinner branches higher in the tree. To her relief, the branch snapped off in Torry's hands and she brought the broken sharp end down into the beast's back. It screamed and writhed in pain, tossing Torry around like a rag-doll. She was just about to drop and make a run for it when a blinding pain blazed through her right shoulder. The beast had reached behind and dug its long claws into Torry. It pulled her up over its shoulder and tossed her almost back to the same spot she had been standing seconds ago.

Torry crashed to the moist leafy ground with a thud and let out a sound that she had never heard come out of her mouth before, something between a cry and a grunt. The impact forced the air from her lungs. She willed herself onto her knees, her chest aching as she struggled for breath. But her breathing was short-lived. The beast was on her, lifting her into the air and squeezing her between its powerful arms. Torry tried to break free, but her feet were off the ground, her arms pinned against her side. The beast raised her up, so close to its face that Torry could feel its warm breath on her skin and hear the saliva gurgling at the back of its throat. Torry closed her eyes so that she didn't have to look at the large green eyes. Then, in an act of desperation, she pulled her head back as far as she could and brought her forehead down hard on the beast's nose. It worked, but at a cost. The manoeuvre startled the beast enough to drop her, but Torry had almost knocked herself unconscious. Her heartbeat was pounding in her head and small speckles of light dance across her vision.

Gasping for breath and shaking her head to cling to consciousness, Torry dived between the beast's legs, colliding with its tail. She groped around with her hand, frantically trying to find something, anything, and then there it was. The branch that she had used earlier must have been knocked free. Torry grabbed it in both hands, and with what strength she had left, plunged the branch into the back of the beast's right leg. Getting to her feet again, she tried to run for safety but had only taken two steps when pain exploded through her head. She felt herself flying through the air and then everything went black.

• • • •

Moving swiftly and keeping to the shadows, Angus remained as quiet as possible, acutely aware of the full moon and the dangers it may bring. Something soon affirmed his fears. Bending under a low-hanging branch as he found his way between two pine trees, he spotted something moving. The moon reflected off its hairy hide. Angus crept forward to the next tree. Crouching with his back to the trunk, he held his breath and listened. It took a few moments for him to calm his heartbeat enough to hear, but soon the sounds of the night came flooding in, the rustle of leaves, the breeze blowing through the branches, and the distant rumble of the ocean. There was also the unmistakable sound of breathing. Something big was close and coming his way. Aware that he had no weapons with him. Angus looked around for what he could use. A strong breeze blew around the top of the trees and then tumbled down, cold on his face as it blew the hair out of his eyes. '*Oh shit,*' he thought to himself, he was out of options now. He was downwind of a werewolf. Time to move.

It was on him faster than he would have liked, and Angus found himself immediately on the defensive. Ducking and dodging hairy, clawed hands, Angus's only hope was for it to make a mistake, but as the seconds ticked by, Angus became concerned that he would be the one to make the first mistake. But then a sound behind the wolf distracted it for a second, and Angus took his chance. He blocked its blow with his left arm and planted a right hook into its snout. As the wolf's head pulled back, Angus dropped Cinder's chain and pendant over its neck. Angus rolled on the ground and picked up a sharp stick. Seconds later, he was holding the stick at the throat of a short, middle-aged man with balding black hair.

'You see that thing around your neck?' Angus asked, pushing the stick into the stranger's neck. 'I want you to track the owner,' he demanded. The balding man gave him a questioning sideways look.

'What do you think I am, a bloodhound?' the man asked. Angus pushed him forward.

'I know exactly what you are, and I know how good your sense of smell is. Now move!'

'Alright, alright,' said the man, raising his hands in the air, 'but I don't need to smell anything. I know the woman that owns this.' He pointed down at the pendant hanging on his hairy chest. 'That is to say, I knew her.'

'Knew her?'

'I'm sorry to say friend, but she's dead.'

'Liar!' Angus pushed the stick so hard that it drew blood.

'Hey!' the man complained, moving away. 'I'm not lying.'

Anger surged through Angus, like wildfire rushing along his veins. If Cinder was dead, if he was too late, there was no reason to keep his prisoner alive. Thoughts of how he would end the life of the animal in front of him, flashed in his head. He could be quick and merciful, snap its disgusting hairy neck, or he could take it slow, it might take dozens of stabs from the stick to rid it of all its blood and Angus could enjoy every scream to help fight off his growing feeling of loss. Then the *thing* in front of him said something that snapped Angus back to reality. 'I know where her daughter is though.' Angus shook his head as if trying to dislodge some invisible blockage from his ears.

'Her daughter?'

'Yeah, the pretty young one, red hair, green eyes.' A wave of relief washed over Angus and he breathed out, only just realising that he had been holding his breath for some time.

'Take me to her,' he said.

'I'm not sure you want to go there.' His captive gave him a questioning look. 'They don't take too kindly to visitors turning up unannounced.'

'I'm not sure you want to go where I'm going to send you if you don't take me,' replied Angus as he pushed the man forward.

'Okay, okay, I'll take you but don't say I didn't warn you.'

They began by marching silently through the trees together, but five minutes later the balding man said. 'Bob.'

'What?' Angus asked angrily.

'Bob, that's my name. Just thought you might want to know.' Angus gave Bob another push in the back.

'I don't care what your name is.'

They walked along in silence for several more minutes until curiosity got the better of Angus. 'Is Bob short for Roberto or Robertus or something?' he asked.

'No, just Bob.'

'Well, there you go,' said Angus. 'I always thought you would all be called things like Demetri and Lucifer.'

'Really? Ow,' Bob started hopping after stepping on a sharp rock. 'That's very stereotypical of you. It would be like me saying that I think you're all called Hamish McDougall or Angus McKenzie or something.' Angus gave him another shove.

'You need to shut up now, Bob.'

Some time passed before Bob broke the silence again. 'I would hate to think what someone would think if they saw us.' He waited for Angus to respond, but when no response came, he continued. 'I mean, it's not something you see every day, is it? Two grown men walking around in the moonlight, one naked and the other in a wetsuit.' Angus didn't reply. He did, however, smile to himself at the idea of how comical his current situation would look.

The surrounding terrain was getting difficult to move through and slowed their progress. They were heading uphill now, and the forest was becoming thicker, making it harder to find gaps between the branches and creating the further inconvenience of blocking out the moonlight.

'Bob,' said Angus between breaths. 'My name's Angus.' Bob began to chuckle to himself. 'Bob.' Angus said again.

'Yes?'

'Shut up.'

'Yes... Angus.' With that, both men laughed out loud.

They were still laughing moments later when they came to the edge of the forest. A large, steep, well-maintained grass area opened up in front of them. Angus could make out a few low garden areas and a cobblestone path that wound its way up the hill like a giant snake lying in the moonlight. At the very top of the hill, a gigantic building rose into the night sky. Three storeys of ornately trimmed arched windows, tall, tiled spires on each corner, and an audacious wrought-iron verandah running along the front. At first glance, Angus thought he must have been looking at a hospital or a resort, but then he realised which way he had walked. He knew about The Big House, everyone around here did, but this was the first time he had seen it up close. 'Are you telling me she lives he...'

He didn't get the last word out. A crunching of leaves behind him was just enough warning for him to spin around and block an oncoming set of hairy claws. He ducked out of the way of the second one, but there was a third, fourth, fifth, and sixth, as well as the snarling jaws that came with them. Angus grabbed hold of the arm of the first beast, twisting it until he felt it dislocate. The beast roared out in pain as he wrapped his other arm around its neck, using it as a shield between him and the others, whose numbers were growing by the second. Angus heard Bob cry something out and felt a mighty thump on the back of his head. He staggered back for a few seconds and just glimpsed Bob's face before he lost consciousness.

• • • •

Someone was making a loud ringing noise just outside her room. *How rude,* Torry thought to herself *I'm trying to sleep,* and now someone was pouring something warm down her neck. She tried to yell at Dom, but there was something in her mouth. Dirt? *What's going on?* She tried to get up and the pain all over her body came flooding in and bringing her back to reality. She wasn't in her room, she was lying face down in the cold, dark forest. *The beast, where is it?*

With a long moan, Torry rolled painfully onto her side. Her right arm was pinned under her and refused to move, so she wiped the dirt and blood gingerly out of her eyes with her left hand. If she had been able to hear over the ringing in her ear, Torry would have heard her attacker screaming and yelling in pain. The branch had gone right through the beast's leg. As it back-handed Torry across the head, the beast had fallen backwards, wedging the branch in a fork of a tree, trapping the leg.

Although she didn't understand why the beast wasn't coming to finish her off, Torry wasted no more time thinking about it. She got to her feet as quickly as her broken body would allow. Stumbling and crashing through the trees, Torry ran off into the night, unsure if she was even going in the right direction. She made it a few hundred metres before cold sweat flooded over her entire body and her legs went limp. Darkness enveloped her, and she fell to the ground again. Her heavy arms shook as she crawled blindly. Finally, her arms gave way and her head fell into the dirt.

# Chapter 12

### Torn

Gunn paced backwards and forwards past the fireplace. His old pipe smouldered in his work-hardened right hand, while the enormous fingers of his left hand pulled at a hole in his grey woollen cardigan. Smoke rose out of his hairy nostrils, momentarily obscuring his eyes that had been darting back and forth between the clock and the front door for hours. Gunn had been growing continually more anxious as the full moon had approached and now, he was beside himself with worry. His instincts told him something was wrong. Sensing something too, Dand had gone in search of his boys and not returned. Over four hours had passed since he had word from anyone. It would be daylight soon. Although it was ordinary for there to be no contact from the others all night, this was far from an ordinary night. Torry was a headstrong and independent girl, but she was also a loving daughter and would know that her father would worry about her. Gunn tried to sit in his chair and calm his mind. 'She's with Angus,' he told himself. 'She'll be fine.' unconvinced, his mind filled with visions of what could happen to the two young people he loved.

Gunn drew one last puff on his old pipe before snuffing it out and placing it down on a table next to his chair. 'All right,' he moaned, his chair and body creaking as he got slowly but purposefully to his feet again. He made his way down the long hallway to his bedroom, his large, booted footsteps reverberating on the timber floor. At the foot of his wrought iron bed was a large metal chest. Chipped dark green paint and black spray-painted numbers giving the box a military appearance. Gunn's large fingers griped at a chain around his stubbled neck, and he withdrew a silver key from beneath his shirt. Lifting the key and chain over his head, Gunn knelt down and slipped the key into a large lock in the chest's front, then pried open the hinged lid. From beneath some old books and maps, Gunn retrieved a Bowie knife with a time-worn wooden handle, a 12-gauge shotgun, and a handful of shells. He placed the gun and ammunition on the end of the bed and pulled a leather cover off the knife. 'Hello old friend,' he said, studying the blade. Gunn locked the chest again and used it to help push himself up off the floor. He was just picking up the last of the shotgun shells when he heard the front door open and Dom's voice calling from the living room.

'Dad! You here?'

Gunn returned to the living room, out of breath. Dom saw the gun in his hand and the knife hanging from his belt. He nodded his approval. 'Alright, now we're talking.'

'Where's your sister? Where's Angus?' the old man interrupted, ignoring his son's enthusiasm.

'I don't know,' Dom answered, his expression changing to one of concern. 'I came back here to ask you where Black is.'

'Something's wrong, boy. I can feel it in my bones. Angus and Tor haven't been back yet and...' He stopped, frozen by the horror that had just appeared in the doorway to his home. A bloodied mess of a person who resembled his 16-year-old daughter had just crawled in the door. She called out two shaky words.

'Red... Queen,' then her eyes rolled back in her head and she fell to the floor, lifeless.

Dom dropped to one knee next to his sister and gently rolled her over, lifting her head. The colour drained from his face. Torry was almost unrecognizable. He placed his ear against her bloody chest. 'She's not breathing,' he cried out, laying her head back down. 'Dad! She's not breathing!' he repeated desperately at his motionless father.

Gunn finally started moving. He dropped his weapons onto a nearby chair before crouching down next to Torry. 'Go get my kit, boy.' Gunn started trying to revive Torry while Dom raced out of the room to get his first aid kit. 'What have they done to you, princess?' Gunn asked as he looked into his daughter's bleeding, bruised, and swollen face, beginning chest compressions. Dom re-entered the room holding an old brown leather Gladstone bag. 'What did she say just before?' Gunn asked him as he got down next to Torry again.

'What?' asked Dom, dazed and confused. Gunn breathed into Torry's mouth, watching her chest rise and fall.

'What did she say, boy?' he asked again, this time grabbing Dom's shirtfront and shaking him.

'Um, Red Queen,' Dom answered, getting slowly to his feet.

'What colour is her pendant, the Cinder girl? What colour boy?' Dom was standing with his hands on his head.

'She's dead,' was all he said in reply.

'Dominic! What colour?' Gunn shouted, searching in his bag.

'Red, red like blood. But Dad, she's dead.'

'You stupid old man,' Gunn said to himself as he continued CPR. 'You only saw it in the moonlight. Stupid old man.'

'What are you talking about?' Dom asked as he sat down next to his father's shotgun.

'The pendant with the blood-red moon never belonged to one of us. It was a, a peace offering to a Red Queen. I was so excited about finding others like us that I forgot about the Red Queen pendant. I sent Angus and Torry out after the deadliest of our enemies, on a full moon, completely unprepared. I might as well have loaded that and asked them to hold it to their heads and pull the trigger.' Gunn motioned to the shotgun next to Dom.

Dom picked up the shotgun and turned it over in his hands, looking back and forth from it to his sister's body on the floor. 'It must have been her mother,' Dom said unable to believe that Cinder could do that to Torry. 'She said it was her mother's pendant.' Gunn shook his head and wiped the perspiration from his wrinkled brow.

'It doesn't work like that boy, a mother's power passes to her firstborn daughter. She can't change anymore after that.'

Suddenly, as if something had switched on in his head, Dom stood up, still holding the shotgun, and walked purposefully over to the doorway. He pulled on a long leather coat that was hanging on a hook behind the door, then walked up to his father's room, filling his pockets with shotgun cartridges. Returning to the front door, he took the knife from Gunn's belt. 'What are you doing, boy?' Gunn protested.

'We let that bitch into our home and treated her like family, and this is how she repays us? By killing my sister?' Dom's voice broke, his eyes warm and wet. 'I'm not just going to sit around here while she might be doing the same thing to my best mate.' Dom got down to the floor again and kissed his sister's head, then ran out of the open front door.

'Dom! Come back here, boy!' Gunn called, but it was too late, Dom had disappeared into the night. Gunn looked down at Torry's broken body. Large tears dropped from his stubbly chin, turning red as they fell on her forehead. 'Please lord don't take my children from me. Please don't punish them for my stupidity.'

# Chapter 13

**Tied to Her Chair**

Angus's eyes opened slowly, his left eye first, his eyelashes casting shadow lines across his vision. His right eye was less willing, sending waves of pain throbbing across the right side and back of his skull. Involuntarily, his hands tried to reach up to his head but wouldn't move. Something was holding them behind his back. Angus blinked his eyes to clear his vision. He was sitting in a dimly-lit room with tall walls covered in bookshelves. Then he saw something that made his heart jump. Sitting in a large armchair a few metres to his left was Cinder. As her face came into focus, a smile spread across Angus's fat lip. 'Aren't you a sight for sore eyes, and a sore head for that matter?' Cinder did not return his smile. She glowered at him.

'And why would *you* be happy to see me?' Her body language suggested anger, but her blood-shot puffy eyes told another story.

'A... a man called Bob told me you were dead.'

'That's not true,' Bob's voice called out from somewhere behind Angus. 'I told you that the woman that owned that pendant was dead.' Angus struggled against whatever was restraining his hands and tried without success to look around behind him.

'Bob! You bastard, I'm going to...' But he didn't get to finish. Cinder had risen from her chair with extraordinary speed and strength and slapped Angus across the face. 'HEY! What was that for?' he asked.

Cinder walked slowly over to the other side of the room, next to some thick green drapes. 'You shouldn't talk to Bob like that. If it wasn't for him, you would be dead already.'

'Already?' Angus asked. 'Does that mean I might still end up dead?' Cinder turned and glared at him again.

'That depends on whether you start telling us the truth.'

'The truth, about what? And who's us?' A look of realisation swept across Angus's face. 'You're one of them.' Angus said, his body becoming tense. Cinder took hold of the drape next to her with a shaking hand, infuriated.

'Them?' she spat. 'What is it that *you* think I am?'

Angus looked her in the eyes for the first time since he became conscious. His smile had completely disappeared.

'You're a werewolf,' he said.

Cinder raised her left eyebrow.

'I am no such thing. I am a Lycan, thank you very much.'

'Or animally enhanced person, if you want to be more PC,' Bob called out.

'Shut up, Bob!' Cinder and Angus said in unison. Angus wanted clarification, but was reluctant to push his luck.

'I don't know... What's the difference?' he ventured.

'Werewolves are things of fiction, giant mindless wolf-like creatures. I am always in control of the beast and I actually like to think I look more cat-like than wolf when I change.'

'Well, there you go,' said Angus, looking down at his feet. 'All the Lycan I've ever come across have seemed fairly mindless,' he added, immediately regretting that he had. Cinder's arm tensed and two curtain rings shot into the air, revealing a thin semicircle of sunlight at the top of the drape before falling and bouncing across the wooden floor.

'You've only ever encountered the males and from what I can see, mindlessness in the males appears to be something both our species share.'

Angus shook his head from side to side and laughed to himself before looking back at Cinder. 'What's this all about, Cin? What do you want me to say?'

Cinder stomped her foot, reminiscent of a small child having a tantrum.

'I know what you are. I want to hear you say it,' she said. Angus looked into her eyes; he could see tears of anger welling. He swallowed, trying unsuccessfully to moisten his dry throat.

'I'm sorry. I don't know what you mean,' he said.

'Arrrrrr!' Cinder yelled at the ceiling. A second jettisoned curtain ring almost hit Angus as it fell to the floor. 'You never go out in the day, you heal fast, and I saw you drinking blood. You're a vampire.' With the word vampire, she ripped the drape away from a tall window. The last sunlight of the day flooded the room and dust-filled beams of light fell across Angus's left side. Angus cringed away from the light, trying to shield his eyes with his shoulder.

'What?' Cinder said to herself as she dropped the drape on the floor.

'I told you he wasn't a vampire.' Came a female voice from behind Angus.

'Is that you, Marraine?' Angus asked, craning his neck and squinting his eyes to look at her as she walked past him. 'What's she talking about?' Cinder was still staring at Angus in anticipation. Marraine placed a hand on her shoulder and walked behind her to face Angus.

'Cinder here, was under the false impression that you, sweetie, are a vampire.'

'A vampire?' Angus laughed but winced because it hurt his head. 'What, did she think, that I was going to sparkle in the sunlight or something?'

'Something a bit more dramatic than that, I'm afraid,' Bob said as he walked around to where Angus could see him, holding up a fire extinguisher.

'What the hell, Cin?' Angus yelled, struggling against his restraints. 'Were you trying to kill me?'

'Isn't that why you came here, to kill me?' Cinder spat back.

'Kill you? I came here to save you.'

'Save me, save me from what?' Angus could see Cinder's chest heaving and the veins in her neck starting to show. He lowered his voice and, as calmly as possible, said.

'Werewolves. Lycan, sorry,' he corrected himself as he saw Cinder raise her eyebrows.

'Perhaps you should tell Cinder what you really are, handsome,' Marraine interrupted, trying to defuse the tension, as she led Cinder back to the armchair.

'I'd rather not, thanks,' Angus replied defiantly. Marraine approached him and leant down to look him in the eyes.

'I don't think you have many other options at this point and it would be better to come from you than me.'

'You know?' Angus looked momentarily taken aback. Marraine smiled and put her hand on his shoulder.

'You would be surprised what I know. I'm not just a pretty face and a smoking-hot body,' she said with a wink. Angus looked slowly from her hand to her eyes.

'If you know what I am, you know that I do have another option,' he said. Marraine crouched down with her hands on her knees like a primary school teacher talking to a student.

'If you're as smart as I think you are, then you've figured out what she is and you've figured out that's not a smart option,' she said, pointing her thumb over her shoulder towards Cinder.

Angus turned to look at Cinder. It was hard to see her now as the same shy girl he had met at Paddy's two weeks ago. 'Okay then,' he said, watching Cinder, who had not taken her eyes off him. 'This is a library, right? Have you got a bible here?' Marraine stood up and gestured for Bob to find a bible. Bob searched the shelves.

'King James or NIV?' he called when he found the right shelf.

'NIV will be fine, Bob,' Angus answered.

'Good,' said Bob, as he walked back, wiping dust off the book's cover with his sleeve. 'The other one was ancient and looked like it might fall apart.' He sat down on the arm of Cinder's chair. 'So, what are we doing with this, some kind of ceremony or something?' Angus smiled and shook his head.

'No, just reading today. Genesis 6, thanks,'

'Um, okay,' Bob flicked through the pages.

'It's at the start, Bob,' Marraine added.

'Got it,' Bob called, sticking his thump in the air. Then he read:

> *When human beings began to increase in number on the earth and daughters were born to them, the sons of God saw that the daughters of humans were beautiful, and they married any of them they chose. Then the Lord said, 'My spirit will not contend with humans forever for they are mortal; their days will be a hundred and twenty years.' The Nephilim were on the earth in those days – and also afterward – when the sons of God went to the daughters of humans and had children by them. They were the heroes of old, men of renown.*

'Numbers 13:33 too please, Bob,' Angus called out. After a few moments of flicking back and forth, Bob continued reading.

> *'We saw the Nephilim there, the descendants of Anak. We seemed like grasshoppers in our own eyes, and we looked the same to them.'*

Cinder laid her head against the back of the armchair and looked up at the high ceiling. 'Ha!' she called out, still looking up. 'What's next, leprechauns?'

'I think I met a leprechaun once,' Bob chimed in as he put the bible down. Marraine glared at him and put her finger to her lips, shaking her head from side to side before mouthing the words.

'Not now.'

Cinder stood up, almost knocking Bob off his perch. 'So, I'm supposed to believe that you're some kind of ancient demigod, giant thing?' she asked, as she walked slowly towards Angus. 'A nef... nerfy... neril?'

'Nephilim,' Marraine corrected her.

'Yes, one of them,' Cinder finished, waving one of her hands dismissively in the air. She stopped a few steps away from Angus, crossed her arms, tilted her head to one side, and raised an eyebrow. 'Sorry, but I find that hard to believe.'

'Ha, ha. What?' This time, it was Angus who laughed. 'You're a werew... a Lycan who thought her boyfriend was a vampire! And you think my story is hard to believe?' Cinder leant forward, pushing her chin out angrily and pointed her finger at his face.

'Firstly, yes, I don't believe a thing you've ever said to me, and secondly,' She came closer, close enough for Angus to see the tears teetering on the edges of her bloodshot eyes. 'If you think you're my boyfriend, then I know you're delusional.' A large tear rolled down her left cheek. 'Not then, not now, not ever,' she choked out as she wiped her face with her sleeve.

Angus tried again to move into a more comfortable position. 'Is that what this is all about? Are you angry that I didn't make a move on you?' Cinder turned her back on him, but he could see her shoulders rising and falling as she took three deep breaths before answering.

'What this is all about is that you are a liar,' she answered as she turned her head just enough to see him in her peripherals. Angus looked down at the rope around his ankles.

'I'm not saying I'm one of the Nephilim, I'm just descended from them. I have their blood running through my veins.'

Cinder walked over to one of the walls of books and ran her finger along the spines, pretending she was looking for something. 'Blood,' she said, absentmindedly tapping a book with her fingernails. 'You haven't explained the blood yet. If you're not a vampire, why did I see you drinking blood?'

Angus turned and watched her as she moved along the books again, keeping her back to him. 'It's not blood. It's, well, it's kind of a long story.' Marraine sat down in the armchair next to Bob.

'None of us are going anywhere, sweetie. You might as well tell the whole story.' Angus's back and shoulders were getting stiff and sore from being in the one place. He tried to wriggle into a more comfortable position, the chair and ropes creaking under the strain.

'How long have I been out for anyway?' he asked, looking out the window now that his eyes had adjusted to the sunlight.

'All day sorry, sweetie,' Marraine apologised. Angus raised his eyebrows in question. 'Making men do what I want is one of the many things I know how to do. That includes keeping them unconscious if needed.'

'The blood?' Cinder interrupted, pretending to be interested in a large book with a lime-green cover and white writing. Angus cleared his throat with a cough.

'Okay then, let's see. Do you know about Pythagoras?' he asked.

'The triangle guy?' Bob asked.

'Yes, the triangle guy, but he was more than that. He was kind of like a cult leader. He believed that everything in the world had balance and order, so much so that he killed one of his followers who discovered something he didn't agree with. Anyway, he was convinced that because he had such a strong mind and a weak body that there must be people out there with the opposite, with strong bodies and weak minds. Anyway, long story short, he found a Nephilim called Milo of Croton, an ancient Greek wrestler. It was by accident really.

Milo held up a burning roof that would have fallen on Pythagoras and killed him. They became best friends and Milo ended up marrying his daughter.'

Cinder pulled a large black book with gold writing off the shelf, flicking through the pages. 'That's a lovely story but you still haven't explained the blood.' Angus shifted uncomfortably, his muscles tensing under his restraints.

'I told you, it's not blood. It's a tonic that Pythagoras made, and my people have developed over the centuries. It amplifies our strength and helps us heal faster.'

'Yes, but what's it made of?' Cinder yelled, slamming the book down on a table and making Bob jump. Angus took a moment to study Cinder's face.

'Vitamins, minerals, hormones and proteins,' he answered. A deep crease appeared between Cinder's eyebrows.

'Why does it look like it does? Why does it smell like it does?' She crossed her arms in front of her chest and stared accusingly at Angus.

'It's mainly bovine plasma and haemoglobin.' Angus replied, squeezing his hands into fists while pushing his feet firmly into the floor.

Later, when Bob talked about what happened that day, he would describe what came next as one of the most frightening few seconds of his life. As the word 'haemoglobin' escaped Angus's lips, it was as if someone had sucked all the air from the room and the world froze in a moment. Seconds ticked by and no one moved until Cinder turned her head slowly to glance at Marraine. Anger, rage, and unresolved bitterness flashed like an explosion behind her eyes. Then several things all happened at once. Marraine dived to get between Cinder and Angus, knocking Bob off the arm of the chair. Cinder, with claws out and teeth bared, leapt onto the table, before flying across the room at Angus. Angus's chair shattered into a pile of wood and frayed rope as he ripped his arms and legs free, rolling to the left just as Cinder landed where he had been sitting. Marraine tackled Cinder to the ground, as Angus struggled with the last of his restraints and grabbed a broken chair leg as protection. Cinder threw Marraine off and crawled towards Angus, lashing out at him with her left hand.

'I know what blood is!' she yelled, saliva shooting from her sharp teeth. 'Don't mistake me for some stupid little schoolgirl!'

Marraine picked herself up and straightened her clothes.

'A little help please, Bob,' she ordered. Bob reluctantly agreed. Picking himself up from the floor, he ran over to help. Angus was able to deflect Cinder's attacks for a short time, but his legs were cramping from being tied up. Cinder pinned him to the ground. Tears and saliva dripped from her face onto his chest.

'I hate you, all of you!' she screamed into his face as Marraine and Bob, now holding one of Cinder's arms each, struggled to pull her off.

'He's not one of them, sweetie,' Marraine whispered calmly in her ear. 'Let go, let go.'

Cinder let go but pulled her arms free. Standing up, looking disorientated, she turned her anger on Marraine. 'Didn't you hear him? Do you all think I'm an idiot? He drinks blood. He basically confessed. And you left me THERE.' She pointed into the distance. 'With them.'

'Sweetie,' Marraine approached her tentatively. 'Sweetie, he's not a vampire. Nothing happened when he was in the sunlight.' She put her arms around Cinder's waist, resting her head on her shoulder. 'I would never do that to you. You're my goddaughter, my friend, and my queen.'

'Queen?' Cinder asked, anger slowly replaced with confusion.

'I'll explain soon, but now I think we all need to rest. It's been a long day.'

Cinder nodded in agreement. Marraine took a step back and wiped Cinder's face with her thumbs, then walked her to the door. Cinder's hand shook on the door handle and Marraine helped pull it open. She turned to take one last angry look at Angus, but as she did, a different, unexpected emotion rose into her chest.

'Is he okay?' she asked. Marraine simply nodded and smiled in reply. Cinder sniffed and wiped the tears off her cheeks with her palm, then left the room.

Angus was still flat on his back on the floor. He breathed rapidly, looking at a hand-painted map of the world that covered most of the ceiling. '*Strange, I hadn't noticed that until now,*' he thought to himself. Bob offered him a hand, and he accepted, pulling himself up into a sitting position. 'Thank you,' he said to the other two, as he rubbed his legs and wriggled his toes to get the feeling back in his feet. 'I didn't think vampires were real, but Cin seems to think so.'

'Oh, they're very real, unfortunately,' Marraine replied, making her way back to the armchair. Angus put one hand on the back of his neck and moved his head from side to side.

'Why does she hate them so much?' he asked. Marraine and Bob exchanged a look that Angus couldn't read. Marraine sat down, smoothed her hair, and straightened her clothes.

'Bob, would you be a dear and fetch us all a drink?'

'Sure,' Bob answered, making his way quickly to the door. 'Water?' he asked.

'Don't be asinine. I need a drink, not a bath.' Marraine said, rolling her eyes. Bob laughed.

'Sorry, red or white?'

'Red would be lovely, thank you.'

Bob opened his mouth to ask another question, but Marraine stopped him with a dismissive wave of her hand. He turned and looked at Angus. 'What about you? Red?'

'No thanks, Bob. I think I should stay away from any red liquids for a bit.' Angus got to his feet. 'Something a bit more amber or brown, I think.' Bob gave him a thumbs up and left through the door that Cinder had exited earlier. Angus paced slowly around the room.

'Would you like to sit?' Marraine offered.

'I think I'll stand for a bit, get the feeling back in my butt,' he answered. Marraine ran her eyes down his body.

'Yes, we wouldn't want to risk damaging that,' she said, stopping at his backside. Angus raised his eyebrow and made his way over to the bookshelves, rubbing his hands on his thighs. Marraine chuckled to herself.

'What?' Angus asked, forcing a smile.

'You,' Marraine answered, 'saying boyfriend. I thought it was going to be all over then. You're supposed to be the smart one.'

'Um yeah.' Angus realised he was wearing someone else's clothes. 'Who got me undressed?'

'Well, I did volunteer, but Cinder overruled me and made Bob do it.' Marraine, replied, with a devious smile.

'I guess that makes Bob and I even,' Angus laughed to himself and inspected the dark blue jeans and baggy black t-shirt.

There was silence for a moment, then Marraine cleared her throat. 'Her father was killed by a vampire,' she announced. Angus stopped and looked down at his feet.

'How does she know it was a vampire?'

'Because she was there. She was just a little girl, and it was there for her. Her father fought it, fought it all night to keep it away from her. Fought it until he was a bloody mess. Fought it until the sun came up and, with his last bit of strength, held onto it and threw himself out of the window. Their bodies got fused together when it burst into flames.' She composed herself before continuing. 'Her father was her whole world, and she had to sit hidden in a wardrobe and watch as he was ripped apart for hours and hours.'

Angus took a book from the shelf, his shaky hands turning the pages, pretending to be interested in the words so he didn't have to make eye contact with Marraine. 'I lost my father in a fire; my mother and sister too.' His throat was getting tight, and he had to force the words out. 'My sister Katie was... They couldn't find her, but they got my parents' bodies out. I remember wanting to see them, but no one would let me. I'm glad now that I didn't. No child should have to see their parents like that.'

'No, no child should,' Marraine agreed.

'How old was she?' he motioned to the door. 'When it, um... When her father died?'

'She was only seven. It almost ruined her, but she's turned out okay, all things considered.' Marraine had the expression of a proud parent. 'Amazing really.' Angus closed the book and placed it back on the shelf.

'Yes, she is,' he agreed. 'Bloody scary,' he added in response to the amused look on Marraine's face. 'But amazing, yes.' He rubbed the red marks on his wrists where the rope had been chafing. 'So,' he changed the subject. 'How long have you known what I am?' Marraine interlocked her fingers and made a bridge for her chin to rest on.

'Well,' she looked up at the painted roof, 'I have known for some time that there was a group of you in town. The men don't come back from their nights out, with cuts and bruises on their own, obviously. But you personally? I didn't know for sure until last night when I got back here to help Cinder. It didn't come as a surprise though; I had my suspicions from when we first met all of you at Paddy's.'

Angus flinched as the door opened. Bob entered, pushing the door with his backside and then closing it again with his foot. He held a large, overfull glass of red wine carefully in his right hand. His left hand was occupied with two amber-coloured bottles, his fingers contorted around their long necks. He handed Marraine her wine first. 'Here you go, M'lady. And...' he reached into his pocket, 'these are for you.' He handed Angus one of the bottles and a bottle opener. Angus studied the opener. The handle comprised one palm-sized metallic ball with two smaller balls spaced a few centimetres part on top.

'Bob? Is this Mickey Mouse?' he asked. Bob grinned and made to reply, but an outburst from Marraine cut him off.

'What is this, Bob? Cask wine?' She questioned, glowering. Angus quickly popped the top of his beer and took a drink. Bob cringed.

'Sorry, it was all I could find,' he apologised. Marraine stormed across the library to the window with the missing drapes.

'All you could find?' she asked, prying open the window and tipping the contents of her grass onto a bed of white roses two floors below. 'Queen biatch has an entire room full of the best wines from around the world!'

'I know,' Bob replied, 'but I spotted her two Haitian bodyguards and didn't want to go into the west wing. I had to get these from the stables.'

Marraine dropped the glass, and it disappeared out of view. 'If they're back, then she's back.' The colour drained from Marraine's olive skin.

'Who's back?' Angus queried, noticing the concern on her face.

'Louvelle. Cinder's.... Mother.' She forced the words out with obvious distaste. 'Bob, you need to find Cinder and take her and Angus out to the stables. I have to go now,' she instructed, hastening to the door.

'You're going?' Bob probed, looking slightly stunned. 'I'm petrified of her, but I didn't think she scared you.' Marraine stopped in the doorway, resting her head against the ajar door.

'I'm not afraid of her, but if she has returned early without me knowing, then someone hasn't been able to tell me. Someone I care about hasn't been able to send me a message. That someone must be in trouble, they're possibly already dead.'

# Chapter 14

**Guys Just Wanna Have Guns**

T*he Big House is... big.* The thought kept going through Angus's head. Bob guided him along a wood-panelled hallway with high ceilings and a handful of doors. At the far end was a trapezoidal atrium. Rows of white framed windows allowed the twilight sun to illuminate a polished timber staircase that led up to the top floor and down to the ground floor. Bob peered down over the handrail before gesturing for Angus to follow him upwards.

The top floor hallway was almost identical to the one below except for the obvious lack of maintenance. Dusty cobwebs occupied most of the ceiling, paint was flaking from the walls in many places, and only about a third of the light globes appeared to be working. Angus could see that Bob was perspiring more than someone should when they've only walked up one flight of stairs.

'This is her room,' he said, stopping in front of the last door and wiping his brow on his sleeve. The two men stood silently, looking at the large timber door.

'Do you want me to go in first, Bob?' Angus whispered. Bob took a step back and nodded in the affirmative. Angus held the brass doorknob in his right hand and knocked gently with the left. 'Cin, it's Black. Bob's with me. Marraine sent us to get you. Can we come in?'

'Just wait!' came a muffled reply through the door. Angus could hear things moving around in the room.

'Are you okay, Cin?' he asked.

'My name is Cinder, and I said to wait,' she yelled, as something in her room made a thud. Angus, still holding the door handle, looked at Bob and shrugged. 'Okay, you can come in now,' Cinder called a moment later.

A cloud of chalk dust greeted Angus as he walked in, making him cough. 'Wow,' he said, looking at the giant white bed, 'that looks comfy.' Cinder was standing in front of the doorway to her wardrobe, dusting her hands off on the front of her pants.

'Well, you'll never find out, will you?' she said without making eye contact with Angus. 'What's happening?' she turned and ask Bob, who was still waiting in the hallway.

'Marraine wants me to hide you two in the stables,' Bob replied. Angus moved slowly around her room, pausing next to her telescope to look out of the window. He then made his way to the head of the bed, leaning against one of the posts as he studied the writing on the chalkboards. Cinder nudged past him and collected a pile of used tissues from her bed.

'Hide? Why do we need to hide?' she asked, throwing the tissues into her wardrobe and slamming the door.

'Lady Gevaudan is back early,' Bob answered, nervously fidgeting with his shirt collar.

'Oh,' Cinder responded, sounding more disappointed than worried. 'She wasn't due back till next week.'

Cinder had wiped most of the walls clean, but Angus spotted some writing still visible behind Cinder's armchair. Arching his neck, he read the writing out loud.

*'The sun came out, and I was taken. Night-time falls. I'm betrayed, mistaken. How can that which gives warmth and light be that which chills my darkest night?'*

Bumping into the telescope and almost knocking it off its tripod, Cinder moved briskly between Angus and the wall. 'Get out of my room,' she ordered.

'Please,' Angus responded, looking her in the eye.

'What?'

'You didn't say please.'

Bob looked on nervously as the other two stood close together, unflinchingly staring each other down. 'Can you come now? Please?' Bob asked finally.

'Sure, Bob,' Angus replied, still holding his gaze firmly on Cinder's right eye. 'Thank you for asking so nicely,' he added, and made his way to the door. 'What would your mother say about you having a boy in your room at night?' he asked as he entered the hall.

'I don't know. All the others haven't lived long enough for me to ask them what she said,' Cinder replied, pushing past him and heading for the stairs.

Cinder led the way out of double glass doors on the ground level of the atrium. Bob jumped anxiously at every sound and pleaded with the other two to move faster and to stop making so much noise. The sun had set, and the moon wasn't yet visible over the top of The Big House. Rows of trapezium-shaped light from the atrium windows lit up a stone path that meandered its way across the lawns. The path led to a flat-roofed brick structure at the rear boundary of the property. Bob tried his best to keep Angus and himself to the shadows, but Cinder stormed off ahead, giving no thought to who might see her.

Cinder had already entered the stables and slammed the door behind her when the others caught up. Opening the door as quietly as possible, Bob gestured for Angus to go inside. He looked around one last time and followed Angus in, closing the door with care.

The inside of the stables was not what Angus had expected. Other than a slight smell, there was no indication that this building once held horses. The stables had been converted into accommodation for the many people – Lycan – that came and went from The Big House. Angus thought the space was reminiscent of a camp dormitory. At one end was a kitchenette with a sink, microwave, refrigerator, and tiled floors and benches. There was a door that Angus guessed led to a bathroom and a sitting area with a brown micro-fibre sofa with yellow cushions, two matching armchairs, and a television. The rest of the space was taken up with ten beds, five along the front wall and five along the back. Each bed had its own grey laminated flat-pack wardrobe and matching bedside table. It soon became apparent that this was where Bob stayed. He flopped down on the unmade bed that was closest to the door in the corner of the room. 'There're drinks in the fridge. Help yourself,' he called out, slipping off his boots and letting them drop to the floor. Angus thanked him and continued into the kitchenette, further studying the layout of the building.

The door they had come in appeared to be the only way in or out. There were no windows, only a set of skylights set every metre or so in the ceiling. '*Easy to defend but hard to escape,*' Angus thought to himself. Angus was glad of the opportunity for another drink; he only had a few sips of the last one before they had to leave the library. 'Would anybody else like one?' he asked, holding up a cold can of cola that he found in the refrigerator.

'No, thanks,' Bob replied, stretching and yawning. Cinder, who had been standing with her hands resting on the back of one of the armchairs, gave no indications that she heard the question. Turning the other way, she moved to the sofa and lay down with her feet up on the armrest.

'Would you like a drink, Cinder?' Angus repeated. Cinder hugged one of the yellow cushions to her chest and closed her eyes.

'If I want something, I'll get it myself,' she grumbled. Angus sat on the kitchen bench and raised his hands in surrender.

'Alright, I was just asking.'

Several minutes passed while Angus finished his drink. Other than his own mouth noises and the hum of the refrigerator, he sat in silence watching the cushion on Cinder's chest rise and fall. His mind wrestled with the juxtaposition of the beautiful young woman before him and the monster in the library that had tied him to a chair and was ready to tear him apart.

Bob had rolled over onto his side and his heavy breathing was rapidly growing into a back-of-the-throat rumbling snore. Angus sat his empty can down gently on the bench and crept closer to Cinder. Sitting down on the armchair closest to her head, he examined her face. Her eyes twitched and rolled under her eyelids. 'Cin,' Angus whispered. 'Cin, are you awake?' When she didn't stir for about an hour and Marraine didn't return, he collected a blanket from one of the beds. After carefully unzipping and removing her boots, he covered her up and tucked her in.

Moving quickly but silently, Angus searched the stables for a telephone. Through the door off the kitchenette, he found a small bathroom and laundry, but no back door. There appeared to be no landline anywhere, but after searching through some of the wardrobes, he found two mobile phones. One phone had a flat battery and there was no charger. The other had full charge but required a pin to unlock it. Angus considered calling the police but couldn't think of any story that wouldn't incriminate his own family. He would have to make a run for it himself. The tree line couldn't be more than ten or fifteen metres away. *'I could be out the door and into the forest in a few seconds,'* he thought to himself. He moved towards the door but stopped as doubt crept in. *'Anything could be out there,'* he thought. *'I wish Dom were here. He would have gone already.'* And then he was... Dom bustled through the door holding Marraine and a shotgun.

# Chapter 15

### The Mother We Share

The night before, Dom had run straight from the farm to the forest. The smell of Torry's blood fresh in his nostrils and the words '*Red Queen*' looping over and over in his head. He had made no attempts to move unheard or unseen, crashing through the forest like wildfire, grief spurring him on and on like hot summer winds. The sooner something found him, the sooner he could repay blood with blood. Stumbling through the undergrowth and gasping for breath, he looked desperately around the trees. 'Where are you, you pieces of shit?' he yelled after catching his breath. The rage pushed him on, running blindly into the darkness again. A dark branch crashed into his face, leaving a line of bloody spots on his stubbled face, adding to the many scratches, bumps, and grazes he had already inflicted upon himself. 'You stupid bitch!' His gravelly voice echoed around the forest. Pulling the shotgun out from under his coat, he smashed the butt into the tree, as if it had somehow deliberately attacked him. The branch that had connected with his face finally gave way under his bombardment and he fell to his knees. 'Come on, you useless bastard,' he said to himself, wiping blood, dirt, and sweat from his face.

Something moved at the top of a rise off to his left. He jumped up and set off running again. Two-thirds of the way up, he slipped on a pile of dry leaves but continued the rest of the way on all fours. At the top of the rise, he rolled over onto his back, his chest heaving. The full moon shone brightly through a gap in the canopy, illuminating his tormented face. Dom stuck his finger up at the moon and retrieved the shotgun from the forest floor, using it as a crutch to help him get back on his feet. Before Dom could register what was happening, a large furry creature with wet teeth and dark eyes launched itself from the shadows, just metres in front of him.

Dom was only up on one knee when he saw the Lycan running at him. 'Great holy mother!' he yelled and let off a shot, the blast echoing through the valley below. Dom wasn't ready for the recoil and ended up back on the ground. A shower of shotgun pellets sprayed across the left side of the beast's face. It clutched at its head, howling in pain. Dom stowed the shotgun. With his ears ringing, he groped desperately for his tomahawks before rolling over and bracing himself on one knee, ready to finish the job. To his surprise and disappointment, the Lycan turned and ran into the forest. 'No!' Dom screamed. 'Get back here.'

Frantically climbing to his feet, Dom chased after the beast. Scratching his face again and again on low branches and tripping over roots and rocks, he desperately tried to keep up. The Lycan was faster than Dom, but the disorientating pain in its face hindered its escape. Dom's shot had blinded its left eye and blood kept getting in its right. Dom came within metres of his prey when it crashed into the trunk of a large willow tree, but his coat-tail became entangled in a blackberry bush.

'I don't need this shit now!' he yelled, feverishly hacking at the bush and sending leather, sticks, and leaves flying. Arms and chest aching, he wrenched himself free and pushed forward.

The ground had been rising steadily for the last few minutes of the chase, but now began to flatten and the trees were thinning out. Before he realised, Dom was running across a flat, manicured lawn and the Lycan was about to escape into a large building. In a last act of desperation, he threw one of his tomahawks at the Lycan's bloodied head. The projectile collected the beast just behind its right ear with a thud before bouncing off. It was not the desired effect, but it was enough to send the Lycan stumbling off balance. Dom was on top of it in three strides, bringing his second tomahawk hurtling down on the skull of his quarry. The Lycan's lifeless body crumpled to the ground, and he collapsed on top of it, pummelling it in the ribs with his bare hands a dozen times for good measure.

Dom rolled off the body and lay on his back, staring up at the clouds that drifted across the night sky. He gasped for breath, as furious tears mingled with Lycan blood, ran down his pale cheeks, stinging the many scratches on his face. As he lay there, he became conscious for the first time that his right ankle was throbbing. He gingerly got to his feet and limped back to collect his jettisoned weapon. Looking around, he found himself on a large grass area next to a cobblestone path that led to a very large three-storey building with a wrought-iron verandah.

Wiping his face with the inside of his coat, Dom hobbled around, trying to get his bearings. Unlike Angus and Gunn, he had no interest in local history, and other than Cinder, no young women lived or worked at The Big House, so Dom had no idea where he was. He retrieved his second tomahawk, still protruding from his victim's head. Placing one foot at the base of its neck to help him lever it out. He was cleaning the blade on the grass when a light on the second-storey came on. Startled, he grabbed hold of the corpse's hairy feet and dragged it as quickly as possible to the tree line, slipping and stumbling on the moist lawn. Dom pushed the now half-human body under some thick blackberry bushes and had just enough time to lie down in the shadows before a female figure appeared at the window. Dom squinted his eyes to see. The person at the window looked like Marraine, but he couldn't be sure. She pulled two large curtains across the window, leaving a thin sliver of light protruding between them.

Dom crawled cautiously out from behind the blackberries and, crouching down to keep himself as small as possible, limped up to the house. After finding a shadowed section of the wall, he hid the shotgun under some rose bushes and started to climb. The decorative ironwork of the verandah made it easy to find foot and finger holds, but the night had made the metal damp and slippery. A shooting pain that ran up his right leg every time he put weight on it further hampered his climb. By the time he made it as high as the window, Dom had almost fallen four times. His shoulders and chest were hot and sore, and his hands were shaking with adrenaline. Shimmying across a narrow ledge with his face against the cold bricks, he was able to get within a few metres of the window but not close enough. Pausing to get his breath and look around for his next move, he started to regret his decision to climb. 'What a stupid bloody idea Dom,' he said to himself between breaths, then looked down at the fall below him.

To his left, just within reaching distance, was a downpipe that ran from the roof, doglegged around the window and down to the ground. If he kept one foot on the ledge, he could lean out against the pipe and see into the window; he would, unfortunately, have to trust that the pipe could hold all his weight. *'What would Black do?'* he thought to himself, but then he realised Angus would not have put himself in this position in the first place. He leant his head against the wall and closed his eyes but opened them again, hearing what sounded like someone tossing a pebble onto the roof. The sound came again, followed shortly by another, then three more times. Dom's heart sank as the sounds grew into a syncopated rhythm and a cold, wet drop struck him above his right eye and ran down his cheek. He had been so focused on climbing he hadn't noticed the storm clouds that had drifted across from the ocean. 'Okay,' he conceded, wiping his cheek with his shoulder, 'time to move.'

Sliding his hands and chest against the wall, Dom reached out for the downpipe. The box-shaped metal flexed and creaked as he wrapped his right hand around it, but seemed to be holding. Seconds later, he was leaning at a forty-five-degree angle, his injured right ankle dangling below him, warm breath from his nose fogging up the window. Once his eyes had adjusted to the light in the room, he could see Marraine walking around what he guessed was a library. Then he saw *her:* the Red Queen. The downpipe creaked in protest of Dom's large hands squeezing around it as he tried to force images of his sister's broken body from his mind. He bobbed his head around, frantically trying to see Angus, but the rain was growing heavier and getting in his eyes.

He shook his head and watched the rain drip from his hair, but as he did, the sky lit up like daylight for a split second, then, boom! Thunder rumbled through The Big House, Dom could feel the downpipe shudder and he almost lost his grip. His heart started racing. Not only did he feel like he was going to fall, but he had glimpsed something in the lightning that concerned him even more than falling. Straining his eyes, he probed into the darkness, hoping that he was mistaken. There was a second flash followed almost immediately this time by another crash of thunder and he was sure now there was no mistake. Walking across the lawn only about forty metres away from him was a large group of werewolves and they were moving his way.

Dom tried desperately to get both feet back on the ledge and straighten up his body. He soon realised, however, that he had managed again to get himself into a stupid position. His arms couldn't push him far enough for him to be upright. If not for his injured ankle, he might have been able to push off the downpipe with his right leg, but even with his leg just hanging in the air, the pain was almost unbearable. Blinking the rain out of his eyes, he searched for another way to get down. He decided that he would have to slide down the downpipe. It wouldn't be easy now that the wall was wet, but it would be quick, and he needed quick. He reached his right hand down to the windowsill and carefully pushed off the ledge with his left foot.

Just as his left knee crashed into the downpipe, another bolt of lightning flash overhead. '*This is great, Dom,*' he thought to himself, '*hanging two-storeys up from a wet metal pipe in a thunderstorm.*' Squeezing his legs against the pipe as best he could, he let go of the windowsill and started to slide down. He immediately realised he was moving too quickly, but gravity had taken over and there was very little he could do to slow himself down. The window below had a shade that protruded at an angle from the wall. Dom groped wildly at the wall to catch hold of the shade on the way past, but he smashed his elbow into it instead. Knocked off balance and his right arm numb, he lost hold of the pipe, fell the last two metres, and landed on his back.

Dom's head had landed in a soft section of garden bed, so he remained conscious; unfortunately, the rest of his body hadn't fared so well. He had lost the feeling in his right hand and when he moved his leg, pain exploded through his coccyx bone. He also had a long gash running up the left side of his stomach, which was bleeding heavily. With great effort and pain, he rolled over onto his right side and tried to inspect the wound on with his fingers. It didn't feel deep, but he knew there was enough blood to alert the werewolves to his location. His hand shook uncontrollably, and he knew he was going into shock. He needed to get warm, and he needed to stop the bleeding. Breathing through gritted teeth to hold back the screams of pain, he forced himself onto his knees. Making a run for it was out of the question. He would be lucky if he could crawl away. Half crawling, half dragging himself, Dom slithered his way back along the muddy ground towards the hidden shotgun; if he was going to get caught, he wanted to take a few of them down with him. With only a few feet to go, the pocket of his coat snagged on something. Pulling angrily at his coat, a large rusty lock and chain rattled free and bashed against something hollow. Using his knee to bang on the ground, he confirmed he was lying on top of two large iron doors. The chain looped around two half-oval-shaped handles locked together at the ends with a solid old padlock. There was just enough room between the chain and the doors for Dom to fit the heads of his tomahawks, and after a couple of attempts, he was able to lever apart one of the links and break the chain. He stretched out painfully, using his fingertips to retrieve the shotgun. Then, with great discomfort and exertion, he lifted one of the doors and squeeze his body through the gap.

Not caring who could hear him this time, Dom yelled and cursed in pain. He wasn't sure how far he had fallen, but he had landed face up on carpet in a dark room. As he lay on the floor, listening for any movement, the feeling returned in his right hand, and he could make a fist without too much pain in his elbow. He rested his head on the ground a few moments longer, happy to be somewhere dry, warm, and, for the moment, out of danger. The warm, wet feeling on his stomach reminded him that he shouldn't stay here any longer. At one end of the darkness, he could see a rectangular halo of pale-yellow light. Assuming that it was a doorway, Dom inched his way towards it on all fours. The floor under him changed from carpet to cobblestone; the smooth, cold surface against his skin was enough to start his arms shivering again. There was a gap of about three centimetres under the door. Dom put his ear down close to the gap. A draught made a ghostly whistle as it rushed under the door, but otherwise, there was no indication of movement. Biting his lip and forcing himself up with his one good arm and leg, his fingers explored the wall for a light switch. Seconds later, a click echoed through the room, and six sets of fluorescent lights hummed and flickered to life. Turning to sit with his back against the wall, Dom blinked and looked around. The long cobblestone room was reminiscent of their gym at home, a well-worn boxing bag hung from the rafters with weights and other exercise paraphernalia scattered around the room. More importantly, on the other side of the door, sitting on a shelf next to a basin, were fresh bandages, rubber gloves, and other first aid supplies. '*Finally,*' Dom thought, '*something's going my way.*'

After swallowing a handful of painkillers and tending to his wounds, the best he could, Dom cleaned the blood off the floor and collapsed on an old leather couch. His eyelids grew heavy, and he drifted out of consciousness. His leg slipped off the side of the couch, the heel of his boot falling heavily to the floor. Dom snapped awake with a cry of pain and surprise; his heart thumped in his ears as he looked around. Slapping his face and wiping drool from his chin, he coerced his pain-ridden and exhausted body to move again. Limping his way further into the room, he found a solid, antique wooden wardrobe. Other than a family of spiders and four long fur coats, the wardrobe was empty. Dom climbed inside, placed one of the coats on the floor as a pillow, and blanketed himself with another. He positioned his weapons under his hands ready and pulled the door closed. As soon as the door blocked out the last sliver of light, Dom slipped out of consciousness. He did not wake again until hours later when the sound of heels on the stone floor stirred him.

• • • •

Marraine paced back and forth, her Stuart Weitzman's echoing their clip-clop off the long stone walls of the repurposed wine cellar. 'Come on, come on, answer!' she ordered into her phone. The fingers of her free hand tapped an accelerando beat on her hip.

As she turned to make her ninth trip away from the door, she lost her footing on something sticky and moist on the floor. Pausing to redial the phone, she inspected the substance on the soul of her shoe.

When Marraine had entered the gym earlier that night, she had immediately smelt blood. Assuming, however, that Cinder had been in here taking her frustrations out on the boxing bag as she often did, Marraine thought little of it. Perhaps if she had not been so distracted, she may have perused the matter further. Therefore, it was not surprising that she was now staring down at three drops of blood and a fourth that she had just smeared with the sole of her pumps. What seemed surprising to Marraine was the consistency of the blood; it appeared to be far drier than she would expect if Cinder had left it here less than an hour ago. Turning and walking back to the door, she finished the call and placed her phone down next to the sink.

An inspection of the bin confirmed her suspicions. Someone had packed it full of paper towel sheets, covered in dry browning blood. A few split knuckles would not create this much blood. Marraine sat leaning against the sink, her eyes moving slowly around the room and her long red nails tapping against the bench-top. She stopped; her eyes focused on the old wardrobe halfway down the long room. She sat still and silent. The only movement was the occasional flaring of her nostrils. Then, with her mind set, she marched over to the wardrobe and flung the doors open.

A cold cylinder of metal appeared, like Jack springing from his box, pushing firmly against her neck. Marraine's pupils had grown into large, black, oval-shaped slits, and her teeth appeared to be getting longer and sharper by the second.

'What are you doing?' she hissed. Dom clambered apprehensively from the wardrobe, careful to keep the shotgun against Marraine's neck, forcing her to take a step back. If it hadn't been for the weapon between them, Marraine might have laughed at Dom's appearance. His unshaven, dirty face, messy hair, and the fur coat draped over his shoulders, reminiscent of a Neanderthal man emerging from the mouth of his cave. Marraine raised her hands submissively, maintaining eye contact with Dom. 'You don't need the gun, sweetie,' she reassured him.

'Don't 'sweetie' me,' Dom forced a raspy reply, coercing his body to stand up straight. 'I know what you are, bitch. I know all about you.'

'That's a shame,' Marraine replied, pouting. 'I've always thought my air of mystery was one of my most endearing qualities.'

'If you don't shut up and take me to Angus, I'm going to splatter some of your endearing qualities all over the walls.'

'Well,' Marraine dropped her eyes to the gun, evaluating Dom's shaky but firm grip. 'Seeing as though you asked so nicely, it would be my pleasure.' Keeping her left hand raised, she motioned with her right hand for Dom to move towards to door. Dom shook his head from side to side.

'You first... Sweetie,' he said.

# Chapter 16

### Ending in Fire

'Hey,' was all Angus could think to say in response to Dom's sudden appearance in the stables. 'How... what... What are you doing here?'

'I've figured out who these filthy, dirty, murdering animals are,' Dom said, pushing Marraine into the room, 'and I've come to get you before they kill you too.' An explosion of dread fell into Angus's stomach.

'What do you mean, 'kill me too'?' he asked. Dom opened his mouth to respond but spotted Cinder sitting up on the sofa, stretching her arms above her head. Dom's dark eyebrows shot up and he whipped the shotgun around to face Cinder.

'That *thing* killed my sister!' he yelled. 'Now I'm going to put it down.' Marraine spun around, throwing her leg in the air. A great bang rang out, followed by a crashing sound.

Angus's nostrils filled with the smell of gunpowder; he could hear Cinder screaming over the ringing in his ears. He turned to help her, but she was already moving towards him. Angus turned back to see Dom struggling to free his right arm from beneath the pointy heel at the end of Marraine's out-stretched leg; still clasping the shotgun in his vice-like grip. Holes of various sizes peppered the ceiling, and a dusting of plasterboard and powder covered the beds.

Bob, who had taken a few seconds to get over the shock of being woken by a gunshot only metres from his bed, ran to grab Dom's other arm. Dom lashed out at him with one of his tomahawks, connecting with Bob's shoulder. Knocked off balance but keeping his footing, Bob grabbed the tomahawk before Dom could take another swing.

As Cinder brushed past Angus, he took hold of her arm. 'Are you alright?' he asked, his eyes darting around her body. Cinder pulled her arm free, paused momentarily to glare at him, and then continued towards the others.

'Let him go!' she demanded. Marraine and Bob, who were still struggling to hold Dom, looked at each other in puzzlement before turning quizzically to Cinder. 'He said something about Torry. What did you say about Tor?' she implored, searching Dom's eyes for some sign that would indicate that she had misheard or misunderstood what he had said. All she found was a well of anger, hatred, and loss.

'You know what happened. You murdered her, you evil bitch!' Dom spat, his neck pulsing with thick veins.

'I... No... I...' Cinder fell to her knees. Her usually pale skin appeared to have become almost transparent. 'Oh Dom,' she sniffed, two glistening lines slowly appearing between her eyes and her chin. 'I didn't... I couldn't... she's my little sister.' She shook her head from side to side, looking at the others in turn, hoping that someone was going to let her know it was all just a sick joke, a prank.

'Liar!' Dom screamed as he pushed Bob against the door. 'It was the Red Queen. It was you. She was trying to help you and you beat her to a bloody pulp, left her to die in the dirt, and then came home to your mansion.'

'I'm not lying, Dom.' Cinder reached out a trembling hand, pleadingly towards Dom. 'Can everyone just stop? Please stop.'

Angus walked cautiously towards Dom, holding his hands up submissively in front of him. 'How about you give me the gun, mate? Just till we get this sorted out.' He took the shotgun from Dom's hand. Blood was dripping from his wrist where he had been struggling against Marraine's heel. Angus pumped the last remaining shell into the chamber and dropped it into his hand.

'What are you doing?' Dom asked, in a tone halfway between confusion and betrayal. 'They're gonna kill us like they killed her.'

'Don't worry,' Angus replied, placing his hand on Marraine's foot, 'if what you're saying is true, I'll help you burn this whole bloody place to the ground. Right now, I think we should all take a seat and figure out what's going to happen next.'

Marraine guardedly lowered her leg. Bob immediately followed her lead, running to the kitchen to find something to stop the blood that was coming from his shoulder and was now covering most of his arm. Dom took hold of his wrist and sat on the end of Bob's bed. Cinder was still on the floor, in a cloud of confusion. Marraine helped her sit on one of the other beds. 'It was Louvelle,' she whispered, sitting down next to Cinder.

'What?' Cinder asked, snapping back to reality.

'The Red Queen – it must have been Louvelle.'

'No, I know my mother's a bit strict, but she's not a murderer. I...'

'More bullshit!' Dom interrupted, getting back on his feet. 'A mother's power passes to her daughter. We all know that.'

'That's true,' added Angus, as he slid his hand into his pocket and ran his fingers over the shotgun shell. Marraine got off the bed and stood between Cinder and the two men.

'That woman is not Cinder's mother.' She announced.

'She's my stepmother,' Cinder clarified, wiping her cheek with her sleeve, 'but I still don't think she...'

'Ha,' Marraine scoffed. 'Sorry sweetie, but it's time I told you some things about mother dear. You boys might want to hear this too.'

Marraine paced slowly along the walkway between the ends of the beds. 'When I first met the Lady Gevaudan, she came to your parents for help. She had come from Bladenboro in North Carolina. Her husband and step-children had been attacked and killed by vampires.' She paused and looked at Cinder. 'Sound familiar?' Cinder nodded.

'Anyway,' Marraine continued, 'she turned up here with a few belongings and a handful of loyal men, and your parents – bless their souls – took her in. About a year later, your mother, your real mother, my friend Annabelle, was very pregnant and came to me with her moon pendant, asking me to take it away somewhere safe. I was far younger and far more naïve. While I was away living it up in Paris, my best friend went into labour early and gave birth to a beautiful baby girl.' She stopped to wipe a single tear from her cheek. 'I never got to see Annabelle again. Complications after the birth, the midwife told me when I got home. I never got to ask what those complications were because after that day I never saw that midwife again either. I did finally track her down this week in Seattle; that's why I was late getting back to you, sweetie.' She smiled at Cinder, who sat perched on the edge of the bed, her lips pursed firmly together. 'Unfortunately, I was twenty-four hours too late. Bear attack, the coroner's report said, very rare for suburban Seattle. So yes, sweetie,' she placed her hand on Cinder's shoulder, 'your stepmother is more than capable of getting rid of anyone that gets in her way.'

Cinder sat, silently studying the damaged ceiling; one of the holes was allowing the night air to interlope on the silence within, the accompanying whistle reminiscent of an old-fashioned kettle boiling. Without making eye contact with anyone, Cinder stood up, slowly walked over to Angus, took the shotgun from him, and placed it down on the end of one of the beds. Continuing to not make eye contact with him, she touched Angus's shoulder gently. 'Can you come with me?' she asked in a hushed tone. 'You too, Bob,' she said louder.

'Cherchez la femme,' Angus said and gestured for Cinder to lead the way.

Without waiting for Bob to reply, Cinder collected her boots from the floor, pulled them on, and marched to the door. 'You two should stay here,' she added, to address Dom's and Marraine's questioning looks. Dom protested, but Cinder was already halfway out of the door with Angus following close behind.

'Doesn't anybody care that I'm bleeding?' Bob asked, as he tried to wrap a pillowcase around his wound. Marraine and Dom didn't respond; they continued to glare at each other as he left the room and closed the door behind him.

It was obvious to Angus that the west wing of The Big House was better cared for than the rest of the property that he had seen. Modern fixtures and artwork adorned the clean, recently painted walls. The scent of fresh apples and crisp linen had replaced the dust and mildew smell of the hallways at the other end of the house. Angus felt guilty that he didn't remove his shoes to walk on the plush grey carpet.

Bob put a skip in his step to keep up with Angus, who had much longer legs.

'Hey,' he said, tapping Angus's arm with his elbow. 'So, do I get a thank you for making sure the others didn't kill you?' Angus leant down and whispered into his ear.

'Thanks, Bob. Just for that, I'm going to kill you last.' He winked and then looked back at Cinder. Bob smiled to himself.

'Shucks Angus, that's the nicest thing you've ever said to me,' he said

At the end of the hallway, they reached two large timber doors. Cinder flung the doors open, storming into the sitting room like a ship crashing through the waves of a turbulent ocean. Her chin set forward and her nostrils flaring. Angus and Bob had to jog to keep up with her. Louvelle was standing with a glass of champagne in her hand. She swirled the golden liquid around the glass and watched the reflections of the flames from the open fire.

'Good evening Cinder, we were just talking about you,' she said without looking up from her drink. 'You should have told me we had a visitor; I would have had some refreshments prepared.' Turning to face them, her eyes moved slowly and deliberately from Angus to Cinder, then back again, her long dark eyelashes moving up and down like dozens of spiders' legs weaving their webs. Angus and Bob stopped just inside the door almost involuntarily, but Cinder continued until she was face-to-face with Louvelle.

'We need to talk,' Cinder demanded, her voice cracking with emotion. She noted a slight limp as Louvelle moved over to a side-table near the leather couches and placed her glass down.

'No, dear, I need to talk, and you need to listen. I've been looking for you, but from what Tibult and Lysander have just informed me, you might have been here since last night.' She gestured to two large bald men standing on either side of the fireplace. Their dark skin and black clothes a stark contrast to the white tones of the rest of the room. 'I left strict instructions when I went away, and it seems those instructions have been ignored.' Louvelle ran her left index finger along the mantel above the fire, a look of disgust spreading across her immaculate face as she rubbed dust between her finger and thumb. 'I give you a measure of trust and you repay me with what? Chaos?'

'She's a grown woman, she can make her own decisions,' Angus interrupted aggressively. Louvelle raised a sculpted eyebrow but didn't turn her attention away from the mantle.

'You need to muzzle your pet, dear. He's cute, but he won't be very petty with his chin on the other side of his head,' she said. Angus stepped forward, Tibult and Lysander responded in kind. Cinder stopped them with a raise of her hand.

'The only one that needs to answer questions is you... Mother!' she spat.

'Excuse me?' Louvelle turned now to look at Cinder.

'Where were you last night and why are you limping? What did you do? What happened to Tor?' Cinder's face flushed with anger and her eyes were glazing with enraged tears. Louvelle raised her eyebrow again.

'I told you, I was out trying to find you, and yes, what do I get for caring? I get injured. I hope you appreciate that. I might be left with a scar.' She looked down at her leg, pouting her lips.

'What did you do to Tor?' Cinder shouted, her chest heaving, fists clenched.

'Do calm down darling, we have guests.' Louvelle picked up her drink and took a sip before continuing. 'What is this *Tor* that you keep mentioning?'

'Tor isn't a thing. She's my family, and someone I care very deeply about,' Angus interrupted.

'Oh, I see,' Louvelle said, placing her glass down again, 'he's one of them. I should have known from the air of ignorance.' She smiled at Lysander and Tibult, who laughed in unison. Louvelle's face became hard, her eyes dark, and she looked directly at Angus for the first time. 'You need to learn your place, boy.'

'My place is between you and the people you want to hurt.' Angus moved closer to Cinder, and Bob followed behind.

Louvelle laughed to herself. 'Oh yes, Uncle Gunn and his merry band of idiots saving the town of Heathcote one chicken at a time. My dear boy, a marionette can't pull on its own strings to move the puppeteer's hands.' She studied Angus's eyes, a smile of triumph spreading across her face when she recognised Angus's confusion. She then turned her focus back to Cinder. 'I think he needs a woman to explain it to him, dear. He is just a man after all.'

'What's she talking about, Cin?' Angus asked, coming to stand next to Cinder. Dropping her eyes sympathetically to the ground, she replied.

'She means that you all think you're here to stop us from hurting people, but in reality, she wants you here, distracted, out of the way so she can go on her trips and do what she wants without you getting in her way.'

'We are in the same business really,' Louvelle added, 'you keep your dumb animals here as a pretence and so do I.'

Angus shook his head in disbelief and growing rage. 'I think you should change, let the beast out,' he said to Cinder.

'No! I don't need to,' she said, turning her attention back to her stepmother. 'Now mother, tell me what you did to Tor. What did you do to my friend?' Louvelle motioned to her two Haitian bodyguards, who moved forward towards Cinder and Angus.

'I don't know why you're angry with me, darling. I was protecting you. If you had stayed where you were told, she would still be alive.'

'How could you?' Cinder screamed, stepping forward and crashing into Lysander's chest. 'She was just a girl.'

'I didn't want to.' Louvelle replied, moving slowly to put the leather couch between her and Cinder. 'If you must know, I liked her; I was impressed that they had finally stopped sending men to do a woman's job. I even tried to be merciful and kill her quickly, but the little thing snagged me and ran off to die in the bushes somewhere.' Cinder felt like her stomach was trying to push its way into her chest. She swallowed hard to get her words out.

'You're a monster.'

'Me?' Louvelle held her hand up to her heart. 'You know nothing of real monsters; I've done everything in my power to make sure of that. This is all on you, dear.' She pointed a long index finger at Cinder. 'We can't have their type,' she pointed at Angus, 'just walking in here and destroying everything I've built for us.' She glared at Angus. 'Actually, while we're talking about that, Bob, take this one outside and dispose of him.' Bob took a step back from Angus and looked down at the ground.

'No,' he replied quietly. Louvelle appeared to grow taller as she took a step in Bob's direction.

'What did you say to me?' she asked?

'No,' Bob repeated himself, daring to be a bit louder this time.

'I am your queen, and you will do as I say.' Beads of sweat materialised on Bob's balding scalp.

'No,' he said again, 'she's my queen now.' He looked at Cinder, 'She turned 21, she wasn't here but we had a cake and everything.' Cinder tried to smile through the anger.

'Thank you, Bob,' she said.

'Don't be ridiculous,' Louvelle responded, slipping into her French accent. 'Coming of age is not enough to make her queen, not if there is already a queen regulating a domicile, which you all seemed to have forgotten, I am.'

'What about a blood-moon pendant?' Bob asked.

'What about a blood-moon pendant?' Louvelle responded. 'Thanks to her stupid mother and my dead husband, that was lost years ago.'

Cinder took a step back from Lysander. 'My parents were not stupid,' she shouted and pulled her pendant out from under her top. 'They were smart enough to make sure you didn't get your hands on this.' Both of Louvelle's eyebrows raised this time, and her pupils doubled in size.

'Salope! Give that to me,' she yelled.

'No, it's mine,' Cinder hissed. 'You're not taking anything else from me ever again.'

Louvelle's usually calm veneer disappeared.

'How dare you,' she cracked, 'after all I have done for you; I treated you as my own daughter and this is how you repay me. I should have dealt with you when I took care of Annabelle or handed you over to the vampires.'

Cinder picked up a vase from one of the side tables and threw it across the room. A shower of china shards exploded with a pop as it hit the wall. 'So it's true then? You killed my mother and now you've killed my little sister too.'

'Oh, grow up, Cinder, that's the way our world works.' Louvelle rolled her eyes. 'Now, Tibult get me that pendant before she breaks something else.' Tibult and Angus both took a step towards Cinder. Bob made a run for the door and Lysander moved to protect Louvelle. Angus took Cinder by the shoulder.

'I think it's time to change,' he urged her again.

'I said no!' she growled, whipping her head around, her eyes like slits of fierce green fire. Then, before Tibult even had time to realise what was happening, she had launched herself at him. She grabbed one of his enormous arms, twirling herself behind his back. The audible sound of something snapping was the first sign that Cinder had caused some damage. A sickening, low-pitched scream confirming Tibult's pain. The scene that followed looked almost comical because of the difference in size between Cinder and Louvelle's huge bodyguard. Cinder, still gripping the incapacitated arm, grit her teeth, grabbed hold of Tibult's crotch, and hoisted him onto her shoulders like a sack of potatoes. After taking three long strides across the room, Cinder yelled and sent a struggling Tibult smashing out through one of the large windows in a mess of falling glass and torn blinds. The cold night air came whistling in, but Tibult fell silent somewhere out in the dark. Angus ran to the window, his jaw involuntarily pulling his mouth open.

'Wow,' he said to Cinder, as he watched her shoulders rise and fall in time with her angry breaths. 'Wow,' he said again.

Cinder held her pendant in her hand and ran her finger over the smooth red stone. 'This is mine and you won't get your filthy hands on it.' She turned to face Louvelle, only to discover that Angus and she were the only two left in the room.

'No, no, no! Why didn't you stop them?' she yelled at Angus.

'Sorry, but I was watching you,' he apologised. 'That was awesome, by the way,' he added. Without thinking, he threw his arms around her and kissed her on the cheek. Cinder's body went rigid. She stood glaring at his arms.

'Seriously?' she asked. 'You're doing this now? There's no time.' She wriggled herself free of his embrace and peered out of the broken window. 'Come on, we need to stop her.'

Cinder pushed past Angus and ran out through the double doors, the hinges groaning in protest as she charged out into the hallway. She had only made it halfway down the length of the west wing when Marraine, Dom, and Bob rushed around the corner ahead of her. 'Did you see them?' she called out 'Did Lysander and my m... Louvelle come this way?'

'We saw a couple of dark figures running across the lawn just as we were coming out of the stables,' Marraine replied. 'We were just coming to see if you were okay. Bob was worried. Are you okay we heard smashing and screaming?'

'I'm fine,' Cinder said, continuing past them, 'but she's not going to be.'

Angus followed her.

'She's fine,' he assured Marraine. 'I can't say the same for the other guy.'

Cinder ran out into the still night air, searching desperately for any sign of Louvelle. The bright moon flooded the grounds with pale light, but the only movement she could see was the gentle sway of the forest trees at the bottom of the hill.

'Which way did they go?' she demanded when the others caught up with her.

'That way,' Bob pointed, 'out the front towards the main gate.'

'No, no, no,' Cinder complained and set off at a sprint, her t-shirt flapping wildly against her back. She ran across one of the large sections of lawn, hurdled a low hedge, and rounded the west-most corner of The

Big House. The main gate came into sight, but her heart sank. Two red taillights disappeared in a haze of dust and the crackle of gravel. Cinder slumped down on the front steps that lead up to the west wing's main door.

'No, no, no, no, no!' she yelled again and with each no she kicked at a cracked piece of the bullnose on the bottom step. When a piece of concrete broke free, she picked it up and hurled it towards the front gate. The others ran around the corner just as her projectile smashed to the ground on the driveway.

'We're too late, she's gone.' Cinder waved her arm towards the front gate. 'It's all true, Marraine, she admitted it. She used and manipulated all of us and now she's going to get away with it.'

'No, there's still a chance,' Marraine said, stepping forward. 'I think I know where she's going, and you should be able to get there quicker on foot. She has a private jet at the airstrip at Tallo's Bluff and the fastest way there is by boat.' She held out her hand to Cinder and helped her stand. 'The marina is just at the bottom of the hill.' Marraine walked back and pointed in the direction they had just come from. 'But by road, she'll have to go the long way around through Heathcote.'

'Let's go then,' Cinder said and went to leave.

'Hang on, hang on,' Angus pleaded. 'There could be a whole army of Lycan out there waiting to stop us. This could be exactly what she wants us to do.'

'Good,' Dom interrupted. 'The more I get to take down on the way, the better I say.'

'Hey pretty boy,' Marraine stood in front of Dom 'some of those Lycan are good friends of mine.' Dom took a stride forward so that he was chest to chest with Marraine.

'Well, if you hadn't noticed, I'm not exactly in the mood for making any more new friends, so your friends better stay out of my way,' he said.

'I'm in your way right now,' Marraine spat back. 'What are we going to do about that?'

'No, stop.' Cinder pulled them apart. 'Dom's right, we can't be stopping to ask questions or second-guessing who's friendly or not.' She put her hands on Marraine's shoulders. 'I want you and Bob to find anyone who is loyal to me and get them to stay out of the way,' she instructed. Marraine placed her hands on Cinder's cheeks.

'Are you sure? There are still a few people here that would love to help.'

'I'm sure. It's not going to be safe for anything with fur and a tail tonight.' Cinder said, taking hold of Marraine's hands and nodded her head. Dom walked over to Angus and patted him on the back.

'Finally, someone's talking some sense. Let's go.' He started jogging towards the tree line. Cinder hugged Marraine and followed him. Angus gave Bob a nod and joined them.

'This is not a good idea,' he said to Dom as they ran into the shadows of the forest. Dom pulled out his tomahawks and looked Angus in the eye.

'I think we've moved way past the time for good ideas.' He pointed his tomahawk towards Cinder. 'She gets it.' Although she was still in her human form, Cinder had the distinct look of a lioness chasing down a meal. It wasn't long before she came across her prey.

# Chapter 17

### Killer Queen

The forest inclined steeply down towards the coastline; the slope quickening their progress but making it difficult for them to keep their footing in the loose plant matter of the forest floor. Three sets of glowing yellow eyes, gambolling in the moonlight, was the first indication that they were not alone. Angus was the first to see them. He pointed them out to Dom and was just about to suggest that they try to sneak past, when Cinder must have seen them, and turned and ran straight for them. Dom followed her lead.

Launching herself off a large rock, Cinder took the closest Lycan by surprise, landing an elbow on the top of its head. Yelping and stumbling backwards, the Lycan slashed out at Cinder with its large, hairy, clawed hand. Cinder easily stopped the attack with her left forearm, before wrapping her hand around behind the Lycan's elbow and pulling it in sharply. The Lycan yelped again, clearly in pain. Cinder took the opportunity to pummel its snout with her other fist, punching it a dozen times in as many seconds. Meanwhile, the remaining Lycan had realised what was happening and were running on all fours to help their comrade, drool flying from their bared teeth.

Dom sprang from the darkness, hip-and-shouldering the first of the running Lycans, sending it tumbling down the slope. The last Lycan launched itself at Dom. Dom ducked to his right but turned quickly to swing violently at the Lycan's left shoulder with his tomahawk. Howling painfully, the Lycan turned to face him, its left arm hanging limply, blood dripping from the deep wound in its shoulder. It tried to swipe at him with its other hand, but Dom's second tomahawk was already swinging in a high arc above his head. The blade came down hard on the dark hairy flesh of the Lycan's forearm, almost detaching the beast's right hand. With both arms incapacitated, the Lycan backed away, but Dom delivered the final deathblow, planting a tomahawk between its ears and splitting open its skull.

The Lycan that had earlier fallen down the hill ran at Dom. Throwing himself backwards, Dom tried to pull his tomahawk from the dead Lycan's head as it fell. He had jammed the blade deep into the beast's skull. His hand slipped from the handle. The third Lycan leapt at Dom, teeth bared, ready to rip open his throat. Dom thrust his second tomahawk between its jaws. Hot breath and foamy spit showered his face as the Lycan's teeth clamped down on the metal blade.

Cinder gave the first Lycan one last uppercut to the jaw for good measure, vaulting its shoulders and snapping its neck as she went. She ran for the Lycan that was still falling to the ground with a tomahawk wedged in the top of its head, pulling the weapon free. With a cry of rage, she kicked the remaining Lycan off Dom, before bringing the tomahawk down on its neck with both hands, removing its head from its body. Dom sat up and watched Cinder wipe the blood from her face with the bottom of her t-shirt. 'Come on, no time to sit around,' she said and tossed Dom his weapon.

Catching up with the others, Angus arrived and caught the tomahawk. He took Dom by the wrist and pull him up. 'Wow,' Dom said, looking around and then watching Cinder run ahead.

'Yeah, that's what I said,' Angus replied, handing Dom his weapon and running after Cinder.

The deeper into the forest they ran, the thicker it became. Angus used his forearm to push a branch of a beech tree out of his path, but lost his footing on a large moss-covered rock. Slipping down onto one knee, he could see under the surrounding branches. To his surprise, he spotted Duncan and Blair in a clearing at the bottom of the hill. Cinder and Dom kept running and even though Angus called out to them, they either could not hear or chose to ignore him and disappeared into the forest. Brushing himself off, Angus hauled himself up, making his way running and sliding down the leafy hill to let Duncan and Blair know they were okay. 'Hey!' he shouted as he came closer.

Duncan and Blair's heads swivelled around, their looks of surprise turning to joy when they recognised Angus. Still smiling, Duncan put up his hand to tell Angus to stop, and then placed the index finger of his other hand in front of his lips. Angus crouched down and surveyed the area, holding up three fingers to indicate that he had seen three Lycan close by. Duncan nodded in reply and pointed to his left, holding up two fingers. Angus crept towards his friends, keeping a sharp eye on the three Lycan he could see. 'Where the hell have you been?' Blair whispered when Angus was beside him.

'Well,' Angus replied, 'long story short, we found the wolves' den and we're chasing the queen now.'

'Who's we?'

'Me and Dom, oh and Cinder, sort of.'

'Sort of?' Duncan questioned.

'I'll explain later.' Angus wasn't sure how to explain.

'Okay then,' Duncan said, looking unsatisfied with Angus's answer, 'here, you might want this.' He picked up Angus's naginata that was leaning against a tree and threw it to him.

'What about Gunn, Dand, or Tor? Are they with you?' Blair asked. 'We went back to the house yesterday morning and couldn't find anyone.' Angus's shoulders dropped.

'You guys don't know about Tor?' he asked. Blair raised his eyebrows questioningly and opened his mouth to ask about Torry, but before the words could escape his lips, a large dark shape crashed through the undergrowth and sent him sprawling into the mud.

Angus leapt to Blair's aid, wedging his weapon under the neck of the Lycan that had him pinned to the ground. He dragged the beast away from his friend, but a second Lycan sprang out of the shadows, mouth frothing and snarling, and lunged at Angus. He had just enough time to swing the first Lycan around to shield himself from the attack before it crashed into him. Stumbling backwards, he collided with a tree but kept a tight hold around the Lycan's neck. The second Lycan bit at his face, but Angus managed to force it back and kick it hard in the chest. With a yelp, the Lycan staggered backwards and toppled over Blair, who was still lying winded on the ground. Angus pulled his naginata tighter around the neck of his captive and pushed his shoulder hard into the top of its spine. The beast writhed frantically as it began to run out of air, forcing Angus repeatedly against the tree. Angus held tight until the Lycan's body became limp and he listened to its putrid breaths, wheezing and gurgling their last. Discarding the body, he ran to help Blair, who was pinned to the ground by the second Lycan.

As Angus threw his leg back, ready to kick the hairy creature off Blair, Blair called out in pain. Angus brought the toe of his boot hard up into the Lycan's ribs, sending in yelping and flailing across the ground.

'Stupid bastard!' Blair yelled, pulling himself backwards along the ground with his arms, his legs dragging along in the mud in front of him.

'You okay?' Angus called out over his shoulder.

'Yep, I'm fine; you just deal with that prick.'

The Lycan regained its footing and made to leap at Angus, but before it could leave the ground, Angus plunged his blade deep into its skull, just above its left eye. Angus placed his foot against his victim's bloody mouth to pull his weapon free. Duncan emerged from the trees and dropped another motionless body on the ground. Its head flopped at an abnormal angle, its long pink tongue dangling from between its teeth. Duncan smiled and patted Angus on the shoulder with his massive hand. 'I guessed we weren't sticking to the no-killing rule. Where's Blair?' he asked. Angus pulled his weapon free and motioned towards Blair with his head.

'Hey,' Duncan called out with a laugh in his voice, 'no sitting around – job's not done.'

Blair sat with his back against the stump of a dead tree, his head resting on his chest. A dark substance covered his left thigh and pooled on the ground beneath him, glistening in the moonlight. The smile quickly dropped away from Duncan's face and he ran forward to shake him by the shoulder. The empty body, which seconds before held his friend, fell into Duncan's arms like a rag-doll.

'Hey, hey get up.' Duncan held up Blair's face. 'We've got work to do. No time to take a nap.'

Angus stood in darkness, the night air cold on the perspiration pooling on his back. His body, motionless, frozen to the spot, but his mind was racing, trying to process the reality of the scene unfolding in front of him. He still couldn't believe that Torry was gone, but this? This made no sense at all. He was just talking to Blair moments ago. He was fine moments ago.

The sound of heavy footsteps and breaking branches alerted him to the fact that there was no more time to think about it. Angus turned to face whatever was coming next, shifting his feet in the damp soil to steady his footing. Duncan sat Blair's body gently back against the stump. He knelt for a few seconds with his forehead sitting against Blair's.

'I'll see you soon, mate,' he said before kissing the top of Blair's head and turning to look at Angus. Standing up slowly, Duncan reached both hands into his coat and withdrew two large machetes. Joining Angus, he let out two long, loud breaths of steam from his nose. Angus could see that the veins on his bald head had tripled in size. His long, dark leather coat was large enough to be a shelter for three normal men, but was now straining audibly under the stress of his large heaving shoulders.

'I think you should go find the others,' he said to Angus without turning to look at him. Angus swept his eyes across the eight, no, nine Lycan that he could see running towards them.

'Are you sure?' he asked. Anger burned in Duncan's eyes as he darted them to the side.

'Go!' He ordered. He was a fearsome-looking man, but this was the first time that Angus had truly felt afraid of him. Angus nodded in agreement and knelt to say goodbye to his friend. He held Blair's hand and watched as Duncan walked slowly but purposefully into the oncoming hoard.

'Come on!' Duncan yelled, beckoning them forward.

Angus placed Blair's still warm hands on his lap and noticed the large bite on the inside of his thigh. As he got up to leave, a Lycan's head landed at his feet, already changing back into its human form. Blood splattered up from where the neck had recently parted ways with its body and dashed across the anchor tattoo on Angus's arm. He studied the words *Pride before your pride*, then wiping his arm down his chest, he reluctantly turned away from his two friends and got to his feet. Running towards the beach, he looked back as Duncan disappeared into a blur of furry limbs and bloodied teeth. Somewhere below, gunshots rang out and echoed around the hillside.

# Chapter 18

### In Need of an Anchor

Angus stopped to catch his breath, his hands shaking and pale on his weapon. He lessened his grip, shaking each hand, in turn, to encourage blood flow to his numb fingers. Three of the Lycan had followed him and he had been running, hiding, and doubling back, for what might have been minutes or hours – he wasn't sure. He had dealt with two of his pursuers simply. Waiting for them to become separated from their companions, Angus had come up on each of them from behind and knocked them unconscious before they would warn the others. The third Lycan, however, had smelled him coming and had put up more of a fight, leaving Angus with scratches and cuts on both arms and a bloody slash above his right eye.

Angus wiped blood from the blades of his naginata on a patch of grass, watching as the hairy corpse at his feet slowly morphed back into a naked, middle-aged man who appeared to be of Asian descent. Retracting the blades, he looked around to regain his bearings.

It was approaching first light, but the sky still showed no signs of sunrise. Angus needed to strain his eyes in the moonlit darkness to see where the others had gone. A chilly wind blew through his hair and rumbling in his ears. When the breeze calmed for a moment, he heard Cinder yelling out in anger. It came from somewhere off to his left, down near the ocean. Angus forced his tired legs to get him moving again. The branches that were scratching against the exposed skin on his face and hands started to thin out. Soon sand and rock replaced the forest. Angus scramble over the rocks and made his way quickly to the firmer wet sand. A few hundred metres down the beach, a long wooden pier jutted out into the ocean. Squinting his eyes, Angus could see movement about two-thirds of the way along.

A man-made stone wall curved its way into the ocean, making a small quay. Angus climbed to the top and ran cautiously along the top of the wall to where it met the pier. He found Louvelle's car abandoned at the side of the road. A scattering of shotgun holes was visible across the rear panel and back door. The rear right tyre sat twisted and punctured in a ditch. At the end of the quay, there were half a dozen vessels moored behind a tall cyclone fence. The only entrance was usually closed off by a tall gate made of heavy vertical bars of rectangular steel. The gate lay in the shallow water, bent at a right angle, a useless lock hanging from one side. Angus walked through the mangled gap where the gate once stood and past a half-a-dozen lifeless bodies. Dom's tomahawk sat proudly wedged in the temple of one of the closer ones. Further along, the second tomahawk protruded from a body that had no head attached or one nearby. The pier creaked under his feet. Waves crashing against the wooden pylons sent sea spray across his stern face, causing his stubbled chin to glisten in the moonlight.

Running past a large Sunseeker yacht with the name 'Calvin's revenge' written in large print along the port side, Angus finally caught up with Cinder and Dom. He was relieved to see them both alive, but the scene before him was not one he would hope for. Held between two grey Lycan, weaponless, was Dom, his clothes torn and his face dripping with blood and sweat. Cinder was less bloody and injured, but no less in trouble. From what Angus could make out in the moonlight, a thick rope bound her hands and arms. Lysander held her, while Louvelle was tying her to a large, disused anchor that was decorating the boardwalk. A handful of other Lycan mingled around, guarding their queen.

'Get this bitch off me, Black!' Cinder yelled when she saw him coming. Louvelle slapped her hard across her left cheek.

'Language, dear,' she scolded, 'a young lady shouldn't use such vulgarity.'

'Let them go,' Angus called.

'Oh, the boyfriend,' Louvelle called back, pulling the knot tight. 'I had almost forgotten about you,' she continued as she dusted off her hands and fixed her hair. 'Your timing is terrible, I'm afraid. I was going to torture pretty boy there to get information out of little Miss Disappointment here.' She yanked Cinder's head back by her hair. 'They might have both survived. Unfortunately, now we need to take care of you too, we just don't have the time.' She looked at her watch, pursed her lips, and moved her head slowly from side to side. 'So, we just need to kill one of them. Or both?' She pushed Cinder's head down and strolled over to circle around Dom, fondling his hair. 'It's the age-old question, isn't it? Your friend or your lover, which do you choose? Bros before hoes, isn't that what you young people say? So, what is it boy, do you save your friend's pretty neck?' she ran her hand across Dom's chest. 'Or do you save the hoe from drowning and watch your bro become a Lycan lunch?' She paced casually back to Cinder. 'Well? We're waiting.'

'I'll take the third option, thanks,' interrupted Angus as he gave Cinder a reassuring smile, then fixed his eyes firmly on Louvelle.

'What third option?' she scoffed.

'The option where I save my friend, get the girl, kill you and all your pets, then go home and have a pint while I listen to Sufjan Stevens,' he said, winking at Dom. Louvelle began to laugh.

'And how exactly do you plan on doing that?' she asked.

'With this,' he said, lifting his naginata.

'What are you going to do with your little stick?' Louvelle jeered, her cold voice thick with laughter. 'I hope you don't expect any of us to fetch it for you.' The two Lycan holding Dom let out a low growl to show approval of their queen's joke.

Dom lessened the grip of the hairy arm across his mouth long enough to call out. 'It's not a stick! Right, Black?' He gestured with his head towards the Lycan over his right shoulder. Angus placed his hands in the correct positions on his weapon.

'That's right,' he murmured to himself. 'It's not a stick, it's a naginata, you stupid bitch.' He yelled. The instant that Dom saw the flash of moonlight on a metal blade, he closed his eyes and pulled his head down to the left. A split second later, he felt a breeze past his ear and heard a whoosh followed by a sickening wet crunch. Angus's weapon sat proudly, hilt deep in the Lycan's left eye socket. The end of the blade was protruding from the back of its head, a hairy skull fragment stuck to the tip. As the Lycan fell backward, Dom broke free and yanked the naginata from its skull. In one fluid motion, he whipped the blade at the opposite end around, catching the second Lycan off guard. Blood spattered up Dom's arms as the partially decapitated beast fell with a thud on the timber deck and convulsed wildly.

The smile dissolved from Louvelle's face.

'What are you all doing standing there? Kill them, you useless fools,' she shrieked. Lysander stood in front of Louvelle while the four remaining Lycan leapt towards Angus. Dom threw the naginata and Angus had to jump out of the way, as the twitching body of one of the beasts fell where he had been standing. He pulled his weapon from the beast's chest, swinging it wildly at the remaining three attackers. The blades becoming a whirlwind of flashes in the moonlight as they connected with claws, jaws, and hairy flesh. Out of the corner of his eye, Angus spotted Dom running to help, but he didn't slow down. He launched himself at full speed at the Lycan that was closest to the edge of the pier. The Lycan let out a howl as Dom tackled it off the edge, and they both tumbled together and disappeared into the dark ocean with a splash.

Angus ducked as a Lycan swiped at his face. Razor-sharp claws ripped into his shoulder and sent him crashing face-first into the ground. The Lycan made a second attempt at his head, but this time, Angus was quicker. Swinging his weapon around in a circle above his head, he sent a hairy hand flying across the pier. Using his momentum to roll behind the last Lycan, Angus slashed its ankles. While the two Lycan thrashed about in pain, Angus retracted one of his blades and brought the blunt end down on their heads.

Angus took a few seconds to catch his breath, then with his blade at the neck of the Lycan with the missing hand, called out to Louvelle.

'Let her go or they die.'

Louvelle laughed.

'Please do, thanks to you they're damaged goods now. You would be doing me a favour,' she said. 'Now, as much fun as this has been, it's time to put that thing down and walk away.'

Angus looked down at the blood-soaked, matted fur of the Lycan unconscious at his feet and then back at Cinder, who was still struggling to get free of her restraints. 'I just want Cinder. Let her go and we can all go home,' he said. Louvelle's lips curled slowly into a malicious smile.

'No one dictates terms to me, boy,' she said, ripping the moon pendant from Cinder's neck and motioning to Lysander. Angus watched in horror as Lysander pushed Cinder and the anchor off the edge. Struggling desperately and screaming curses at her stepmother, Cinder toppled head-first towards the black ocean. Angus ran, but she had already disappeared under the crashing waves by the time he reached the edge of the boardwalk. Taking a deep breath, he dropped his weapon on the pier and dived in next to the tell-tale bubbles rising to the surface.

Cinder's heart was pounding, and her eyes were stinging from the salty water. Wriggling desperately, she tried to free her arms, but without her pendant, she was already growing larger, pulling the ropes tighter. Suddenly, there was another set of hands pulling at her restraints. She could just make out Angus's face in the murky dimness and then his lips were against hers. *Now he kisses me?* she thought to herself, but he wasn't kissing her. He held her nose and forced air into her mouth. Some salty water went down her throat and it took all of Cinder's concentration to not open her mouth and cough it out. Finally, she managed to get one of her hands free. She desperately tried to paddle her way back to the surface, but with her legs still tied to the anchor, she continued to sink down among the rocks and seaweed.

Coughing and spluttering, Angus was back at the surface. A wave crashed against the back of his head, sending salty foam into his eyes and ears. He gasped in another deep breath and ducked back under the water. The water was shallow enough that he could still make out Cinder's form on the ocean floor in the moonlight, but it was deep enough that he had to swim down to her. Long claws had formed at the ends of Cinder's fingers. She started trying to claw her feet free. It was difficult in the darkness to tell the difference between rope and seaweed, so she began frantically swiping at everything. Her lungs were aching to breathe, and her muscles were shaking with pain.

Angus found the ropes around Cinder's feet and started trying to pull her free. In her panic and desperate slashing, she scratched him across his already wounded shoulder. Four deep cuts opened up and a cloud of blood filled the water. In shock, Angus breathed in a mouthful of water. The burning in his lungs and the pain in his shoulder forced him back to the surface. Coughing violently as water spewed from his mouth and nose, he used his uninjured arm to hold on to one of the large wooden pylons. His chest heaved, drawing in desperate, rattling breaths as his mind raced to come up with a plan.

Laying exhausted among the weeds as they swayed gently around her, the urge to breathe was too strong for Cinder to fight any longer. Her mouth involuntarily shot open and cold water rushed into her lungs. Her throat shuddered as her vocal cords tried to close off her airway and the surrounding darkness grew thick and warm. Shortly, however, the darkness melted away like smoke in a breeze and she was looking up at the roof of the library at home. She sat on her father's knee, her head against his warm shoulder, listening as his deep voice rumble reassuringly around in his chest.

For the third time, Angus dived back under the water. This time, he ignored the ropes and made straight for the anchor. One of the flukes was resting on top of a large mussel-covered rock. Angus lifted it onto his shoulder, then finding a flat sandy spot to plant his feet, he lifted the anchor and Cinder onto his back. Cinder's face was still just below the waterline, so, mustering what strength he had left, Angus trudged towards the shore. His knees felt like they might buckle under him with each step, but at least the weight kept his feet on the ocean floor. Four steps later and Cinder's head was above the water, five more steps, and her head and chest were in the chilly night air, waves splashing against her cheeks. Unfortunately for Angus, the more of Cinder's body that appeared above the water, the less her buoyancy helped him lift her; by the time her whole torso was free, Angus was bent over, almost crawling on all fours. Finally, his own head was out of the water and he could breathe again. His limbs felt heavy and limp. Flashes of light blurred his vision, but he could see the shoreline just metres ahead of him. Soon the white flashes turned to dark patches as the beach faded out of view. Eventually, he was walking blind and all he could do was to continue putting one foot in front of the other, hopeful that he was still heading out of the water. A cold shiver ran over his entire body and his legs refused to continue; the anchor slid from his back. He stumbled around for a moment, then fell face down in the sand.

Drenched and coated in sand, Cinder resembled a giant fur-ball, coughed up by the ocean. One of her feet was still tied to the anchor, but the rest of her body lay sprawled in the sand looking up at the moon. Other than the rapid and distressed rise and fall of her chest, she remained motionless. Her throat and lungs felt like they were on fire, and tears of pain and anger pooled at the top of her cheeks. She turned her head slowly towards the ocean, releasing the tears to trickle down onto her nose and lips before dripping on the sand. Blinking to clear her vision, she was just able to see Louvelle's boat hopping its way across the top of the waves towards the private jet that would already be prepped and waiting to take her... *anywhere.*

'Black?' Cinder tried to call out, but her voice sounded muffled and crackly. 'Black!' she called again. A wave crept up the beach towards her, lapping teasingly against her right arm before retreating into the ocean. While the rest of her remained still, her eyes darted about, trying to see Angus. When she couldn't see him anywhere, she forced herself to sit up. Moaning and shaking, she rolled over onto her side and pushed her torso off the ground. She saw Angus lying face down in the shallows, just out of her reach. Motionless. 'BLACK!' This time, she screamed.

Cinder tried to get up and run to Angus, but realised that she still had one foot tied to the anchor. Cursing and screaming, she pushed against the ropes with her other foot as she tried to pull her way free. Wet fur ripped from her ankles, but her foot was working its way out. When the rope burn started to take the top layers of skin off her heel, she closed her eyes and dug her claws into the sand. Clenching her long sharp teeth together, she gave her leg one last yank, pulling her bloodied heel free as the rest of her foot followed. Scurrying across the sand like a hermit crab and pulling herself free of what remained of her torn clothes, Cinder fell on Angus's side, shaking him and calling his name. When he didn't respond, she rolled him over and tried to give him CPR. Salt, tears, and sand covered her furry face and her mouth was now on the end of a tooth-filled snout. She was also not sure how hard to push on his chest without causing him harm.

'No, no, no,' she whimpered between messy, ineffective breaths into Angus's mouth. A mix of anger and grief was building in her chest and she was running out of breath again herself. A large set of hands gripped her shoulders tightly and pulled her away from Angus. She was just about to lash out at the new arrival, when she saw Dom's pale stern face next to hers. Dom knelt next to her, wiping the water from his face and hair.

'You do the chest, I'll do the mouth,' he ordered, placing Cinder's hands back on Angus's chest. 'Gently,' he added.

Dom pulled Angus's head back, wiping his hands on his wet shirt, before cleaning out Angus's mouth with his fingers. Holding Angus's nose, he breathed three large breaths into his mouth. Cinder could feel the rise and fall of his chest under her palms.

'Okay,' Dom said with a nod and counted, 'one, two, three, four, five,' as Cinder rhythmically pushed down on Angus's sternum. Dom listened, but there was no response.

They repeated this process over and over, and as the tide receded, so did Cinder's hope. Dom's determination and continued barking of commands was all that kept her going. Eventually, she could see that even Dom was willing to concede defeat. He had begun with an expression of determination, but his face now hung with blurry-eyed disbelief. How could his sister and his best friend die in front of him in the one night?

'Argh,' his raspy voice screamed into the night, frightening some sea birds from their nesting place in the dunes. He breathed three more breaths into his best friend's lungs and fell into the sand next to him. Cinder made ready to compress his chest again but felt it moving by itself, slowly up and down.

'Dom, DOM!' she called. Dom sprang up again and put his ear to Angus's chest.

'It's beating,' he announced triumphantly and lay with his head listening to the most welcome sound he had ever heard. Angus opened one eye and coughed.

The sun had just risen over the horizon, sending the darkness into its shadowy hiding places.

'Thank goodness,' Cinder said as she rose slowly to her feet, her back to the sun and the ocean. 'I don't want him to see me like this.' Angus rolled his head towards her voice. Cinder cast a silhouette against the sun. The first light just hitting her, sparkling off the drops of water on her fur, creating a golden aura around the edge of her body. Cinder's large, emerald green eyes glowed from inside the silhouette. He tried to speak, but he was too quiet for them to hear.

'What was that, Black?' Dom asked, leaning closer. Cinder fell back on her knees next to him.

'What did he say?'

'Beautiful, he said, it's the most beautiful thing he's seen... He could be talking about the sunrise – he hasn't seen one for a while.' Dom said. Cinder was starting to look more like her human self. She was smiling, but her smile quickly turned to an expression of concern. She mustered what energy she had left and ran, falling a few times in the softer sand. Dom watched as she disappeared into the shadows of the tree line. Too exhausted to call out to her, or care where she was going, Dom looked back down just as Angus's eyes closed again.

# Chapter 19

## They Are Night Zombies! They Are Neighbours! They Have Come Back From the Dead! Ahhhh!

Gunn sat on a grey vinyl chair, picking dirt from under his fingernails. 'I hate hospitals,' he told Angus for the second time in ten minutes. 'It's the smell, like disinfectant, mucus, and dead flowers.' Angus forced a smile and nodded in agreement. He knew Gunn had every reason to be uncomfortable in hospitals, but he had been reminding his family, doctors, nurses, or anyone that would listen several times a day for the past two weeks.

The sounds of heart monitors and I.V. machines hummed and bleeped in the background as Angus sat on the end of the hospital bed in the Heathcote Community Hospital or the H.C.H as the locals knew it. It was a stretch to call the H.C.H a hospital. It was just a glorified medical centre with two small wards and a surgery, surrounded by beautiful gardens and amazing ocean views.

'Hi Zombie Boy,' came a small croaky voice from beside Angus.

'Hey Zombie Girl,' he said to the occupant of the bed. Gunn had been calling them 'Zombie Boy' and 'Zombie Girl' on account of them both returning from the dead. Bandages still covered most of Torry's head, but the swelling in her face had gone down enough that she looked like herself again. Her bruises were now mostly yellow, with only a few spots of purple and red. The doctor had placed her in a coma because of how much swelling she had around her brain, and she had only regained consciousness a week ago. The pain medication still made her sleepy, so she spent most of her days going in and out of consciousness. Her right arm was in a cast, so Angus took hold of her left hand, careful not to bump her I.V. drip. Torry squeezed his index finger.

'Have you been here long?' she asked, forming a smile as best she could.

'Just a half-hour or so,' Angus returned her smile. 'I was here yesterday, but you didn't wake up. Sorry I didn't come to see you earlier; I've been trying to find Dom.'

'Dad told me he'd gone. I thought he would have called by now.'

'No, no call. I don't even think he knows you're okay.'

Torry pulled her hand away.

'I'm sorry, Black. Sorry I let you down, I wasn't strong enough,' she said, looking away. Angus turned and moved his leg onto the bed so that he was looking at her straight on.

'What are you talking about you let me down?' he asked. 'Your dad and I have just been talking about how amazing you were.'

'But I almost died,' Torry said, looking from Angus to father. Angus placed his large hand on the white hospital blanket over her shin and looked into her bloodshot eyes.

'As far as we can tell, you're the only one of us, man or woman, who has faced a Red Queen alone, and lived to talk about it. Don't let anyone ever tell you you're not strong enough – you're made of steel and stone.'

'Thanks, Black,' she said as a single tear rolled down her left cheek. 'Bloody morphine's making me a sook.' She wiped her cheek on her shoulder. 'Anyway,' she said to change the subject, 'did you find anyone else while you were looking for Dom?'

Angus stood up and removed a blue plastic folder that was hanging from the end of the bed. 'I'm not sure who you mean,' he said, flicking through Torry's charts.

'Last time I saw you, you were running off into the darkness to find Cinder.' Torry said, moving slowly and painfully into a sitting position. Gunn stood up and helped her with her pillows. 'I just want to know if you told her what you needed to,' she continued.

'And what would that be?' Angus asked, hanging the folder back on the bed.

'How you feel about her, silly.'

'Oh, okay, and how do I feel about her?' Angus asked. Gunn and Torry exchanged knowing looks.

'You love her, of course,' she said.

'Love?' Angus laughed. 'How is this love? Since I've met her, I've lost my best friend and her family have tried to kill me. I've nearly died a handful of times. Hell, she's even tried to kill me. I'm not sure right now if I actually hate her. I don't know if I want to kiss her or strangle her.'

Gunn chuckled to himself, his large chest moving up and down.

'My boy, I couldn't have described love better myself.' He walked over and placed his rough hand firmly on Angus's shoulder. 'People make the mistake of thinking that love and hate are opposite things, and one can't exist with the other. The fact is, they are just simply two sides of the same coin.' He continued walking over to the window but appeared to not be looking at the view but picturing a scene in his mind. 'Your Aunt Emily and I were together for 35 years, and I'm fairly sure she wanted to kill me for 34 of those.'

'Why did she stay with you then?' asked Angus.

'Because,' Gunn said, 'she would also have died for me and me for her. That's love, boy: the actions, not the feelings. And from the sounds of it, you already proved you would die for this girl.'

'I don't know. People have died!' Angus said, rubbing the stubble on his chin. 'I think this whole thing was just a big mistake.' Gunn turned back from the window, raised his large eyebrows, and looked Angus in his eyes.

'Mistake? Ha, mistakes are how we learn, and mistakes are the things we look back on and laugh.' He turned and looked at Torry, smiling. 'But boy, let this silly old man tell you something: if you want to know what will keep you awake at night, wondering when you're an old man like me, it's the mistakes you didn't make. Go make some mistakes, boy.'

'Even if that is the case,' said Angus, taking a seat on the vinyl chair, 'she ran off on me and I haven't been able to find her. She hasn't been back to her house since that night.'

'That's because she's been here, stupid,' interrupted Torry.

'Here?' Angus looked around the room as if he might see her hiding in a corner.

'Yes here. Where else would you expect a big sister to be when their little sister is in the hospital?' Torry said. Gunn nodded and smirked. Torry threw a pillow at Angus, the best she could without pulling on the stitches in her back.

Angus got up and put the pillow back on her bed, leaning in close and looking into Torry's eyes.

'Is she here now?' he asked.

'Yep,' Torry said. 'She told us she was going to have a nap in the gardens.' Angus smiled and kissed Torry on the forehead.

'Thanks, I'll see you soon,' he said.

'Good luck,' Torry called out to him as he turned and left. Angus looked back and gave her one last smile and held up both his hands, showing her his crossed fingers.

# Chapter 20

### The End of a Tail

The hospital sat on a large flat area on a hill behind the main esplanade of Heathcote. Falling away sharply on the west boundary, it overlooked the police station and a fish and chip shop. The building itself had an orange brick exterior and brown-tiled roof and only took up about a quarter of the property. Gardens that were maintained by community groups, sprawled across the remaining area of the flat. A handful of tall palm trees were casting long shadows from the twilight sun over manicured green lawns. Angus's feet crunched away the tranquillity as he strolled along one of the red gravel paths, snaking its way through beds of ferns, rhododendrons, and orchids. He was glad of the sounds of crickets, distant seabirds, and the rumble of the ocean, because he was sure if it were any quieter, the sound of his heart pounding against his chest would be audible.

Cinder was sitting on a green wooden bench in front of a cold stone wall, tucked between two large ferns. She was looking out over Heathcote and the pink twilit ocean that stretched out to the distant horizon. When Angus walked around the corner, he noted she was wearing the same clothes as the first night she and Marraine had met them at the beach. A lifetime ago.

Cinder turned to look when she heard Angus's footsteps on the stones. 'You found me,' she said, turning back to look at the view.

'Yes,' he replied, 'it turned out easier than I thought it would be.' Cinder continued to watch as a group of three birds, black against the background, floated over the ocean and dived behind the white foamy crests of the breakers.

'I don't usually get to look out over Heathcote from this end, and from so close,' she said. 'It looks beautiful, innocent.'

'That's what I thought when I first saw you,' Angus said, sitting down next to her. Cinder gave a half-smile and laughed, looked down at her feet, then back at the view.

'You know, I think I can see my house from here,' she said, squinting her eyes to look through the trees atop the hill at the far end of the beach.

'I think you can see your house from the moon!' Angus teased. This time, a full grin curved Cinder's cheeks and flashed in her eyes. She whacked Angus playfully in the chest.

'Well, I am a queen. I deserve a palace,' she joked, resting her hand on his lap.

'There's a good view of Mr. Loo's backyard from here,' Angus said, happy that things appeared to be progressing positively. Cinder turned and looked at him quizzically.

'What?' she asked with laughter in her voice.

'Mr. Loo's yard.' Angus pointed out the large backyard of a shop that fronted onto one of the streets that ran uphill, perpendicular to the esplanade. A line of fruit trees ran along one of the age-greyed pine fences. Along the opposite fence was a small building with a rusty, corrugated iron roof. 'Surely you know the story of Mr. Loo's chickens?' he asked. Cinder still looked confused.

'No, I think I've heard you mention it, but I don't know what you're talking about.'

'It's legend around here, and it involves some of your people.' Angus said. Cinder raised an eyebrow at the 'your people' comment, but Angus continued before she could make her protest.

'The Loos have run that fish and chip shop forever and old Mr. Loo, who was the grandfather of the owner now, used to sell fruit and vegetables from his garden and fresh eggs. The story goes that he had issues with feral animals taking his chickens, so one night he hid in his chicken coop, armed will a large kitchen knife. Around midnight he heard something moving outside the coop and from his hiding place, he could see a large furry tail in the moonlight. Pulling out his knife, he brought it down on the animal's tail and cut it in half. To his surprise, he heard a man's voice cry out in pain. Hearing the mysterious animal run away, he grabbed the half a tail as evidence, only to have it shrivel up into a piece of skin in his hand. So, there you go.' Angus nodded towards Mr. Loo's shop again. 'That's where all the rumours about strange beasts in the area started, and that's why my family eventually moved here. You don't know anyone with half a tail, do you?'

'No, no. Before my time, I think,' Cinder replied with a grin. 'People must have thought he was crazy.'

'Most did, but there was also a group of believers with similar stories. Enough to get my grandfather's attention.'

'Your grandfather?' Cinder asked. 'You haven't ever mentioned him before.'

'I've never met him,' Angus said, shrugging. 'I think he might be still alive; he had a falling out with his kids. I don't really know the details.'

'I don't know anything about my grandparents,' Cinder said thoughtfully, a wave of sadness falling over her face. 'I don't really know much about my parents even.'

Angus could feel her grip on his lap tightening. He placed his hand on hers, and she relaxed her grip.

'Why did you leave? You know... after,' he asked. Cinder turned her body towards him and looked him in the eye.

'If you didn't notice, when I change, I get a lot bigger and... well, my clothes don't. So, I was only seconds away from being naked in front of you and Dom. Not something I'm ready for yet.'

'Maybe that's more a second date thing,' said Angus hopefully. 'At least we got to kiss on our first date.'

Cinder reached out and patted him reassuringly on his chest. 'If you're calling resuscitating you a kiss, then I'm sorry to say, I think you and Dom got to second base. I had very little to do with it,' she said. Angus laughed, studying her face. He had never met someone that looked so different every time he looked at them.

'I didn't lie to you, you know?' he said.

'What?'

'In the library, when you had me tied up, you called me a liar. I didn't. I didn't tell you the whole truth, but I didn't lie.'

'I did,' Cinder admitted, looking down at the ground. 'I lied about my age, who I was, where I lived. I had no right to get angry with you. I just thought you were one of them and I freaked out. I was coming to tell you... tell you the truth, and I was just so excited that I had found someone I trusted to tell and then I saw you drinking that stuff at the fire and... I just couldn't think straight,' she said, taking her hand off his lap. Angus started laughing out loud. Cinder looked up at him in surprise. 'I'm pouring my heart out here and you're laughing?'

'Sorry,' Angus said, 'I just realised that you must have seen Dom naked. That would disturb anyone.'

'I don't know about disturbed. It made me feel something.' Cinder teased.

'Oh, is that right?' Angus asked.

'It was pretty good, really,' Cinder answered.

'Whatever.' Angus pushed her shoulder. Cinder smiled and looked down at her feet, wiggling her toes.

'I lied about having other men in my room too,' she confessed. 'You were the first, the first that I wanted.' Angus leant in closer and mirrored her foot-studying and toe-wiggling.

'Was it all you'd dreamed it would be?' he joked.

'It wasn't really how I had pictured it, no. I never imagined Bob being there for starters.'

'Yeah,' Angus agreed. 'Being drugged and tied up by two women and a balding man, then having to hide from someone's mum in the stable. That sounds more like something Dom would be into.' They both laughed in agreement then sat enjoying the view and each other's company in silence.

Turning her head and resting it on Angus's shoulder, Cinder stared into his chocolate brown eyes. The stars had begun to peek through the branches behind him. A cool breeze blew across her cheek and a loose lock of hair fell across her freckled nose. Angus took it in his fingers and gently tucked it behind her ear. Cinder could feel her breathing quicken as she watched his lips quiver and felt his rough fingertips on the back of her neck. Angus dropped his eyes away from hers and looked at his feet again.

'Hey!' Cinder said, reaching out and pushing his chin up with her fingers. 'Are you going to kiss me or what?'

'Um,' was all he could manage to reply, dumfounded.

'Whatever, I'll do it myself.' Cinder said, grabbing the hair at the back of his head and pushing her lips hard against his. Keeping their lips connected, she closed her eyes and moved slowly up onto her knees so that her head was above his. When she opened her eyes again, all that existed in that moment were his warm lips and the deep brown pools of his eyes. She pulled away slowly, holding his lower lip between hers. Angus wrapped his arms around her and pulled her close again. Cinder pushed him away and looked at him in mock surprise.

'You know I just realised,' she said, 'on a clear night like tonight, with no moon, we might be able to see Uranus.'

• • • •

Continue Cinder and Black's journey in book 2
    Hearts and Diamonds

# REWARD

## The Maikranz Method

In 2009 author D. Eric Maikranz, offered a reward to readers of his novel "The Reincarnationist Papers". This novel has now gone on to be the inspiration for the Hollywood movie "INFINITE" by Paramount Pictures. You can read full story at https://ericmaikranz.com/

This was the reward offered by D. Eric Maikranz.

As the author of this work, I offer you the reader, the opportunity to redeem a cash award for introducing this work to any literary agent, publisher or producer that offers an acceptable contract to the author for this work. The reward offered is 10% of any initial book advance or option contract for film or television series up to a maximum of $10,000.

Via this reward, our mutual goal is to introduce this work to literary/publishing professionals or producers. Many are likely familiar with the term "6 degrees of separation," the theory that anyone on the planet can be connected to any other person on the planet through a chain of acquaintances that has no more than five intermediaries. This is what I aim to accomplish here with your help

With his blessing, I now offer you the same reward. Please send any leads or contacts to maxxvictorbooks@gmail.com.

Thank you and happy hunting,

| Page

# Don't miss out!

Visit the website below and you can sign up to receive emails whenever Maxx Victor publishes a new book. There's no charge and no obligation.

https://books2read.com/r/B-A-WVYN-JGHNB

**BOOKS 2 READ**

Connecting independent readers to independent writers.

# About the Author

Maxx Victor is an Australian author, musician, and secondary school science teacher, who has achieved award winning success with his short stories. A dedicated husband and proud father of two, he is also highly involved in his local arts community; performing in bands and producing and directing amateur films.

Maxx's author journey began at a very young age. As a child with dyslexia, reading and writing were a constant struggle. To help, his father implemented the nightly routine of reading Titin and Asterix comics and Biggles books to Maxx and his brother; installing a lifelong passion for reading. Maxx's mother also encouraged him to write stories (some which he has kept to this day).

During his secondary school years, Maxx unearthed a love for music. He regularly wrote poetry and song lyrics, as well as scripts for plays and short films. Something again sparked the curiosity for writing stories when Maxx's children were toddlers. He frequently created impromptu, twisted fairy-tale bedtime stories, with his family members as the main characters. Maxx now writes teen fiction and hopes that his writing can inspire young people to be defined by their passions and talents, not by the things that the world will tell them are impairments.

Read more at Maxxvictorbooks.com.